da nuts

Rich Kisielewski

WolfSinger Publications – Security Colorado

ACKNOWLEDGEMENTS

Many thanks to my wife Liz and my favorite kids Tara and Brian—they are my team of readers and editors who keep me honest and turn my work into mostly readable English. Your constant support is what keeps me going.

Chapter 1

Eighteen years old. A mere eighteen years old. Impossible to believe, but he had played over a quarter of a million hands of poker by the time he had reached his eighteenth birthday. Evidenced by the size of his bank account, he had won a lot more of those hands than he had lost. All of that meant nothing when he turned up unconscious in his hotel room on the morning of the first day of the "Under 18 World Championship of Poker" tournament.

~ * ~

Maybe I should jump back a few steps and let you in on what's going on here. My name is Harry, because I'm told an aunt promised to lay some bread on me if my mom named me Harold. I don't believe it one little bit because I didn't see a single dime and, to my knowledge, neither did my moms.

Oh yeah, it's Harry, or should I say Harold Mickey Shorts, which wasn't my given name when I was ushered into this wonderful world of ours. My original name didn't cut it in my eyes and the Mick, Mr. Mantle, is my all-time favorite ballplayer. Plus, my original last name was way too long. Wearing tee shirts and shorts is how the Big Guy upstairs intended us to dress, so that's how I came up with my new and improved name—"Shorts"—which just happens to be a great conversation topic for the ladies.

By trade, I guess you would call me a private investigator, but I'm not your ordinary run-of-the-mill, every day private dick. Kizmet Incorporated is what my card would say, if I had one. Max, my son, called Kizmet Incorporated and asked if he could hire a cracker-jack private investigator, if they had one. He's a funny kid sometimes and he needed my help. When I'm asked for help, you best jump back, because I'm coming through to do anything in my power to mend what needs mending.

And so the story begins…

Chapter 2

"Waz up, Max my son," Harry asked when Max answered the phone.

"Is this Kizmet Inc. calling in reference to my inquiry?" Max responded. "Or," he continued, "might it be my number one poppyson calling just because I happen to be his bestest and most favorite son?"

"Could be both, could be neither. One never know, do one?" Harry responded.

"One sure don't, do one?" Max replied.

"So, waz up?" Harry asked again.

"A business meeting to discuss the possible hiring of Kizmet Inc. to handle a delicate matter that has materialized," Max replied.

"Ah, but by who?" Harry asked. "And to what end? What's this 'delicate matter' you speak of?"

"Me," Max replied. "Well, that's me and about a hundred other guys my age, or a little older. We have money and it is an actual case we want you to investigate. You could cut us a little slack and charge us the discount rate if you are feeling generous."

"We can talk about the rate later," Harry started. "What's going on? What's this case you're talking about and how are you involved?"

"How about I have my girl call your girl and we'll do lunch," Max replied.

"That would be great," Harry replied. "Unfortunately, I don't have a girl and your moms will kick your ass if you ask her to call me."

"Two very good points," Max replied. "Me and two buds at your place in an hour?" Max asked.

"Done," Harry replied. "I'll get the booze and you bring the dancing girls. Deal?"

"Deal," Max answered.

"Deal my ass," Harry said. "Just show up in an hour and we'll talk business."

~ * ~

The doorbell rang and Harry let Max and his two buds into his apartment. Three kids looking to hire Harry Mickey Shorts, private investigator extraordinaire; if only in his own mind. The world was getting weirder every day; at least Harry's world was.

"So, Max, what's going on?" Harry asked when they were all seated in his living room. Since the room wasn't that big they were all fairly close together. The three boys didn't have to look far as they stared at each other trying to decide who would speak first.

"Dad, this is Robby," Max finally said pointing to the taller of his two companions. "And that's Jimmy. They're both from town."

The boys barely took a peek at Harry. Yeah, I guess you could say they were a bit on the shy side, or terrified.

"Glad to meet you guys," Harry told them.

"Should I get everyone a beer before we get started?" Max asked with a straight face.

"Yeah, root beers all around," Harry replied with an equally straight face.

"If you insist," Max said as he got up to get the drinks.

"Do I need to frisk you guys?" Harry asked the two boys when Max was gone.

Panic began to show in their eyes as they looked anxiously for Max to return.

"Maybe put you both up against the wall, spread eagle your legs and give you the once over."

"Cut the shit, pops," Max said as he returned with root beers all around. "They're scared enough just being involved with this. Getting them to come up here with me was chore enough. You make them shit themselves and I'll have to listen to their sorry asses forever."

Harry smiled.

"It's all right, guys. My dad thinks he's hysterical at times. He's only playing with you," Max assured them.

Robby and Jimmy started to breathe again.

Harry laughed and said, "Grab a drink and I'll put some tunes on. Music to construct cases by I call it."

"Means we're gonna hear some of his old shit is what he's really saying," Max told his buds.

Harry smacked Max behind the head as he went over to put on some of his best "old shit" on the turntable.

Chapter 3

Van Morrison's Moondance filled the room to the delight of at least Harry. Max approved without showing it. Both Harry and Max knew.

Harry's collection of vintage vinyl albums numbered in the 700-800 range with just about every album in good to excellent condition. If it didn't play, it didn't stay was the approach Harry took to his music collection.

"So, who's gonna spill the beans here?" Harry started.

Robby looked at Jimmy and Jimmy looked at Max who was looking at both of them at that very second. They had already decided beforehand Max would be the spokesman, but Max wanted to make it look like they hadn't talked about it beforehand. Look confused and prey on the old man's sympathies for his favorite son. They were talking about real money here.

Harry knew exactly what they, no, what Max was doing.

Finally Max spoke up.

"We would like to retain the services of Kizmet Inc. to investigate the unusual circumstances surrounding the untimely and unfortunate events that befell Clinton Rensford."

The room went quiet.

Harry waited, but it remained quiet.

Having waited long enough, Harry spoke in return.

"If that's all I'm going to get from you, I'll ask several questions if I may?"

"You may," Max responded.

"Thank you. Who's 'we'? What unusual circumstances? How untimely and unfortunate? What events? Who's Clinton Rensford? Isn't Van grand?"

The last question confused Robby and Jimmy.

"Appropriately contrived questions," Max started. "I'll take them in order if I can. If not, I'll improvise. Robby and Jimmy will fill in some holes as we go along."

"They talk?" Harry asked.

Max cocked his head, thought a second, then realized Robby and Jimmy hadn't spoken a word yet.

"Yeah, they talk," Max replied.

"Good to know. Go on," Harry said.

"As you so deftly say on occasion, why don't we jump back a few steps here and lay some groundwork for the explanations to your questions. Copasetic?" Max asked.

"Wholly copasetic," Harry answered.

"You're familiar with the poker craze that has taken over the imagination and wallets of many a man and woman in this country and across the many seas?" Robby started.

"He does speak," Harry said.

"He does," Max concurred.

"And quite well if I may say so," Harry added.

"You may," Max allowed. "Debate team."

Robby continued.

"There is the World Series of Poker and every other form of Poker Championship that has invaded TV and the casinos. You also are surely aware of the on-line poker mania that exploded almost overnight. You may also know there are minimum ages for participation for all of the above activities."

"I'm with you so far," Harry chimed in.

"Wonderfully concrete of you," Jimmy picked up. "Max informed us you were capable of absorbing the essence of the dilemma with a minimum of factual interaction."

"What the...?" Harry was about to blurt out before Max caught his direction and interceded.

"Jimmy is President of the Shakespeare Society and also captains the chess and computer clubs."

"Freakin nerd-ass," Robby said not quite under his breath.

"This freakin nerd-ass will kick your freakin brainiack geek ass if you say that again," Jimmy blurted out.

"He's got a brown belt, too," Max told Harry.

"Excuse me, but if I'm going to have to endure more of this, this young man's take-over of the older man's world, I'm going to have to remove the root from the equation and go to the purest form—St. Pauli Girl," Harry interrupted.

Chapter 4

Order now restored and the aforementioned St. Pauli Girl properly placed in front of Harry, they continued.

Max retook the lead.

"So much brains between the two of them and they fight like two little girls sharing one doll."

"We do not," they both said in unison.

Everyone laughed at that and the tension left the room.

"In answer to your first question, the 'we' is a group of kids our age who worship the ground Clint walks on. That's Clinton Rensford—I'll get to him later. To understand where we are coming from, you have to know about the underground poker phenomenon that has swept through the kids of America," Max began.

"Not just America," Robby interjected.

"I sit corrected," Max agreed. "I should have said the underground poker phenomenon that has swept through the kids of America and many other countries as well. It is an online poker site restricted to kids between the ages of sixteen and eighteen—male or female. More guys for sure, but the girls are getting more prevalent every day. We, the under sixteeners, we can watch but we are prohibited from playing."

Max sensed his dad was somewhat confused at this point.

"Sounds kinda absurd like Rod Serling Twilight Zoneish absurd you're probably thinking," Robby chimed in.

"You know Twilight Zone?" Harry asked him.

Three looks.

Dumb questions Harry understood.

"Let me lay it down for you," Jimmy said. "Right about three years ago, well maybe less than that actually, a message starting showing up on some web sites that kids in the fifteen to seventeen range would frequent. There was the first blurb and then nothing. Word spread and everyone wanted to know what the deal was."

"What did the message say?" Harry asked.

"I figured you'd ask that so I brought a copy with me. Didn't want to get it wrong since it's probably the first clue," Max said.

"We'll see about the clue thing, but shoot," Harry replied

"Okay, here goes," Max said. "Kids aged sixteen to eighteen can earn college money legitimately…play your way to free college tuition…more to come soon…."

"That's it?" Harry asked.

"That be all," Max replied.

"Huh," Harry grunted.

"Nobody knew anything else; where it came from, who sent it, what it meant?" Harry continued.

"Nada to each of your w's or anything else for that matter," Max answered.

Jimmy and Robby nodded in agreement.

"Weird," Harry said.

"Kinda like Rod Serling Twilight Zoneish weird," Robby said.

Harry gave Robby a sideways look and then said, "What happened next?"

"That's the weirdest part," Robby said. "Nothing happened next. Nothing for the next three weeks."

"Kids just figured it was somebody goofing on the bracket and forgot about it," Jimmy added.

"Goofing on the bracket?" Harry asked.

"Yeah, goofing on the bracket," Max repeated. "You know, goofing, jerking us around, playing with us. The us, the bracket, was the kids in the fifteen to seventeen age bracket and the younger ones who would be getting there pretty soon. Everyone thought it was just some dimwad goofing."

"And it wasn't? Harry asked.

"No it tweren't," Max replied

"Tweren't?" Harry mimicked.

"Beverly Hillbillies rerun," Max replied.

"Piss break and refill time," Harry said as he got up and left the room.

Chapter 5

New SP Girl in hand, Harry was ready to listen to more of their tale. The tale was going to have to get a whole lot clearer, plus a whole lot faster, to keep his interest.

"So...." Harry prompted.

"So," Max started anew, "the boards lit up like a Christmas tree when the next message hit. Again, it was a one shot quickie that had everyone talking and firing emails all over the net."

"What'd it say?" Harry asked.

"I don't have a copy of the second one," Max said. "It hit and I never saw it. But, paraphrasing, it went something like 'Gamin for bucks—tuition style' and little more. Nobody could figure out what it meant, but you mention money and college tuition and kids jump back and take notice," Max continued.

"Where?" Harry asked.

"What?" Robby said.

"No, where?" Harry replied.

"What's he..." Jimmy started to say.

"Where. Where was the message posted is what I think he's asking. Right?" Max asked his dad.

"Right. Where?"

"Oh," Robby uttered.

"In response to this one dude's blog that lots of kids look for all the time. He must have known it'd get plenty of play and spread fast and far," Jimmy said.

"He right?" Harry asked.

"Sure as shit," Max answered. "Kids as far away as California, Canada, and some overseas kids posted responses almost right away. The noise didn't stop for a week."

"And nothing further from the mystery poster?" Harry asked.

"Nada, squat, bupkiss..."

"I get the point, Max," Harry interrupted.

Harry thought and sipped his beer.

"Lemme recap this if I can," Harry finally said. "Someone posts a message to a site kids utilize and it peaks their interest. Everyone wants to know what's up, but nobody knows. A few weeks later a second post hits in a different online venue and a country worth of kids plus kids overseas get all jazzed. Still nada on who's doing the posting, or why?"

"Correctamundo," Max confirms.

"I'm solid so far; what next?" Harry asked.

The three stooges look at each other, nobody saying boo.

"Max?" Harry prompts.

"Well, nothing again. Nothing for another couple of weeks. Then, the dam opened up and emails were everywhere. Every site kids frequented, and some underground ones as well, had emails all signed by a BrianK. Nothing more, just BrianK."

"What'd they say?" Harry prompted again.

"They all said basically the same thing," Jimmy said.

"Yeah, the same thing," Robby agreed.

"They did," Max also agreed.

Shaking his head, Harry said very slowly, "Now that I know they all said the same thing as all three of you have confirmed, I will repeat my question—'What did they say?'"

"Oh. And again, I'm paraphrasing, but the gist of the messages was a new site was gonna be available soon that every kid wouldn't want to miss. It said college money would be available and every kid between the ages of sixteen and eighteen would be eligible to get a chunk of it. It said something like 'Play to Pay your way through College' and more info would be up soon. And it was," Max finished.

"It was what?" Harry asked.

"Up soon," Robby replied.

"A week later," Jimmy added.

Quiet.

"And?" Harry prompted again.

"And," Max went on, "the next communication that was posted everywhere you could post a message kids would see said, 'Pay for college for as little as two hundred dollars if you're feeling lucky—or good'."

"Interesting," was all Harry said in reply

Chapter 6

The boys watched Harry drain his beer and head into the kitchen. When he returned he walked right past them and out onto the deck off the living room. About two minutes later they decided he wasn't coming back so they followed him out onto the deck.

Harry was leaning on the railing with his back to the boys when they came out onto the deck. The deck sat above the driveway the wound past the main house and down to the street. Harry spent a good bit of time out on his deck especially in the good weather.

"Took you that long?" Harry asked when they finally showed up.

"Robby and Jimmy were busy ransacking the house," Max replied.

"We were not!" they both said in unison.

"Relax," Harry said. "Max is just jerking your chain."

"You're such a prick," Robby threw in Max's direction.

"Thank you very much," Max replied. He was obviously quite pleased with himself.

"All right, let's move on if we can," Harry said.

The Pauli Girls were gone since Harry was now drinking a Sierra Nevada Pale Ale.

"So, our mystery e-mailer, the elusive BrianK, sucks in every living and breathing kid with promises of hard earned cash for college tuition. Sounds too easy and too good to be true," Harry tells them.

"Maybe to you, and maybe it was," Jimmy starts, "but to all the kids we know, they practically wet themselves with the thoughts of free money for college. Don't get me wrong, a lot of the kids in town don't have to worry about college. The town's got money trees growing in every other back yard, but some of us won't be able to go where we want if we don't get big time scholarships, or free money like BrianK was promising. And there aren't that many towns like Manhasset in the rest of the country. Some, but lots more kids like us than richbee's."

"I know where you're coming from, Jimmy. Max here better bone up on his studies or get a major infusion of big time athletic ability very pronto," Harry replied.

A slight nod confirmed Max knew where his dad was coming from.

"What happened next?" Harry continued.

Max took the lead again.

"It took a few days and then the big announcement hit the e-waves. All the normal sites kids everywhere would frequent had the same announcement appear almost simultaneously. The directions were very simple: if you wanted to accumulate funds to be used for your college education, go to www.pokcolmon.com and follow the easy instructions."

"Pokcolmon.com?" Harry repeated.

"Yeah," Max continued. "Turns out it was short for 'poker college money' and had very strict guidelines on who could play, parental sign-offs needed, what documentation was needed to gain entrance to the site, how much could be "donated" by each participant over specific time frames and the security measures required that could lead to forfeiting one's bankroll if you were caught abusing those security guidelines."

"Poker?" Harry asked.

"Yeah, online poker, just like the other online poker sites you see advertised all the time. The catch was this site is only for kids between the ages of sixteen and eighteen."

"How does it work? Have the rules changes since it started?" Harry asked.

"To get into the site and play in the daily games, plus weekly tournaments, you need to fill out an application for a credit card and submit it to a web site. The information needed included your name, address, birth date and Social Security Number with copies of the information in a .pdf file verifying all of the information. Your parent(s) signature(s) approving your participation and application for the credit card, plus their identical information and personal guarantee had to be included in the .pdf file submitted."

"A credit card?" Harry asked.

"Yeah, a credit card issued in the parent(s) name(s) that allowed you to make a donation to the 'US College Scholarship Fund' controlled by BrianK," Max told Harry.

"Let me get this straight," Harry began. "The kid—using a

credit card in his mom or dad's name makes a 'donation' to some fund that allows him to play poker and accumulate money toward a college scholarship of sorts?"

"You got it," they all said in unison.

"And the kid can't play without their parent's permission and signature stating so. What guarantee are the parents giving?" Harry asked.

"I forgot to mention," Max said. "You have to be nominated by three kids already in the fund along with their parent's signature or you can't even get in to play in the first place. The guarantee—the parents, and by extension the kids, guarantee the kids won't cheat, and if they do and are caught, they forfeit everything that is in their "account" and they are barred from ever participating again for life. Their name will be broadcast on every site imaginable as a "cheater" and their parent's names will be included, too."

At that moment the phone rang and Harry went inside to get it.

Chapter 7

Arriving back out on the deck properly re-beered, Harry started the conversation anew.

"How much money are we talking about? It can't amount to much, can it? At least it can't amount to enough money to warrant you guys hiring a cracker-jack P.I. such as me at exorbitant daily rates."

The three guys looked at each other. Robby took the lead.

"Here's how it works," Robby started. "The maximum allowable donation per individual is two hundred dollars per month for which you receive a tee-shirt at a cost of twenty-five dollars. The assumption is the twenty-five minus the cost of the tee shirt and mailing costs goes to the BrianK organization. There is no other fee and there is no rake during games, so BrianK's profits come from the up-front twenty-five dollar donation minus subtractions. You can only donate once per month, so if you lose your one seventy-five on the first day, you are shit out of luck for the rest of the month."

"By rake you mean a cut of each hand taken out of the total pot by the house, or BrianK's organization who are behind the fund in this case," Harry confirmed.

"Correct," Jimmy said.

"So, if some kids donate a net of one seventy-five per month to the fund, even if they do it all twelve months, that's only a maximum of twenty-one hundred per kid, per year. That can't amount to that much, can it?" Harry asked.

"It sure can," Max said. "It doesn't happen, but if every kid donated the maximum twenty-one hundred per year it would come to over two hundred million."

"Say what?" Harry asked.

"Right now there are just over one hundred thousand kids worldwide registered to play. At only one seventy-five per player, that would come to over seventeen million dollars a month."

Harry stared at Max in amazement. He looked at Robby and Jimmy and they shrugged their shoulders in return.

"At those numbers this is big business," Harry said. "And the

BrianK organization is taking in millions even after their expenses are covered. Isn't anyone questioning the twenty-five dollar slice they are taking off the top, tee shirts or no tee shirts?"

The three boys looked at each other and then back at Harry. Max again took the lead.

"If you're doing good, you only look at the bank account you are amassing and your college tuition being taken care of. If you aren't, for only two hundred dollars you are back in the game and on your way to free college. If your parents say that's enough, they pull the plug and you're out."

"And BrianK?" Harry repeated.

"Nobody cares what goes on behind the scenes or how much money BrianK's people are making. It's the game, man, it's the game," Robby said.

Jimmy chimed in, "And the parents of the kids who are building up these big bankrolls are loving every dollar of it. The losers, well there's always next month."

"Where do you guys fit in?" Harry asked.

"When you join and make your first donation there is a "First Timer" tournament scheduled for the fifth of every month or the first Saturday after the fifth day. That is the only "first hand" access we—the "Too Young Kids" or TYK's—have to watch the real fund kids play," Max said.

"Plus," Jimmy said, "there is a general web site that anyone having a "TYK" password can access and watch the results of regular tournaments. We don't see the actual play as it is going on, just the hand results as soon as they are completed."

"What about collusion?" Harry asked. "With that much money up for grabs you have to believe some kids will figure out how to manipulate the game."

"Nope," Max replied.

"No,' Harry replied. "Never mind the kids—parents, uncles, plain old crooks will steal the rest of the kids blind."

"Nope," Max repeated. "A sophisticated computer program tracks every player, every move, in every hand. It tracks who plays with who, how often, who wins and who loses, how and when they fold their hands and who's left in the hand when they fold; raises and re-raises, and more additional factors than you could imagine. Every possible angle is covered. You cheat—you're caught! You're caught—sayonara college money! You forfeit the entire bankroll in your account and you're shamed all across the web big time."

"This is amazing," Harry said. "Why isn't it publicized? Why isn't it spread across every newspaper, every TV channel country-wide. Never mind country-wide, world-wide even?"

Max thought for a second, and then said, "Because nobody's sure it's actually one hundred percent legal."

Chapter 8

The kids were gone and Harry was left sitting on his deck looking down at the yard behind the main house his garage apartment belonged to. Fine looking it was, too.

Sandy, who lived in one of the apartments in the main house, had come out during Harry's talk with the boys and was sun bathing at that very moment. Sun bathing in all her splendid glory.

Harry loved watching Sandy's splendid glory, every inch of it. Nothing better than sipping a cold beer and enjoying Sandy's splendid glory. Well, maybe there was at least one thing Harry could think of. It was even better when Sandy's knockout of a daughter was home from college and joined her moms: it was then a multitude of splendid glories. A P.I.'s work was never done.

Hearing the words, "What are you looking at, Harry?" brought him out of his trance.

"Why what else, you," Harry replied.

"Is that all you plan on doing—looking? Sandy asked.

"Unless you have a better suggestion," Harry tried.

"While I gather my things, I suggest you walk down and open the door to your apartment. I suggest you then walk back up the stairs and get the can of whipped cream out of your refrigerator. I further suggest you meet me in the back of your apartment and prepare to utilize that can of whipped cream for things we know we will both thoroughly enjoy," Sandy suggested.

"An excellent stream of suggestions," Harry said. "I shall proceed forthwith.

"Yes, Harry, I'm expecting a good deal of width proceeding forth. And I so love your width proceeding forth," Sandy finished.

~ * ~

They were resting against the wall in Harry's bedroom, their pillows propped against the wall. The fan in the back window had them almost dried off again.

"Planning on staying around for a while, Harry?" Sandy asked.

"Don't want me to go forthwith?" Harry joked.

"Oh don't worry, you'll be doing more forth width very soon, empty whipped cream can or not. I just want you to stay around so I can admire that pretty face of yours. Plus some other things, too."

"Ah, other things. Forth width," Harry repeated with a smile.

"Not yet, Harry. Answer my question first. Are you going to be staying close to home for a while?" Sandy repeated.

"Don't know," Harry said getting serious. "Max and his buds have something they want me to look into and I may have to do a little road work to check it out. I'll know soon."

"Hope it's not for long. Just to be safe, we better practice your...I can't say it again," Sandy laughed. "Just get over here and bang me silly. And, may the forth-width be with you."

Chapter 9

"Big Mel, my favorite EBIL. How the hell are ya?" Harry asked.

Mel, Harry's ex-brother-in-law, hence EBIL, was seated behind his desk in his real estate office on Plandome Road in Manhasset, Long Island. That's in New York for those of you who are semi-geographically challenged. Harry happens to share space in the back of the office and uses it as a business mailing address.

"I was fine and dandy until your ugly puss showed up," Mel replied.

"Be careful, the fragile ego," Harry replied.

"Fragile ego my ass," Mel answered. "Your ego is the size of Wyoming and harder than a…than a…ah fuck it, why do I bother," Mel replied.

"Harry!" came a squeal from the back of the office.

"Bunny!" Harry attempted to squeal back.

Bunny Malone was Mel's able bodied assistant. Her body was the primary able part with the rest of her assistant skills constantly in doubt. But, what an able body she did possess.

"I've missed you, Harry," Bunny told him. "I haven't seen you since, well, since last week."

"That was only four days ago," Harry informed Bunny.

"I know, but I still missed you," Bunny said as she moved past Harry and swept a glancing lip brush across his cheek.

Johnson jumped to attention in case there was additional brushing to come.

As traditionally occurs when Harry enters the premises, Bunny stopped at the file cabinet and bent over to get some supplies out of the bottom drawer. Her long shapely legs and cute tight ass were clearly defined for all to see; well, at least for Harry and Mel to observe. The short skirts Bunny favored didn't hurt the show one bit.

Harry caught himself before the "oh baby" escaped his lips.

Regaining his senses, Mel asked, "What do you want, Harry?"

"The joy of your company and the pleasant, ah, smile of Bunny Malone," Harry tried.

"Yeah, right," Mel replied. "Now, I repeat, what do you want, Harry?"

"What else would I want, Mel baby. Intel," Harry told him.

"What now?" Mel asked.

Bunny sat and read a glamour magazine. There must be a picture of a house somewhere in the magazine that would count as market research.

"Max come talk to you recently?" Harry asked.

"Me?" Bunny looked up and asked.

"Ah, no, Bunny. I was actually asking Mel."

"Oh, okay," Bunny replied as she went back to her magazine.

Mel and Harry both shook their heads simultaneously in amazement.

"About what?" Mel asked.

"This poker thing."

"Poker?" Mel replied.

"You jerking my chain?" Harry asked.

"One of my small enjoyments in life," Mel answered.

"It thrills me to be here for you, big guy. Now, the kid been here?"

"Yeah, we talked. He didn't tell me much but it seemed to be important to him," Mel said.

"Know anything about this fund? The guy BrianK behind it? Online poker in general?" Harry asked.

"No. No. A little," Mel replied.

"Helpful, aren't we," Harry said in return.

"You asked, I answered."

"Any thoughts on who I might be able to score some intel from?" Harry tried.

"Not my area, Harry. I got enough problems without pissing away money playing online games," Mel said.

"Anyone else you happen to know I might try asking."

"No, maybe. You gonna help Max?" Mel asked.

"Is the Pope Catholic? Yeah, he's my kid. I'll do what I can for him and his buds. Don't tell him I asked. Okay?" Harry said.

"Sure," Mel assured him. "Now beat it, I got work to do."

With that, Mel picked up the New York Times and started reading the sports pages.

"Later, Bunny," Harry threw in her direction.

"I'm counting on it, Harry. Just not too much later I hope."

Harry smiled the smile of the knowing man.

Chapter 10

Harry had two directions he could go in to get some much needed information before he made up his mind on helping Max and his buds. The first was Mr. M. Randle Trundle.

Trundle, or Randy as Harry called him, was the CEO of a major New York City conglomerate. Trundle Industries had more interests in more things than you could shake a stick at. Harry had handled two cases for Trundle and both were handled in a manner that pleased Mr. Trundle. He was on retainer to Trundle Industries, and Trundle personally, which allowed him to take on cases like Max's for little or no fees. Plus, Trundle Industries had more tools and toys at their disposal than God his/herself.

Harry firmly believed you should always hedge your bets when you can. One never know…

The second option Harry could turn to would be foolproof, but expensive. The Web Dudes could get any information on anything you could imagine if the information existed. Jaxy, head Web Dude, was the best there is, ever was, or ever will be. You can take that to the bank and count on your interest compounded secondly.

Cheap would do for now Harry decided.

"Ms. Timmons' office, may I help you?"

Sexy voice Harry thought to himself. A new one, too.

"Yes you may. Is Ms. Timmons available?" Harry asked. "And your name would be?"

"Who may I ask is calling?" sexy voice replied.

"Harry Mickey Shorts. And your name would be?"

"I'll check. Please hold," was all Harry got in reply.

Ms. Timmons was the personal assistant to M. Randle Trundle. She also was one fine foxy package that to date had eluded the grasp of Harry and his almost never failing charms. Close, but no cigar, much to Harry's dismay.

"Timmons," was all she said when she came on the line.

"Shorts," Harry said in reply.

"Funny, Harry. You haven't called in a while. I thought the scourge of my life was finally gone for good," Timmons said.

"I'd never abandon you, Ms. Timmons. We still have unfinished business we need to attend to," Harry answered.

"Dream on, Harry. What do you want?"

If Harry was capable of getting a complex, the "What do you want" could give him one.

"Besides you, I need some intel. Any chance I can use the company's brains or do I have to go through Randle?" Harry tried.

"Mr. Trundle is in London, so you couldn't ask him if you wanted to, or I let you. Why I don't know, but I'll try and help you if I can. What kind of intel are you looking for?" Timmons asked.

"The HMS charms are getting to you, aren't they?" Harry tried.

"The HMS Pinafore has a better chance of getting to me, Harry. Intel? Kind?" Timmons answered.

"It's not that straight forward," Harry started. "I need a computer person to help me track down an online gaming site and follow its path from start-up to current day. I need someone to get me everything available on the person/people/organization behind said gaming site. I need the money trail from initial "start-up cost" backing, annual financials and where the money is, plus an accounting (with disbursements) of the "fund" that was set up as the basis for the site. That's for starters," Harry concluded.

"For starters?" Timmons echoed.

"Yeah," Harry replied. "I'll need some heavy legal research and opinions at some time later on."

Silence filled the line.

"Timmons? You still there?" Harry tried.

"I'll get back to you," Timmons said right before the phone line went dead.

Damn her for doing that Harry thought to himself.

Chapter 11

The Bayport Schooners are a Double A baseball team in the Eastern League. They play their home games in, where else— Bayport, Long Island. Harry had been a player coach for them a few years back and liked to catch a game whenever he could. Today they had a game and catch it he could.

"Yo, Mel," Harry yelled to his favorite EBIL as he entered his place of business. The reason he yelled "Yo" at Mel was so he could hear him. Mel happened to be sound asleep behind his desk in the rear of the office.

"The fuck, Harry," Mel blurted out as he came awake. "Why do you have to be such a fondugotz."

"The Sheik of Arabeek was just here looking to buy five houses for his United States harem and wanted you to be his personal real estate guru. He and his posse were leaving just as I came in. A fondu what?" Harry asked.

"Never mind, Harry. And stick that sheik bullshit where the sun don't shine," Mel oh-so-fondly told Harry.

"Hey, I'm going out to Bayport to catch the Schooners this afternoon. You wanna go?" Harry asked.

"You know what, business is slower than an eighty year old turtle in a pile of goo and I could use a dog and a couple of beers. Let me call Shack and see if he's up for a game. Maybe we can tool out there in style if he opts to blow off the afternoon as well."

"A stretcheroo from the Shack Limo stable perhaps?" Harry hoped out loud.

"Why he likes you I'll never fathom, but if Shack tags along, you can expect we'll be going in style."

~ * ~

Harry was ready and out the door as the stretch Escalade pulled into the driveway heading toward his garage apartment. The driver opened the door and Harry found both Mel and Shack in the back. They already had a long neck in hand.

"Shack, my man. Good to see ya. How they hanging, dude?" Harry asked Shack.

"Life is as it should be, Harry. And yeah, been too long," Shack replied.

"Enjoying the fruits of your labors I see," Harry chided Shack. "Or at least the millions you bank from the hard work all the minions that toil for Shack Limousine, Inc. bring in."

"Millions my ass," Shack spat back. "If I had two nickels to rub together I'd be ten cents ahead of the game."

Mel almost spit out his beer when he heard that one escape Shacks lips.

"Fuck you, Mel. Let's go see some baseball," Shack said.

They all clicked long necks to that.

~ * ~

The Schooners scored two runs in the bottom of the first and two more in the third. The rookie wonder-kid pitcher Harry had introduced Mel and Shack to before the game had a no hitter going through four innings. Harry still had access to the clubhouse and used his friendship with the Schooner's Assistant General Manager to get Mel and Shack the grand fifty cent tour.

The three of them were sitting in the owner's box right behind the first base dugout. M. Randle Trundle, or Trundle Industries to be precise, owned the Schooners—sure helps to know the big cheese.

Between bites of his dog and sips of beer, Mel asked Harry, "So, you gonna take Max's job?"

Harry finished chewing the last bite of his dog and said, "I'm doing a preliminary look see. If there's meat on the bone, I'll look into it for him."

"You have a gut on it yet?" Mel asked.

"A gut feeling, yeah," Harry replied. "One I can't rely on yet. Once I get some intel I'll be in a better position to tell you."

"Don't hang the kid out to dry," Mel said. "He seemed to pretty hopped up about this thing. He and his buds coming up with the cash to hire you took some doing and showed some major cahones."

"Yeah, I agree," Harry said. "I'll do him and his buds right if there's something to it. Gotta give him his due for standing up for what he believes in."

The crack of the bat grabbed their attention. They watched the ball fly over the left field fence and all three runners round the bases. The Schooners were on their way to a major romp to the delight of all in attendance.

For some reason even he couldn't figure out, the Schooners rarely lost when Harry came out to see them play.

Chapter 12

"Max, Robby, Jimmy. How you boys doing?" Harry asked as they were deciding where to sit in Harry's living room. Max jumped for the recliner which was directly across from the music system Harry had assembled. It was his favorite spot in the room. The other boys finally gave up and sat in the first chair they came to.

Quietly the sounds of, "All right, I guess" came from Robby and Jimmy. Max just shrugged in Harry's direction.

Quiet ensued.

"So," Max finally said.

"So?" Harry answered in the form of a question.

"So, are you going to take our case?" Max continued.

"Well," Harry started, "it's been almost a week and I'm not much further along than when we talked the first time."

"Why not?" Robby was brave enough to ask.

"Well, I'm still waiting on some info I asked for. Plus, I don't know what the case is. What do you boys want me to look into? What happened that has your shorts in a bunch?"

Robby and Jimmy looked at Max.

"He's old," Max told them. "He says old shit like that."

"So?" Harry asked.

"So, here it is," Max said. "The first 'Under Eighteen World Championship of Poker' tournament was scheduled to begin that morning."

"The what championship? What morning?" Harry interjected.

"Jesus, dad, I'm getting to it," Max replied.

"He's involved, too," Harry said.

Robby and Jimmy looked at Max who was obviously pondering Harry's question as well.

"No, Jesus is not involved. If you just sit there and listen, I'll get to it all," Max told Harry. "The first 'Under Eighteen World Championship of Poker' tournament was the culmination of two years of play for the sixteen-to-eighteen year olds who initially started the fund play and all the new players since then. Anyone who participated during the two years could enter the tournament if they had at least one dollar of "winnings" in their account."

"How many kids, where, and when?" Harry asked.

"There were a little over three thousand entrants in the tournament from the United States and more than five hundred from abroad. It started a month ago last Saturday at one of the big hotels in Atlantic City."

"That's a lotta kids," Harry said.

"Yeah, plus parents and friends," Max added. "The hotel cut everyone a major break and got you similar deals in other hotels on the strip if you couldn't get into their hotel."

"Brought in some big bucks for AC I would think," Harry commented.

"Yeah," Robby agreed. "It also provided major exposure for some of the people who may not have had a taste of that life before. Plus, they had side tournaments during the whole week for the adults who attended. Specials shows, big performers for the kids and the adults, the whole gamut."

"How much money are we talking about?" Harry asked.

"Entry fee was two hundred fifty dollars per kid. You could either subtract it from your account balance or put it on your credit card as a one-time exception to the two hundred dollar a month rule," Max explained.

"You're getting close to a million bucks with those kind of numbers," Harry said.

"With entry fees, contribution from the BrianK organization and a five hundred thousand dollar donation from the hotel hosting the event, the total amount that would be divided in additional scholarship money was one point five million dollars," Jimmy told Harry.

"One and a half million dollars?" Harry said in amazement.

"That's right, a lotta bucks," Max confirmed.

"Wow!" Harry exclaimed.

"Yeah, wow is right," Robby said.

After thinking about that for a few seconds, Harry said, "So, since there was that kind of money being made available and you guys couldn't participate, I'll ask again. What happened that has your shorts in a bunch?"

Max spoke for the boys. "The tourney favorite, Clint, or I should say Clinton Rensford, turned up unconscious in his hotel room on the morning of what was to be the first day of the tournament. We want to know what really happened."

Chapter 13

"Tell me about it," Harry said to Max and the other two boys. "Who's this Clint kid and what makes you want me to look into what happened?"

Max again took the lead.

"What we know about Clint comes from the boards we frequent. He's the guy that gets the most hits on the "fund" web site BrianK set up to spread news about the regular play, the tournament results, and other site's doings. All the kids that play are regulars on the site."

"You guys, too?" Harry asked.

"Yeah, we can surf it and read what's being said, but we can't contribute. You have to be a player to actually post to the message board," Robby replied.

"Go on," Harry said.

"Again, this is all from what we heard through the board. Clint was supposed to be number one in his senior class in a high school somewhere in Pennsylvania. He's a math/computer wiz and he only got one question wrong on his entire SAT's "on purpose" so he wouldn't be lumped in with the kids that got a perfect score. He supposedly does weird shit like that all the time. Not for the attention, just because he wants to, and he can."

"He in it from the beginning?" Harry asked.

"If you believe in the rumors," Robby said, "he started playing online when he was twelve using another account; some say his older brother's, some kids say his father's. Either way, a kid that claims to be his best friend from home says he had played over a quarter million hands of poker by the time he had reached his eighteenth birthday."

"How much had he accumulated in his fund account?" Harry asked.

"Big money," Max answered. "He had the largest account balance of anyone at just under a hundred and eighty thou. You have to remember, the limit allowed for any one player is two hundred thou, so he was almost maxed out. BrianK set a parameter when the rules for the game were originally established and calculated fifty thousand per year for three years plus fifty-K in tournament play—a maximum of two hundred thousand in tuition dollars for any one player paid directly to the college of your choice. You had to prove enrollment to have the money funded to the school—directly to the school."

"What would have happened if Clint had played in the tournament and won enough to push him over two hundred thousand dollars?" Harry asked.

"Good question," Jimmy answered.

When nobody said anything else, Harry asked, "And?"

"Oh," Jimmy continued. "Just before the tournament started, me and some other kids wondered the same thing, so I read the bylaws word by word and found a clause buried in the fine print at the end. Paraphrased it says, 'If any one player accumulates more than two hundred thousand dollars in winnings, the excess will be credited to his/her account in a "limbo fund" for future educational endeavors above and beyond the college level.'"

"Meaning?" Harry asked.

"Nobody's sure," Max started, "but we're guessing it could go for graduate school, law school, medical school, like that. That's just a guess, though."

"So in reality there was no cap. Anybody ask this BrianK about this apparent loophole in the rules?" Harry pressed on.

"Nope, not that we know of," Max answered.

"Anyone else close to the max limit?" Harry asked.

"Not even close," Robby said. "The next highest total was just over ninety-five thousand dollars by some kid named Richie from the Isle of Mann."

"Isle of Mann?" Harry said.

"Yeah, Isle of Mann," Max answered. "Funny, too; Clint was always urging the kids from abroad who planned to go to school in the United States to get involved and keep on playing. Like he wanted their money to increase the amount in play."

"Interesting," Harry said. "And he never made the tournament you say. Turned up unconscious the morning of the tournament?"

"Yep," Max answered.

"You guys really think there's something screwy going on here?" Harry asked.

"We don't know," Max said for the group. "But, we want to

find out and we're willing to pay for it."

"Okay, lemme see what my initial inquiries bring out. If there's something to go on, I'll see what I can do. That seem fair enough to you guys?" Harry asked.

"Solid," Jimmy replied.

"Solid?" Robby said. "Where the hell did you get solid from?"

"You know, solid, like right on, dude," Jimmy said.

"Like right on, dude?" Robby mimicked.

"Yeah, my old man's gonna do us a solid and you've got shit for brains, Jimmy," Max said laughing.

Jimmy got up and walked out of the apartment in a definite huff to the sounds of gut-splitting laughter coming from Max and Robby.

Kids, Harry thought to himself.

Chapter 14

At 6:40 am the following morning, Harry was awoken by the screeching ring of the telephone that happened to be two inched from his head.

Somehow managing to get the phone off the hook, Harry said into the receiver, "The hell you doing."

"Good morning, Harry," Ms. Timmons said. "I didn't wake you, did I?"

"The hell you think?" Harry stammered.

"Good. I have your information for you and will present it when you come in today for lunch with Mr. Trundle."

"The hell you talking about," was Harry's reply barely opening one eye.

"If you choose not to have lunch with Mr. Trundle today, I can inform him you are too busy to join him at his kind request. I'll just dispose of the information Trundle Industries has composed at your request as well," Timmons droned on.

"Timmons, don't be a pain in my ass at six forty in the morning."

"It's actually six forty-five now, Harry."

"Excuse my tired ass," Harry answered. "What time?"

"Why, six forty-five, Harry. Didn't you hear me?" Timmons said with a slight chuckle in her voice.

"Someday," Harry answered.

"So you keep saying, Harry, so you keep saying. Lunch will be at twelve thirty in the tower and Charles will pick you up at eleven thirty."

Dead air was all Harry heard after that.

Harry was asleep before the phone even hit the hook.

~ *~

At precisely 11:30, the violet limousine of Trundle Industries came up the driveway toward Harry's garage apartment. Every time Harry saw the violet limo, his first thought was, "Who in their right mind owns a violet limousine." Answer—someone who doesn't give two shits what anyone thinks. Follow-up to the initial answer—M. Randle Trundle.

"Harry," Charles said as he opened the door to the limo.

"Charles," Harry replied. "How you be, my man?"

"Better than a hound dog asleep on a shady porch on a breezy summer day," Charles replied.

"That good?" Harry inquired.

"That good," Charles replied.

Charles was the personal driver for M. Randle Trundle. When he wasn't needed by Trundle and Harry was to visit Trundle Industries, or travel on Trundle Industries business, Charles was his man. Plus, Charles loved doing it.

"Let us scoot," Harry said.

"Scoot we shall, Harry. You need anything for the ride?" Charles asked.

"Just you and me and the violet chariot motoring toward the big white way," Harry replied.

Charles smiled and off they went.

~ * ~

Thanks to Charles, Harry was sitting in the waiting area outside Randle's office at 12:10. Much to Harry's dismay, Ms. Timmons did not greet Harry when he arrived as she normally would. Seeing Timmons was as much fun as seeing Randy. The beauty sitting behind the reception desk wasn't bad on the eyes either.

Precisely at 12:30 the door to Trundle's office opened and two men emerged followed by Trundle himself. They looked familiar, but Harry couldn't place them immediately. Trundle shook their hands and they headed for the elevator. Trundle then turned and started back toward his office as if Harry wasn't sitting there waiting. When he got to his door he hesitated and then turned back toward Harry.

"I was just playing with you, Harry," Trundle said with a broad smile. "Get in here and let's wet our whistles."

"And here I thought I was being relegated to 'wait outside his office for the big guy' status," Harry said.

As Harry entered Trundle's office he cocked his head to one side and listened for a few seconds. Recognition came to him and he said, "Cool. Been to Ireland recently?"

"Why yes, Harry. I just returned from a stop in Ireland after some business in England."

"That the Coors I hear?" Harry inquired.

"Very good, Harry. You approve?" Trundle asked.

"Very much," Harry answered.

"Good. How about a JFL before lunch, Harry?" Trundle asked.

"A JFL?" Harry said. "How do you know about JFL's?" Harry asked.

"Sit, Harry. I'll get us some drinks and tell you a little story."

Chapter 15

As soon as the drinks were delivered by Trundle's executive assistant, Trundle started in on his story.

"I'm sitting in your typical one hundred year old pub in Dublin with two business associates having a few pints and I overhear this guy sitting at the bar order a JFL. The bartender's this crusty old Irishman who looks like he served the first pint when the place originally opened. He looks at the guy and says 'A what?' back at him."

Trundle stopped to have a taste of his JFL. Harry did the same.

"So, the guy tells the bartender it's a half-n-half. Stella Artois for the lighter side of the combo along with your standard Guinness. The bartender tells the guy he's daft—he's never heard of such a thing. The guy proceeds to tell the bartender he was sitting in an Irish Pub in Queens, New York called Patrick's Pub and overheard this other guy ordering it. The guy told the waitress a buddy he knows in Atlanta turned him onto it. It's called a JFL is what he told her."

"You kidding me, Randle?" Harry asked.

"I kid you not," Randle replied. "So, I turned to the guy sitting at the bar and asked him if he knew the Patrick Pub's guy's name. He said he thought the waitress called him by Shorts."

"True story?" Harry asked.

"No bullshit, Harry. Was it you?"

"Well, yeah, it's me. It actually happened just the way he told it," Harry confirmed.

"It's a small world," Randle said. "Here's to your guy in Atlanta, Harry, and a happy JFL to us both."

~ * ~

Lunch completed, Harry and Trundle went out onto the balcony adjoining Randle's office. As soon as they had gotten comfortable Ms. Timmons joined them.

"Mr. Trundle. Shorts," she said as she entered.

"How wonderful to see you, Ms. Timmons," Harry replied.

Timmons smirked at Harry as Trundle smiled quietly. He so loved to see Harry at play.

"We can go over the reports you asked for as soon as I finish my business with Harry, Mr. Trundle," Timmons said.

"You and I are going to get busy?" Harry said to Timmons.

"Harry," Randle said in Harry's direction.

"Business, Harry," Timmons repeated. "I said when we finish our business."

"I'm sorry, Ms. Timmons. Sometimes my mind goes totally blank and I don't hear straight in the presence of such sheer beauty...."

"Harry," Trundle cut him off.

Without hesitating, Timmons started right in.

"The information you asked for went two ways, Harry. Some wasn't easy to get at all, some of it was readily available for anyone to find. The easy stuff first: the site you are looking for is "www.pokcolmon.com" and is the only one of its kind. Easy enough to find, but the security is top of the line. If they don't want you in, you don't get in. And remember, Harry, we have some of the best hackers in the world working for Trundle Industries. They must have a very good anti-hacker working for them as well."

"Interesting," Harry said.

"Not to worry, Harry. It was just a cursory first pass and our guys have assured me they can get in," Timmons told him.

"Good to know," Harry said.

"The group behind it is called CPT, Inc. which is short for College Poker Tuition Incorporated. BrianK, the individual that seems to be the mastermind behind the idea, is a lawyer who has passed the bar in New Jersey and Pennsylvania. He's also known in some circles as somewhat of a computer wiz himself. He is credited with writing a good bit of the computer code behind the fund site set-up with the help of a college buddy by the name of Kevin McCullough. Our guys are familiar with the college buddy's work. A team of programmers would have picked up the slack at some point and performed the bulk of the code work. Long time poker professional Alberto "Y-Man" Yannone was an advisor to the BrianK group and helped with the original site design and set-up. He can be seen on occasion popping up in the marketing scheme still being employed by the group."

"That's good work, Ms. Timmons," Trundle said.

"Thank you, Mr. Trundle," she replied.

To Harry she said, "There are more details in the file, but those are the key pieces of information from what you requested. If you need anything else, we will be happy to look into it further."

"Thank you," Harry said looking at the file. "This should be good for now. It gives me somewhere to start and enough rocks to turn over."

Turning toward Trundle, Harry said, "Thanks, Randle. I appreciate your company's help with this."

"Harry, anything and everything Trundle Industries has is at your disposal. Just ask and it's yours," Trundle told Harry.

Harry looked at Timmons.

"Harry," Trundle said.

Chapter 16

Randle told Harry Charles was available to drive him back to his apartment in Manhasset, but Harry declined the offer. He didn't get into the city that often, or at least not nearly as often as he would like. The world is at your disposal and all is contained right there in New York City. It's such a shame more people don't avail themselves of its riches.

Of course, there are parts of the city and activities that go on that give the city its bad reputation. Every city has them; New York's just get magnified and blown out of proportion. Harry for one was glad he had the opportunity to use it to its fullest.

Harry spent the next two hours strolling through midtown streets and eventually he made his way down to Greenwich Village. Man, he missed the city when he stayed away too long.

~ * ~

The Long Island Railroad deposited him at the Manhasset station and Harry walked the couple of blocks to his apartment. He had glanced at the file Trundle's people had put together for him during the ride, but he wanted to fully consume it in the privacy of his apartment with a cool one at his side. Well, several cool ones to be more precise.

The file took a solid hour to pour through and then Harry read through it again much more slowly. The gist of the information was exactly what he had been told by Ms. Timmons on Randle's balcony. Some additional background on BrianK pointed Harry in a direction to start. How the mastermind behind the tuition fund got his name was conjecture, but sounded as good as any story Harry had heard before. And you have to remember Harry had heard quite a few stories in his short lifetime.

It seemed BrianK has a somewhat famous sister who goes by the name TaraK. No first name, no last name—just TaraK. You see the connection—BrianK and TaraK. The story in the Trundle package of information intrigued Harry. It went something like this:

An insurance appraiser was in a bank for a settlement. As he walked by the office of one of the bank's executives, he saw a picture hanging on the wall. The appraiser also dabbled in the art world, both buying and selling works of unknown artists. The picture on the wall was a TaraK original when TaraK was just that, an unknown artist among so many unknown artists. The appraiser knew different though. He saw the raw talent in the simple work. Now, TaraK originals go for a minimum of fifty thousand dollars, that is, if you can even get one. It's the same TaraK featured in the most recent VW Jetta commercial running on all over the TV.

So what you say?

So, that same bank executive's last name started with a K and he is now the President of a Midwest banking conglomerate. The same banking conglomerate that happens to have a credit card company as part of its portfolio of financial holdings. Coincidence you say; maybe. Too much of a coincidence you're thinking—also maybe. A possible coincidence worth looking into—definitely. A possible coincidence worth looking into that just so happens to be located in the middle of the country—now that's priceless.

The middle of the country is important due to the fact Lee's Summit, Missouri also happens to be in the middle of the country. You now probably have running through your head the question "What's in Lee's Summit, Missouri?" So, I'll tell you.

Doc.

Or, one Kate Martin as she is commonly known by if you're into first and last names. To Harry, she is just Doc. Also, she happens to be on Harry's mind way too much for him not to hop on out there and see what will be.

I realize you need a hint on this one, so I'll get a beer and refresh your memories from one of Harry's prior excursions.

Chapter 17

M. Randle Trundle, Harry's primary benefactor and, as you have seen, CEO of a major New York conglomerate, engaged Harry in an attempt to solve a problem. During that investigation Harry met a most interesting individual of the opposite sex who caught Harry's fancy in a serious way.

Kate Martin, or Doc as she is known by most, took an equally serious liking to Harry. The result was a short but torrid tango that left Harry wondering and Doc wanting. Harry wondered whether this could be the real deal and Doc wanting it to be. When Harry left he said they would get back together and this seemed like the right time to do it.

The rest, as they say, may be history.

~ * ~

Harry pranced into Mel's office and immediately set to work.

"Mel, my main man, my man of all men, the best damn…." Harry started.

"So as to alleviate the need for you to continue to blow smoke in the area where I shit, what do you want, Harry?" Mel asked.

"I couldn't just be here to commend the…"

"No, Harry, you couldn't, and you aren't. Now, I repeat myself, what do you want?"

Looking thoroughly put off, Harry said, "You ever play online poker?"

"Online poker? Do I play online poker? Harry, get this straight. I play poker once a month on a Friday night at the country club so I can drink beers and smoke cigars with the boys. I don't win and enjoy making my monthly donation to enjoy the night out. I don't have one of those email address things people talk about. I don't go on the computer period. So, I ask you, what possesses you to ask such a dumb ass question?"

"Concise, complete, and to the point. That's what I like about you, Mel. No bullshit. No reason to play along and let the person you are speaking with believe a conversation is taking place. Spew forth, shut 'em down. I repeat, that is what I like about you," Harry replied.

"You're still here so I assume you still want something. Does your question have anything to do with the kid's case?" Mel asked.

"Yeah, it does," Harry answered. "In the vast array of adventures I have experienced, online poker has never made it to the 'do dat' stage. Since you don't know jack about it, you happen to know anyone that might?"

"Why should I help?"

"I need to do some research and it's for Max. I would prefer not to go through him to get a quickie education in online poker," Harry answered.

"If I get you someone, will you leave me alone?" Mel asked.

"Yes," Harry replied.

"Consider it done, then. I'll have someone call you."

"You da man, big Mel," Harry said.

"Now will you leave so I can get some work done?"

"Sure, I'm gone," Harry replied.

As he was leaving the office, Harry looked back to see Mel placing his feet on the desk. Sleep-work was about to commence, EBIL style.

~ * ~

As Harry was going up the stairs to his apartment, he heard the phone begin ringing. Getting to the phone on the third ring, Harry hit the speaker button.

"Shorts," he said.

"Tank," came back over the speaker.

"Ah, Tank?" Harry answered in question.

"Yeah, Tank. Mel asked me to call you."

"Oh, sorry, I didn't expect him to get someone to give me a call that soon. This about online poker?"

"Yeah. What do you want?" Tank asked.

"How about a quick lesson and maybe a session online to show me the ropes?" Harry asked.

"For Mel, done," Tank answered. "Meet me in an hour."

Tank supplied the address and was gone.

Chapter 18

The address Tank gave Harry turned out to be a rather nice house in the Munsey Park section of Manhasset. It was a nice house on a non-descript street. You'd never know what you would find inside if you hadn't been in it.

Harry rang the bell and the door opened almost immediately.

"Shorts?" the man that opened the door asked.

"Yes," Harry answered.

"I'm Tank. Come on in," he said as he moved aside for Harry to go past.

"Whoa," escaped from Harry's mouth before he could catch himself.

Another man Harry hadn't seen as he entered the house was now pointing a rather large gun at Harry's face.

"Don't worry, man," Tank said. "I'm just gonna frisk you to make sure you're not wired. Problem?"

"Ah, no, no problem at all," Harry answered. "I just wasn't expecting some guy to stick a small cannon in my face. Go ahead, search away," Harry told Tank.

"Mel's cool, but I gotta protect myself," Tank told Harry.

Search completed, and a thorough search at that, Tank led Harry into a room that would have been the living room in most homes. The decorating motif consisted of poker tables, a fully stocked bar, and a bank of computer screens on long tables that filled one full wall. And, well, there wasn't anything else. Nothing on the walls, no other furniture, nothing that would make you think you had stepped into a "home" as we all would know it. Just poker shit.

"I'd show you the rest of the place," Tank said, "but most of the other rooms look pretty much like this one."

"This is cool," Harry told Tank.

"Drink?" Tank asked Harry.

"Beer would be good," Harry answered.

Tank looked at the guy with the small cannon who immediately left to get the drinks.

"I got about an hour before I have some people coming over.

So, what is it you want to know?" Tank asked.

"Online poker," Harry told him. "How does it work, how do you get to it, and what do I need to know about it so I don't get fleeced?" Harry asked.

"You know how to play poker?" Tank asked.

"Played my share," Harry answered. "No expert, but I can hold my own."

"It's what they all think," Tank laughed in return, "till they're broke and begging for credit. Okay, come on over here and I'll give you a lesson in the basics."

Tank led Harry over to the table on the right and told him to sit in front of one of the screens. He showed him how to log onto the site and used one of his own user names and passwords to get Harry up and running.

"The basic premise is the same as regular poker," Tank began. "The rules are the same, betting is the same, winning and losing is the same. Only difference is you don't get to look at the people you are playing against. With this site you can play in cash games, multi-table tournaments or Sit-N-Goes."

"Sit-N-Goes?" Harry queried.

"Just another name for a one table tournament that usually has nine players sign up before it starts," Tank explained. "Some have six."

"The poker is straight forward?' Harry asked. "No gimmicks?"

"Most of the popular games are available," Tank said. "But, No-Limit Poker is the main game played online. Same as you see on TV with the World Series of Poker, World Poker Tour and the rest of them. You put money in your account and you can play up to that limit at any time. You lose it, you replenish your account."

Tank showed Harry the basics needed to navigate the site and put him in an online room within the site that had a small game of No-Limit Poker being played. The Big and Small blinds—the amount of money the two players to the left of the dealer put up to start the hand—were five (Small Blind) and ten (Big Blind) dollars. The blinds rotate around the board and each player has his turn to ante the blinds.

Harry played for a little over a half hour and lost close to seventy-five bucks. No-Limit wasn't his main game, but he understood how it was played. You could lose a great deal of money very quickly if you were playing for heavy stakes.

Realizing Tank had "people" coming soon, Harry got up to hit the road.

"Thanks, Tank," Harry told him.

As Harry was pulling out some bills to reimburse Tank for the money he had lost using his account, Tank waved Harry off.

"Mel's done me some major solids, man. Consider it my gift to a novice poker player. Maybe you might want to come by some time and get in on a game here. Mel vouches for you, that means you be welcome here any time."

"Thanks, man," Harry told him. "I'll consider it and give you a call if I'm interested."

"Just tell Mel and he'll get me word, okay," Tank told Harry.

"Cool," Harry told Tank. "And thanks."

"Anytime," Tank replied as he showed Harry the door.

Chapter 19

It was a tradition for Max and his sister Briande to plan an entire day out with their dad—Harry. The kids thought up what they would do, they made the arrangements, and Harry would pay. So what else was new? It was called their "Saturdays" together and the kids loved it. Truth be told, Harry wasn't sure who loved it more, the kids or him.

"Max, my main little and getting bigger all the time man," Harry started off the phone conversation. "Next Saturday still a go?"

"Saturday's still a go and wait till you see where we get," Max replied.

"The usual hint, kiddo?" Harry asked.

"Yep—nada," Max replied.

"As I expected," Harry added. "Briande cool with this one?"

"Cooler than a cucumber in a summer salad," Max quipped.

"That cool you say. Your moms home?" Harry asked.

"Yeah, hang tight, I'll get her. Saturday at nine sharp," Max said as he put down the phone to get Harry's ex.

Harry and his ex-wife, Sherry, had been on a better than average wavelength of late. You might almost say they were getting along, but it hinged on Sherry most of the time. The rolls in the sack they had going on lately didn't hurt the equation any.

"Harry, what a surprise," Sherry said when she came on the line.

"I was talking to Max to see if next Saturday was set and figured I'd see if you were around," Harry answered.

"Nice of you to think of me," Sherry purred.

She wants something Harry thought to himself.

"Everything good, Sher?" Harry tried.

"Everything is fine, Harry, but thanks for asking," Sherry responded. "As long as I have you on the phone, I was wondering if you wanted to come over on Sunday and I'll cook you some dinner?"

She wants something Harry thought to himself again.

"That sounds great, Sherry. What time do you want me to

come by?" Harry asked.

"Well, the kids are going on a trip with the school and will be gone all day. They leave around ten in the morning and won't be back until late."

"Late?" Harry inquired.

"Yes, Harry, late. The bus isn't scheduled to get back to the school until around ten that night. They're going to some state park in New Jersey with a lake and they're having a cook-out for dinner. Could be after ten even," Sherry informed Harry.

Harry was beginning to get an inkling of what Sherry wanted.

"You thinking maybe an early dinner?" Harry continued.

"Yeah, I was," Sherry answered. "An early dinner and whatever happens after that."

"Sounds great, Sher. An early dinner and whatever happens after that," Harry confirmed.

"See you around five then? Unless you want to come over and hang out for the afternoon, Harry. Maybe do something before we eat to stir up an appetite?" Sherry asked.

"Anything in particular you have in mind?" Harry said.

"I'm sure we can come up with something, Harry. Don't you?" Sherry said in return.

"If history repeats itself, I'm sure we can, Sherry. I'll see you on Sunday," Harry concluded.

"Okay, Harry. Come any time, and often," Sherry laughed as she rang off.

What came to mind as Harry thought about Sherry's sendoff was: batten down the hatches and hide the women and children.

Chapter 20

When you get spoiled by traveling in style, Trundle Industries corporate jet style that is, commercial travel in the back of the plane pales in comparison, big time. Since Harry had experienced the finer end of the travel spectrum, he was "paling" in spades as he headed out to the heartland of this US of A.

Harry landed in Topeka, Kansas only a slight bit behind schedule. The Mustang convertible he picked up at the car rental lot brightened his spirits immeasurably. Top down, Springsteen blaring on the radio, he was off.

Without anything in particular scheduled, Harry was free-forming it as he liked to say. He had a name, a city, a company name and some additional intel from his main Web Dude, Jaxy.

There will be more to come on Jaxy and his Web Dudes later I'm sure.

Topeka National was the name of the bank that belonged to a larger financial conglomerate. As established in the information Trundle's people had compiled, it was a financial/banking conglomerate that happened to have a credit card company as part of its portfolio of financial holdings. Plus, they were heavy into the education loan business through another of their subsidiaries. You add credit cards and college tuition loans together and it starts to smell of BrianKdom.

Today's agenda called for visiting the target bank and asking questions, gaining information, forming contacts. In essence— snooping Harry Mickey Shorts style. It was one of Harry's favorite pastimes.

The directions Harry got at the car rental counter turned out to be perfect. The bank was right where it was supposed to be. If you follow directions, that can happen some of the time. Other times, not so much. Harry parked in the lot next to the bank and proceeded inside.

It wasn't the biggest bank Harry had ever seen but, there again, it wasn't the biggest town Harry had ever been in, either. Entering the bank it was more wide open than Harry had expected, perhaps a bit homier, too. Or as homey as a bank can be

Harry thought to himself.

There was an information kiosk just inside the main entrance to the bank. Harry decided to avail himself of their services and walked up as confident as could be.

"Excuse me," Harry said to the pretty young thing manning the kiosk.

"Yes, sir, how may I be of service today?" she responded.

Harry shook the combined young thing plus service thoughts from his head.

"Names Sherman, Danny Sherman," Harry started. "I'm new in town and my people should have already been in contact. I'm going to need somebody who can handle a multitude of new accounts both for me personally and my company as well. You have somebody that can do all that?"

"Of course," sweet thing said while looking not too sure about it as the words came out of her mouth.

"Good. That's good," Harry said. "I like to handle my finances on my own and can't stand having to go through different people for different things."

"Let me get the right person for you," she said as she picked up the phone.

Two minutes later a man came walking from the back of the bank in Harry's direction. Harry's first impression as he approached was that he was a Midwestern bank guy. Nice suit but nothing special, plain glasses on a plain face and nothing else to distinguish him from a million other guys. Well there was one thing that did set him apart—his name tag said Ron Schlecht.

"Mr. Sherman, I'm Ron Schlecht. How can Topeka National be of service to you?" he asked.

"Got a multitude of things I'm going to need. Where can we talk?" Harry asked.

"Right this way," Schlecht said.

They walked back the way Schlect had come from originally and entered a good sized office off the main corridor.

"Please, have a seat Mr. Sherman," Schlecht said.

"Thanks, Ron. Can I call you Ron? You can call me Danny."

"Ron is fine, Danny. Now, how can Topeka help you?"

"Well, I got some businesses here and there and I'd like to run the revenues through your bank. We give all our customers credit cards to charge their purchases from us directly. Should be nearly ten, maybe fifteen thousand I would guess if I was to give you a ballpark. We good so far, Ron? You with me?" Harry asked.

"So far Topeka can handle what you have mentioned. Anything else?" Ron asked.

"My philosophy is to treat all my employees like family. I help all their kids with college tuition if they need it. One service fits all you might say. You got anyway to handle that, Ron?"

"The Topeka Corporation has a credit card arm and a subsidiary that deals strictly in educational loan services of all kinds, Danny. I believe we can service your needs quite efficiently at more than equitable market rates."

"Big enough to handle my "size" needs?" Harry asked emphasizing the "size" part.

Ron smiled and said, "Not to brag, Danny, but we handle one particular venture with over one hundred thousand individual credit card holders. We also have a college tuition fund that supports something close to the same number of potential recipients. We're big, Danny, real big. But you already knew that, didn't you?" Ron tested.

"Maybe I did, Ron, maybe I did. Like to know who and what I'm dealing with before I deal with them," Harry responded.

"Fair enough, Danny. Let me show you around our office and then we can talk about getting you familiarized with the Topeka National way of doing business."

"Sounds good, Ron. I'll be back out here in a few weeks and we can sign on the dotted line then. My people will send you all the specifics," Harry said.

"Sounds fine, Danny."

"Now, show me the big guy's office with the TaraK originals I've read about," Harry said. "I like to meet the head man when I do business with a company."

"Right this way, Danny."

Chapter 21

Tooling down the highway with the top down, Lee's Summit, Missouri and Doc in his immediate future, Harry replayed his visit to Topeka National over in his head. Ron had fallen for his pitch hook, line and sinker envisioning big bucks from Danny Sherman and his array of company and personal holdings.

Confirmation was what Harry needed and confirmation was what he got. Topeka had a credit card arm that had one account with over one hundred thousand individual cards issued. Add to that the tuition loan program that matched BrianK's fund to a "T" and Harry had his information. The TaraK original hanging on the wall of the Bank President's office combined with varying pictures of his two kids at different ages was the clincher.

BrianK used Topeka National as the source for his operation's set-up and the location of the fund's deposits. If Harry was right, the Bank President was also the father of the fund mastermind and facilitated the use of the bank's operational units. He may also have provided the original seed money to get the venture started. Whether he was still involved remained to be seen. But one thing was sure, Harry would have to find out a great deal more about Topeka National and its current president.

~ * ~

Board Room Farms was one of the most successful breeding operations in the country. Their racing stable was ever increasing and could compete with the best around as well. To Harry, though, the best asset Board Room Farms possessed was its head veterinarian—one Kate Martin. Or, as she was better known to all who knew and loved her, Doc.

Harry had barely stepped out of the car when the lasso flew over his head and pinned his arms by his side.

"What the hell?" Harry blurted out.

"Wanted to make sure you didn't get away too fast," came a familiar voice from behind him.

"Doc, I won't be doing anything fast for the rest of today and into tonight," Harry said.

"That's all I needed to hear," Doc answered.

Harry turned and removed the lasso. As he was slipping it over his head, Doc locked both arms around his waist and buried her head in his chest.

"Miss me?" Harry asked.

"You bet your cute little ass I did," Doc replied.

"Then let's say we get this cute little ass of mine someplace warm and cozy and get reacquainted," Harry said.

"That's the best thing you've said since you got here," Doc replied.

"But, I just got here," Harry answered.

"That may be true, but it's still the best thing you've said since you got here. Plus, that cute little ass of yours should have been someplace warm and cozy long before now."

"Then, let's get to it," Harry said.

"It is ready for the getting, Harry. It has been ready since the day you left," Doc told Harry.

"Then get, little doggie," Harry teased.

They got.

~ * ~

The sun had gone down while Harry and Doc did their reacquainting. Sitting with their backs to the headboard in Doc's bedroom, Harry asked Doc what she was hard at work thinking about.

"You. Me. This ranch and what I do," Doc started. "I've been thinking about life without the horses and Board Room Farms, my volunteer work at the animal hospital. Life as I've known it for as long as I can remember. I like my life, Harry. It makes me happy."

"There's a whole lot to like, Doc. No reason you shouldn't," Harry responded.

"Yeah, but there's you, if there is a you, or a we?" Doc added. "You're not going to come out here to Lee's Summit, and I don't know if I could be as happy somewhere back east."

Harry didn't answer.

"That all you have to say, Harry?" Doc asked.

"I don't have an answer right now, Doc. It's not an easy one to have an answer for. And I've thought long and hard on it. But I'm here now and that has to mean something. At least for now, today, right this minute. Tomorrow will have to bring tomorrow and we'll see what that is."

"You're right, Harry, you came," Doc said.

"I did," Harry agreed.

As Doc reached over and shut out the light, she said, "And I get the feeling you're about to come again real soon."

Chapter 22

The plane was packed and Harry was stuck in the back of the bus again, sky travel style. The joys of travelling Trundle Industries style were never more apparent than at times like this. But, shitbum Private Investigators travelling on their own dime can't afford the luxuries of the rich and famous or Corporate Honchos.

The kid that wouldn't stop crying, no make that wailing, was about ten rows up and just far enough away so as not to make Harry want to jump out of the plane. Two guys had already threatened to open the emergency exit and jump. Luckily the flight attendants intervened. Harry was fairly close to trying his luck at a parachute-less jump if he could only figure out how to avoid the lovely ladies of the aisle.

Resigned to his present fate, Harry's thoughts wandered freely as he tried to concentrate on the new Michael Connelly book. Hieronymus Bosch was one of his favorite characters, but Topeka National and Doc dominated his brain vision.

If Harry was correct, and all initial indications pointed in that direction, the BrianK camp had an extensive and powerful organization behind them. If President K. of Topeka National was the force behind BrianK, lending both his guiding hand and financial wherewithal, it would seem to be a legitimate enterprise on first glance.

First glances can be deceiving Harry had learned. Perhaps BrianK was on his own now.

Who, what, when, where and how would be the next task. Harry knew them well. They were the basis for all investigations and necessary if one was to fully understand what one was up against. It seemed like Harry was going to take Max's case and he would have to be the one to crack it.

Who is BrianK and who else is involved within his operation? What is he after and what is he getting out of it? When did he start planning it, when did it actually get formed, and when does he plan to get out? Where is BrianK and where is home base for his operation. How did he get the backing and how does he plan on keeping the vultures away—if he does?

Who are these kids that plunk down their money and who says they can? What possesses their parents to let them do it and what happens if/when they constantly lose? When do they get in and when do they get out—voluntarily or otherwise? Where are these kids from and where are the "winnings" going? How can all these kids expect to get to the pot of gold at the end of the rainbow and how does BrianK keep them thinking they can?

Finally, and perhaps the most important question Harry needed to find the answer to was, why?

The second half of Harry's thought wanderings weren't as straight forward. When he was with Doc he was higher than a kite; he's floating on air; he's foot loose and fancy free; he's...you get the picture. The problem is she's there—in Lee's Summit, Missouri—and Harry can't see himself settling down in Lee's Summit, Missouri. City slickers don't go country all of a sudden. Love can move mountains, but unfortunately Harry wasn't even sure he was truly in love, true or otherwise. He didn't even know if he understood what true love was or if he was indeed capable of love. He was and had always been Harry Mickey Shorts— wanderer extraordinaire.

Love may be able to move mountains, but perhaps not Harry Mickey Shorts.

So, "what's one to do?" Harry asked himself. One solution was to find out if there was possible movement on the other side of the mountain. Harry would invite Doc to come east and visit him and let her spend some time seeing how the other part of the world lives. There were horse farms on Long Island, some not too far away in Pennsylvania. If Harry couldn't live in the middle of the country, maybe Doc could live on one of its coasts.

It was worth a try and Harry felt in his heart he needed to give it his best shot. Or, those hot dogs he had consumed at the airport were giving him tremendous heartburn. Either way, Doc coming east was worth a shot.

Max, Briande, Sherry, Big Mel, Ms. Bunny Malone, neighbor Sandy, Trundle and Ms. Timmons were all shadows in the back of Harry's mind as he hatched his plan. Shadows he would have to deal with, skirt, and survive if Doc was to be in his life. If she wanted to be. If he wanted her to be. If it was to be. To be or not to...never mind.

Is she the one after all this time? I don't know. Get her east and give it a whirl. That was your first HMS Question, Answer, Solution (QAS), this one airplane style.

Mama walked by with the wailing kid who happened to be wailing up a storm at that very minute. Harry got up after they went by and headed for the emergency exit. He was saved when the captain came on and said they were about to land.

Chapter 23

Having arrived at his home base in Manhasset, Harry moved on to the next step in his loosely developed plan.

"Maxie boy, fire up the PC and let's have a look at this college tuition fund site of yours," Harry told Max when he called him the following morning.

"You're hot on the trail, Sherlock?" Max asked.

"Pissing away your money like it's going out of style," Harry told him.

"We'll be expected a full accounting of your expenditures, Mr. Shorts," Max replied.

"Yeah, right," Harry replied. "You just watch the mailbox every day and sooner or later that full accounting of my expenditures will show up. For your own good, I recommend you don't hold your breath while you're waiting."

Harry heard Max let out a long breath.

"Funny. Now what do you have that I can look at?" Harry asked.

"We can go three ways," Max told him. "I can show you the 'pokcolmon.com' site itself and we can watch some play going on. Remember, the portion of the site I have access to only shows me what happens after the hand is done. I do know some guys from school that play and maybe I can get them to let you watch some real live play."

"Maybe we go that way if we need to sometime down the road. Not yet, though," Harry said. "What are the other options?"

"Second option is we buy the Under 18 World Championship of Poker DVD that just came out. It has a pretty good amount of play from the tournament including the last table. I know who won, so I haven't bought it yet. Christmas present material I figured," Max said.

"Who gets the revenue from the DVD sales?" Harry asked.

"I'll give you one guess," Max said.

"The one, the only, BrianK?" Harry guessed already knowing the answer.

"Bingo, poppyson one," Max confirmed.

"Okay, third option?" Harry tried.

"There are regional tournaments going on right now that only high school seniors who are registered at 'pokcolmon.com' can enter. It gives them a last shot at making some one-time big bucks and building up their tuition accounts before they graduate. No matter how old you are, when your senior class graduates, it's sayonara time, baby."

"What if you turn eighteen before you graduate?" Harry asked.

"That was a big question early on," Max confirmed. "A mouthpiece from BrianK's organization issued an addendum to the official rules that said you could continue through the actual day in June of the year your senior class graduates as long as you don't turn eighteen before January 1st of that year."

"If you do?" Harry continued the thought.

"Then you're officially done on December 31st of the year you turn eighteen."

"That's it; you're all done?" Harry asked to make sure he understood this particular rule.

"Yeah, they're done except for the year end tournament BrianK instituted last year just for those kids. The tournament was held on the last weekend of the year with the usual two hundred dollar entry fee. It was held in Kansas somewhere and drew almost three hundred kids including a dozen from overseas, plus a busload from Canada," Max said.

"Topeka, Kansas?" Harry asked.

"Yeah, I think that's where it was. A convention hall in Topeka," Max confirmed. "Sounded like a strange place to have it but, nobody questioned it, and kids signed up and went."

"Not as strange as you would think if you knew what I know, Maxie boy," Harry thought to himself.

"Where and when is option three?" Harry continued.

"You're not going to believe this, pops, but it is scheduled for a weekend later this month in Hershey, PA. It's scheduled in the old Hershey Arena next to the new Giant Center where the Hershey Bears play."

"You kidding me, kiddo?" Harry asked in disbelief.

"I kid you not, kiddo," Max replied.

"Road trip?" Harry said.

"Damn right we're going on a road trip," Max replied.

Harry's mind quickly traveled from Hershey, PA to Mechan-icsburg, PA, his prior exploits involving a small insurance company called MechInsCo., and a very special lady.

Chapter 24

Sunday morning arrived like any other Sunday morning in the world of Harry Mickey Shorts. This one didn't include a hangover which was unlike many others he had endured. Routine took over.

The Sunday paper was waiting for him at the door to his apartment. He walked back up the stairs, paper in hand, and got himself a cup of coffee. With everything he needed, he went out onto his deck and prepared to spend the next hour lost in no place in particular. From the sports pages right through to the classified section, Harry would read just about every word of the Sunday paper. What was happening in the United States and the rest of the world was of equal importance to what used golf clubs were available for sale on the local market.

Information overload—Harry Mickey Shorts style.

Two cups of coffee and one Sunday paper later, Harry headed back into his apartment to get ready for the day's activities. He still wasn't sure what he was in for, but a visit with his ex-wife waited.

At twelve noon, Harry rang the bell to Sherry's house. He had stopped and picked up some goodies for lunch and a treat for the Airedales. They barked immediately upon hearing the front doorbell sound off.

The door opened and Harry couldn't get a "Hi Sherry" to come out of his mouth. Perhaps it was the fact Sherry was standing there in her birthday suit that got him. Perhaps it was the fact he always had a quick intake of breath whenever he saw his ex-wife in all her unclothed beauty. All at once he realized it was both of the above topped off by the pink shower cap she was currently wearing.

"Hi, Harry," Sherry said without any apparent problem at all. "Come on in. I was just getting out of the shower when I heard the doorbell and thought it might be you."

Finally mustering the ability to speak, Harry said, "What if it wasn't me?"

"Then there would have been one very lucky guy standing on my porch," Sherry answered.

"That make me a lucky guy?" Harry asked.

As Sherry turned and walked back into the house, she replied, "That remains to be seen, doesn't it Harry."

Watching Sherry walk away, Harry saw all he needed to see and was pretty sure he was going to be a very lucky guy before the day was over.

~ * ~

Sitting at the kitchen table, both of them now fully clothed, Harry dug into perhaps his favorite sandwich of all time. More than a quarter pound of warm pastrami and a slice of melted swiss cheese was piled between two pieces of lightly toasted marbled rye bread, a light smear of mayo complimenting the sandwich beautifully. Wise BBQ chips and a bunch of sweet gherkins filled the rest of his plate.

Sherry had the same minus half the amount of pastrami, the mayo, the chips and the gherkins. A quarter piece of a sliced dill pickle was all that accompanied her sandwich.

"That all you going to eat?" Harry asked Sherry. "And by the way, I still don't think you had to get dressed just to eat lunch. I kind of liked the view I got when I first arrived."

"This will be just fine, Harry," Sherry started. "I don't want to spend the next week in the gym working off the pile of food you're stuffing in your face. And as for my clothing, I make it a habit to wear clothes when I eat. What happens with them when I'm done eating is another story."

Harry looked up mid-bite to see Sherry smiling that come-and-get-it smile she knew drove Harry wild.

"Can I at least finish my sandwich?" Harry pleaded.

Sherry finished the last bite of her sandwich, dabbed her lips with her napkin, then stood and said, "Suit yourself, Harry. Its one-thirty now and the kids will be home around ten. That leaves us less than eight hours to be on the safe side. If you think you can afford the time to finish your sandwich, go ahead. On the other hand, you could wrap it up and take it home with you. Every minute counts when you factor in the new hot tub I had installed on the back porch last week."

"Hot tub? Back porch? Barely eight hours?" Harry repeated.

Sherry's shorts hit the floor as she walked out of the kitchen with "Barely eight hours" trailing behind her.

Harry walked to the back door and threw the rest of his sandwich to the Airedales in the back yard. Passing the kitchen table on his way to the back of the house, and Sherry's bedroom, Harry grabbed the last gherkin from his plate.

"Could come in handy," he said to no one who might be listening.

~ * ~

Harry wasn't sure he could move if his life depended on it. At four-thirty they had hit the hot tub and arrived back in the bedroom some time before seven. He thought he remembered four times, but he could have dreamt one while they napped briefly before adjoining to the hot tub again.

"It's getting late, Harry. You need to be out of here before the kids get home," Sherry reminded Harry.

"I got ya, Sher," Harry replied. "I'll get up in a minute."

"Since we don't have much time, why don't I help you get up, Harry," Sherry said.

With that, Sherry slipped under the covers and helped Harry "get up." They then thoroughly enjoyed the fact Harry was now up and continued to enjoy the up…with the down…with the up…with the down….

Chapter 25

The following Tuesday Harry got his clients together for another brainstorming session on the case. Since he was now committed for the long haul, whatever facts they could provide would be useful in determining his next steps in the investigative process.

Harry greeted the boys when they got to his apartment.

"Jimmy, Robby, Max. Thanks for coming by on short notice."

"Dad," Max started, "we're here. Let's get it going so we can get to the oh so important things we have to do."

Harry looked slightly confused.

"Just busting your you-know-whats, poppyson. We have nothing else to do and nowhere else to be. Ask away," Max said.

Robby and Jimmy nodded.

"Okay," Harry started. "Since the primary concern is what happened to Clint, or Clinton Rensford to be precise, let's focus on who and what he is."

"Who and what he is?" Jimmy repeated.

"Yeah," Harry said. "Who is he? What is he? What do we know about him? What should we know about him? What about his parents, family? Who are his friends? What does he do besides play poker? What does he like to do besides play poker? Yeah, who is he, what is he?" Harry said.

"You want to know all that?" Jimmy asked.

"Who knows all that?" Robby asked.

"We want to know all that. You and the rest of your buds who fronted the big buckaroos this case will cost want to know all that and much more. Could be a hundred thousand dollars by the time we're done," Harry told them.

"Holy Shit!" Robby blurted out.

"Relax, Robby," Max told him. "My dad's just playing with us. Aren't you?" Max asked nervously.

"Yeah," Harry laughed, "I'm just playing with you."

A collective sigh of relief was heard in the room.

"So, gimme the who's and what's."

Max thought for a second and then started.

"We already told you how smart Clint was, ah, is. Top of his class and way over the top on the brainiac scale. It's common knowledge on all the web message boards that Clint has full ride scholarship offers from over a dozen of the top schools, Ivy League included. But, he wants to go to Carnegie Mellon and he wasn't offered any scholarship money to go there. He's bitched about that on his web page over and over again.

"Even though his parents are loaded, they're afraid he'll piss it away playing poker instead of getting an education. The poker "fund" money is going to be used for his tuition at Carnegie Mellon. That comes from rumors on several web pages from kids that say they know him."

"That's interesting," Harry said. "And see, that's some of the what's and who's we're looking for."

"He's also an athlete," Robby added to the discussion.

"Athlete you say? What sport, or sports?" Harry asked.

"He is the star pitcher on his high school baseball team. Rumor has it he has some scholarship offers for baseball to go along with the academic scholarship offers. One school in particular is waiting for his "YES" but he's jerking them along and making them wait," Robby added.

"Now this one is total rumor so far, but one site has a blurb saying he was suspended from his high school team twice for missing practices on Saturday mornings. The rumor was he was playing poker until all hours of the night and he wasn't able to get it going in time to make the scheduled practice. He even missed one game so he could play in a big online tournament," Jimmy chirped in.

"Any piece of this alleged rumor say why he would be holding off on telling the school yes or no?" Harry asked.

The boys looked at each other.

"Well," Max hesitated, "I didn't see it personally, but it was going around that there's this rival school star pitcher that lives in Clint's part of Pennsylvania and he wants to go to the same school. Clint's never used his name on his site, but it has been insinuated he hates a player, a pitcher, on a rival school team. The same rival school team. If you believe this rumor, there's only one scholarship left at this particular college and he's number one on the top of the waiting list for that last scholarship if another "star" pitcher doesn't take it."

"What happened between them?" Harry asked.

Before the boys could answer, the phone rang and Harry got up to answer it.

Chapter 26

Back from his phone call, a pee break, and securing liquid refreshments for himself and the boys, Harry settled in to continue the discussion.

"So, what happened between them—Clint and this mystery star pitcher?" Harry repeated.

"Either nobody knows or nobody's talking," Max said. "Clint never went into any specifics on his personal site from what we heard and any mention of the feud was devoid of specifics."

"And the scholarship is still hanging?" Harry asked.

"Far as we know," Robby confirmed.

"You know the school?" Harry asked.

"Nope," Max answered.

Harry looked at Robby and Jimmy. They shook their heads in the negative.

"Okay, let's let that go for now. I'll do some digging and see what I can come up with," Harry said.

He took a sip of his Sierra Nevada and the boys took a slug of their root beers.

"The tournament," Harry said next. "Let's talk about the big tournament where Clint turned up unconscious."

Nobody said a word.

"Cat got your tongues?" Harry asked.

Still nothing.

"Okay, same deal. Give me the who's, the what's, the "what happened" at the tournament that you definitely know about from start to finish."

Robby took the lead this time.

"Everybody, and I mean everybody, was hyped up over the tournament. The kids registered to play couldn't wait to get there and get started. Plus, it was spring break and all their friends were going to be there to cheer them on. Clint was a god and would be there in the flesh for everyone to see and meet. He was a poker god to anyone who was a part of pokcolmon.com. Maybe you might even get the chance to be the one to knock him out of the tournament they all thought."

"The message boards and kid's personal sites were going non-stop day and night. You'd wake up and see a posting from kids in England, Canada, even a kid coming to the tournament was posting and talking trash from Australia. It was wild, better than…" Max added.

"Better than…?" Harry repeated.

"Never mind," Max replied.

"So, the tournament," Harry prompted.

"They had a pre-tourney thing the night before it started. Go over some rules and let everyone pull their table and seat numbers from this huge fish bowl they had set up in the middle of the room. Clint got to go first so the rest of the field would know what table he was at. Most hoped they didn't get the same table as him to start off the tournament, but a couple of lame-heads were saying they were going to knock Clint out and wanted to get at him right from the get go," Max told Harry.

"Yeah, real pineapple brains," Jimmy added.

The two other boys looked at him compelling Jimmy to look down at his shoes and be quiet.

"Anyway," Max continued, "the Friday thing ended and everyone went up to their rooms to get a good night's sleep. The boards had stories of the parents hitting the tables and partying until the wee hours. One of the fathers hit a slot machine for a twenty-five grand payout. It was wild they were saying."

"Who was saying?" Harry asked.

"Kids that were there. They had their laptops and used their web pages to keep the rest of us who weren't there informed the whole time," Robby said.

"Saturday morning was one of the worst weather days of the year. It just poured like buckets all morning. The kids that weren't staying at the host casino had a bitch of a time getting there. And then it happened," Max said.

"Clint?" Harry asked.

"Yeah, Clint," Max confirmed. "When the tables started to fill up, Clint was a no-show. Ten minutes before the first cards were to be dealt he still wasn't anywhere in sight. One kid in the gallery posted a message saying BrianK was frantic. He had been calling Clint's room on his cell and getting no answer. He started yelling for someone to get upstairs, find Clint, and get his ass down to the tables.

"The tournament was scheduled to start at nine o'clock and every other seat at every table was now occupied. Clint was the only player who wasn't there at nine. A kid that was posting flashed a message saying the guy doing the pre-start announcing got up and said there was an emergency. The start of the tournament would be delayed until ten o'clock. They shouldn't leave the area in case there was a decision to start earlier."

Robby added, "The emergency turned out to be a shit storm in the making."

Chapter 27

"What happened next?" Harry asked.

Max looked at the other two boys and took the lead in continuing the story.

"The same kid posted again at nine thirty and said there was another announcement only a minute before telling the room they would start in fifteen minutes. He then said that one of the players, Clinton Rensford, was ill and would not be participating in the tournament."

Jimmy said, "The kid that was posting for us said the room exploded. Next thing you knew there were postings from twenty or thirty other kids all saying the same thing. They said shouts of 'Where's Clint?' and 'What happened to Clint?' could be heard all over the room."

Robby picked up the story next.

"The announcer guy came back to the podium and quieted the room. He informed all participants they should be at their seats to begin play at ten o'clock sharp. BrianK then took the podium and told the group that while Clint would be unable to take part in the tournament, he was okay and would be fine. All questions that were shouted at him were waved off by BrianK's people and he left the podium without saying anything else."

"It wasn't until the lunch break that postings with any additional information on Clint started to hit the web. We found out Clint had been found unconscious in his room when they went up to get him," Max said.

"Who actually found him?" Harry asked.

The boys looked at each other and they all shrugged.

"We don't know that," Max said. "It must have been BrianK or his people, I guess."

Harry thought for a minute before he continued.

"Let's move on to something else and come back to Clint again later," Harry said. "The tournament started at ten o'clock like they said it would?"

"Yep," Max answered, "and instead of us telling you what happened, we bought the DVD so you can watch it for yourself.

Fire up your laptop and let's watch some poker."

~ * ~

Harry had no idea what he was in for when they fired up the DVD showing the inaugural Under 18 World Championship of Poker Tournament—No Limit Holdem Poker. Much to his surprise it turned out to be a top quality product with excellent coverage. It was as good as the World Series of Poker coverage he watched on ESPN. As it turned out, the credits proved why. The same company that does the World Series of Poker did this video.

"Here we go," Max said as the first hands were dealt on all tables.

Harry interrupted the DVD and asked, "With Clint out, what was the expectation in terms of who would do well, or win maybe?"

Robby answered this one.

"Several players in the tournament were low on the pre-tournament account bankroll list, but they had high expectations in the tourney. Word is they were in the 'need money for college bad' category and practiced forever in the free game part of the pokcolmon.com site. One of them had turned sixteen in the six months before the tournament date but he didn't have money to put up monthly and play regularly."

"How'd they do?" Harry asked.

"Their site names were Tiny22 and BobbyBoy. Nobody is sure of their real names or where they came from. Seems nobody knows them at all and you don't have to fill out the data fact sheets if you don't want to. Most kids do, but they didn't."

Harry repeated his question.

"Let's wait and see," Max replied.

~ * ~

The number of tables surprised Harry. There were nine players to a table and the hands went pretty fast. It seemed all the kids playing were well versed in the rules and there were very few snafus visible. Harry said as much to the boys.

"Remember it is a DVD," Max said. "The other kids in the gallery reported on all the stupid things that went on and had us laughing all the time. One kid who wanted to go ALL IN on a hand and bet all his chips pushed his chips right over to the other kid that was also ALL IN. Would have been better if he at least waited until all the cards were dealt. He lost anyway."

There were some interesting hands and spirited play.

Tiny22, one of the supposed favorites going in with Clint out of the running, had a rough start. On his third hand he had Big Slick—AK of diamonds—and he raised pre-flop (before the table saw the three card flop). The player on the button (the dealer) called his raise. The flop was 6 4 of diamonds and A of clubs. Tiny now had a pair of A's and an A high flush draw—he raised two thousand. The kid on the button called his raise again.

Tiny looked perplexed on the screen, or at least as perplexed as a sixteen year old kid playing No Limit poker for big stakes can look.

The fourth card (the Turn) laid down on the table by the house dealer was the 4 of hearts—giving Tiny two pair. Unsure of his opponent's cards, Tiny checked. His opponent thought for a good two minutes, then checked as well.

The fifth and last card (the River) was the 7 of diamonds giving Tiny an A high flush, otherwise known as a nut flush. Having "the nuts" meant you had the best hand possible for that particular hand. In this case, a flush at least from what you could readily see.

Tiny played it slow obviously hoping to suck in his opponent and made a small two thousand dollar bet. Without hesitation he was called and raised another two thousand.

Tiny was stuck and had no choice but to call the additional two thousand dollar raise. When his opponent turned over his hole cards and showed a pair of sevens giving him a full house, Tiny looked like he was going to cry. The camera held the close up on his face for what seemed like five minutes; in reality it was really only about fifteen seconds.

Tiny said "nice hand" and looked at his chip stack that was now down to four thousand chips from the ten thousand chips he and everyone else had started with.

Tiny22 had a tiny stack.

~ * ~

Harry and the boys watched the first day of play and saw an A high straight lose to a flush, one boat (full house) lose to a higher boat, and a girl from Canada go ALL IN with three Jack's only to lose to three Queen's. End of tournament for her and that should have made all the boys sigh in unison—she was one of the eighteen year olds and quite a looker.

The day had started with a little over thirty-five hundred entrants and ended with just under nine hundred less. The make-believes were falling by the wayside and the players were ready to go to war.

Chapter 28

The boys had headed home which left Harry to watch the rest of the tournament by himself. The boys said they would catch it later since they already knew who won.

Beer at the ready, Harry turned to day two of the tournament. Day one hadn't produced any run aways, so the field at the top was pretty even going into day two. The other pre-tourney favorite was one of the leaders after the first day of play with a little over one hundred sixty-seven thousand dollars in chips. Harry also figured out where the name BobbyBoy came from when he saw that fifth place was occupied by BobbyGirl with close to fifty thousand in chips.

BrianK started off the second day by welcoming everyone still in play and thanking those that had been wiped out on day one for coming and supporting the pokcolmon team. He then said he had a special guest who wanted to say a few words to all the players. Stepping out from behind the curtain at the back of the stage was their god—Clinton Rensford.

The place blew apart when they realized who it was. They stood and clapped. They whistled. Just about every other noise humanly possible could be heard. In short, they showed their love for their god.

Clint waved them quiet and waited for the noise level to get to a point where he could yell over them. When he had quiet, he pointed to BrianK and told them how BrianK personally looked after him in his time of need and that the entire pokcolmon.com organization had been there for him. He then said, "You guys are the luckiest group of kids in the world. You have a man like BrianK to provide the opportunity of a lifetime and it just keeps on coming. Plus, I'm not in this tournament to kick all your asses and take all the money."

The place went wild again.

"Enjoy your game and may the cards light up your lives," Clint told the group.

As he left the stage, every person in the room stood and cheered.

The kid sure knew how to work a crowd.

~ * ~

Day two was more of day one only one day later. Some of the day two highlights were:

In the first hour there were twenty five ALL INS that sent twenty additional kids on their way.

Tiny22, one of the tourney faves who started off day one in a deep hole, played himself back into contention; he wound up with fifteen thousand in chips to start the day and would be in the top 250 by days end.

The conservative play of day one went out the window and reckless abandon abounded.

By half-way through day two a clear leader emerged having accumulated a stack surpassing the million dollar level. He quickly went to two and then three million picking off one ALL IN stack after another.

BobbyGirl remained the top female by the end of day two. She also was involved in the best hand of the day that Harry was able to watch.

~ * ~

Play had started at nine o'clock that morning right on schedule. They played throughout the day and into the evening. Breaks were short and they had one hour for lunch. By seven thirty that evening the kids looked like they were shot. Zombies would have looked better than some of those still at the tables.

The hand that stood out occurred in a back corner table with five guys and four girls at the table. In general, the guys had more of the chips but a few of the girls were holding their own. Harry was sure the boys would have preferred the girls holding something of theirs, but let's not go there.

Here is the point where you get the Harry Mickey Shorts free of charge tiny bit of education for the slightly uneducated in the group. The player to the left of the dealer puts into the pot something called the "Small Blind" and the player to his left puts in the "Big Blind." To stay in the hand you have to at least match the big blind.

In some games every player also puts in an "ante" every hand before the start of play. Other games it isn't until later on when the entire table has to ante on every hand. Right now there is no ante included in the hands.

The hand produced spirited play from the beginning. The kid to the left of the big blind ($1000) raised it up to five thousand—a raise of four thousand. The next two players folded which brought the bet to BobbyGirl. She counted out the five thousand in chips and placed them in front of her stack. As she was pushing them into the middle of the table she said "I'll raise" simultaneously. The kid to the right of the big blind protested immediately saying she couldn't raise as she had already put her chips into the pot.

"I said I was going to raise, Michael," BobbyGirl could clearly be heard saying in response to the kid's protest.

"Chips are in the pot, you can't raise no matter what you say," Michael responded.

The rest of the table was mute.

The dealer raised his hand and called for the director as BobbyGirl and Michael began yelling at each other. Play throughout the room stopped to see what the commotion was about.

From the right of the screen you saw BrianK himself coming over to the table trailed by Clint Rensford. Harry had been surprised to see Clint making the rounds from table to table throughout the day. He was clearly working the tables and encouraging everyone to have fun and play well. As he left each table you could hear his "May the cards light up your lives" trailing behind him.

Harry hit the pause button so he could take a leak and get himself some more liquid refreshment.

Chapter 29

"What's the problem?" BrianK said as he reached the table.

All nine players at the table started to talk at the same time. The dealer spoke directly to BrianK and indicated one player at the table—he pointed to Michael—had protested an attempted bet by another player at the table—he then pointed to BobbyGirl.

The rest of play in the room had virtually stopped. Harry thought it odd this would be covered on the DVD, but watch on he did.

Speaking directly to Michael, BrianK said, "What was the nature of your protest?"

As he was asking the question, another man moved closer to the table to hear what was being said.

"She tried to make a raise after pushing her chips into the middle of the table thus calling the original bet," Michael said. "I saw somebody on ESPN do the same thing and they wouldn't let him raise then either. If the pros can't do it, she can't do it. That's only fair, don't you think?"

BrianK thanked Michael and then turned his attention to BobbyGirl.

"And your response to his protest?" BrianK asked her while flashing her a huge smile.

Clint walked over behind her and put his hand on her shoulder as if trying to calm her down. Harry was beginning to wonder why Clint was all over the place and all over the DVD as well.

BobbyGirl seemed momentarily flustered, then said, "I said I was going to raise as I put the required chips in to match the original bet. I did it together."

The man next to BrianK then spoke up.

"I'm sorry, but you need to announce your intent to raise before you place any chips into the pot. Based on what I have heard, I believe Michael has a valid point and your bet will have to stand as a call only."

BobbyGirl was clearly upset while Michael smiled victoriously as if to say, "Take that you girl you."

The man who voiced the ruling said to BobbyGirl, "I can

take a look at the tape and verify what happened if it would make you feel better."

BobbyGirl half-smiled and said, 'No, that won't be necessary. I'll be more careful in the future. Thank you anyway."

The DVD coverage moved away from that table to show play beginning again in the rest of the room. It also showed BrianK and Clint moving down the aisle together toward the front of the room. The man who took charge and made the ruling disappeared.

Coverage moved right back to the table with BobbyGirl almost immediately. The next two players folded and that left the button, small and big blind players. The button kid with "I'm Sonny" on the front of his tee shirt looked around the table and then announced loud and clear he was raising it to a total bet of ten thousand. The small blind folded and the big blind called reluctantly putting an additional nine thousand in chips in the pot.

Michael quickly called as did BobbyGirl leaving four players in the hand.

The flop came down K of diamonds, Q of spades and 4 of spades.

Big blind checked and Michael began counting out chips. He announced a bet of fifteen thousand as he glared at BobbyGirl. She glared back as she called the bet. The dealer folded, but to Harry's surprise, the big blind also called.

The Turn card was the A of hearts.

Big blind checked again and Michael promptly bet forty thousand.

BobbyGirl checked her hole cards and asked the dealer what the bet was to her.

Michael said, "Didn't you hear me. I said the bet was forty thousand."

BobbyGirl looked at the dealer and again asked what the bet was to her.

Michael stood and looked like he was about to jump across the table until an arm was placed around his shoulder and Clint was seen whispering something in Michael's ear. Michael sat down and didn't say a word.

The dealer informed BobbyGirl the bet was forty thousand to her.

She looked at her hole cards again and looked directly at Michael as she said in a voice players two tables away could hear, "I raise."

She counted out one hundred thousand chips and said, "I raise to one hundred thousand if that is permissible, Michael?"

Clint's hand was now resting on Michael's shoulder.

Without hesitation the big blind threw in his cards leaving it up to Michael to call BobbyGirl's raise.

"I call," Michael said as he counted out sixty thousand chips and splashed them into the pot.

Splashing is when a player throws, instead of placing, their chips into the pot. Splashing can cause the chips to mix with the pot, making it impossible to tell how much money was put in without a recount. It is common knowledge you do not ever splash the pot, not only will it slow the game down, it is a fast way to annoy your opponents.

Even Harry knew splashing the pot was bad etiquette.

BobbyGirl went tsk, tsk.

The River card was the K of spades.

Michael asked the dealer for a count of BobbyGirl's remaining chips. When he was told she had seventy-four thousand left, Michael bet exactly seventy-four thousand and placed them nicely in the middle of the table.

BobbyGirl smiled at Michael and said, "That places me all in if I call, and since I'm already pot committed, I guess I have no choice but to call."

She moved her chips into the pot making the total pot somewhere around a half a million chips and said, "I call."

Michael confidently turned over his cards showing the A and 10 of spades giving him the nut spade flush.

Big blind gave Michael a high five when he saw Michael's cards.

BobbyGirl blinked twice and then turned over her cards. The A and K of clubs gave her a full house—A's over K's—beating Michael's flush.

The four girls at the table stood, pointed at Michael, and said in unison, "Eat shit and die, loser boy."

Harry noticed Clint was now nowhere in sight.

Chapter 30

The rest of day 2 was calm after the BobbyGirl and Michael brouhaha. Play went until eight that night and there was a bunch of tired and hurting puppies when play was adjourned.

The day 2 wrap-up report from Suzie, BrianK's P.R. mouthpiece, indicated the field was now reduced to less than one thousand players. With the scheduled escalation of the blinds for day 3 play, and the institution of antes by all players in addition to those higher blinds, players would be falling very quickly throughout the day.

Before signing off, the mouthpiece, and a very good looking one in Harry's opinion, introduced a special guest segment. She said they would be including these special guest segments right through the end of the tournament.

The first guest was none other than the subject of Harry's inquiries, Clinton Rensford.

"Good evening, Clinton," Suzie started.

"Call me Clint," Clint responded with a big smile for the camera.

"Okay, Clint. Tell us how you are feeling after your ordeal."

"I'm feeling fine. It was certainly a scare but BrianK and his people were great. They got me medical attention immediately," Clint said.

"Any idea what happened? Are there any lasting effects?" Suzie asked.

"No, I have no idea how it happened. I just didn't wake up and the medical personal didn't have any clues either. It was just lucky it happened here and BrianK cared enough to come looking for me."

Harry began feeling like he might barf.

"One last question and then I'll let you go," Suzie said. "How do you feel about missing the opportunity to play in the tournament?"

"It's a bummer," Clint said. "Not playing after all the anticipation and planning is very disappointing. But, even though I'm not playing, BrianK has asked me to stay around and be a part of the tournament committee on an unofficial basis. Plus, he very generously topped off my account to get me to the two hundred thousand dollar level."

"Wow," Suzie said, "That is generous of him."

The camera showed Clint smiling in response and, as if on cue, an arm being draped around his shoulder.

The camera panned back to show BrianK standing next to Clint.

"Clint is an important part of the pokcolmon family," BrianK said. "He's been with us from the start and our aim is to reward the young men and women who helped us become the success we are today."

With that, the screen faded to black and then block letters spelling out DAY THREE came on the screen one letter at a time. They faded away and the chip standings as of the end of play on day 2 popped up on the screen. BobbyBoy was the day 2 leader by over two million chips; Richie from the Isle of Mann was in second with BobbyGirl as the leading girl in seventh place.

Harry was thinking that if he was a betting man, he might place a bob or two on a BobbyBoy and BobbyGirl showdown for the title. He'd probably throw in Richie from the Isle of Mann if he was going to box the triple. Which brought another thought to mind: what are the kids playing for? Scholarship money in their account was the obvious answer, but how much? How many spots are they going to pay, and how much does the eventual winner get?

As if on cue, Suzie's smiling face appeared on screen. She announced another guest segment before the start of day 3 of the tournament.

"With us today we are pleased to have two of the giants from the professional world of poker—Alberto "Y-Man" Yannone and his sister Sally. Welcome Sally, welcome Y-Man," Suzie said.

"Thanks, Suzie," Sally said. "It's a pleasure and a great honor for my brother and I to be here today. These kids should be very proud of what they have accomplished and we're obviously thrilled to see poker being promoted by pokcolmon and BrianK to the younger generation."

"I understand you have an announcement you'd like to make at this time?" Suzie prompted.

"Yes we do," Y-Man said. "BrianK has asked us to come on

this morning and announce the payouts for the tournament. The top three hundred and fifty places will cash and the winner of the tournament will receive a top prize of one hundred and fifty thousand dollars deposited in his or her scholarship account. Second place will receive one hundred thousand all the way down to one thousand for the last fifty places. The total payout will be a cool one million dollars in scholarship money awarded."

The roar that could be heard off camera when Y-Man made the announcement was deafening. The camera panned around to show the players jumping around in the background hugging each other.

It came to Harry in a flash: BrianK was going to make a fortune selling these DVD's at twenty-nine ninety-nine a pop.

Chapter 31

Play on day 3 started out fast and furious. The small stacks were all trying to get back in it with ALL IN big plays and the big stacks were happy to oblige. Their chips were as good as anybody else's. The two Bobby's continued to build their stacks while Richie hit a cold spell and stayed about even for the day.

By the lunch break the tournament was down to less than five hundred players. A short two hours later and the number got down closer to four hundred. Everyone started watching play throughout the room knowing the top three fifty would cash and they didn't want to miss out by being one of the last ones to go bust.

You play to win the whole magilla, but you don't lose out on a chance to cash.

An ALL IN by a medium stack at Richie's table gave him a chance to bounce another player and get back to building up his own stack of chips. There's something in poker called "runner runner" when two cards, the last two placed face up on the table by the dealer, give you the winning hand. Richie got runner runner hearts on the Turn and River to make a heart flush and bust the medium stack who was a kid from Great Neck, Long Island. It's a town one over from Manhasset.

How'd Harry know the kid was from Great Neck? First, as we have come to know, he's a crackerjack private investigator extraordinaire. Second, the kid had on a Great Neck High School Track tee shirt.

By the afternoon break the count of remaining players in the tournament was three hundred sixty-five. Once fifteen more players went broke the remainder would cash and add to their scholarship pokcolmon.com accounts.

During the break, Suzie came on screen with her next guest segment spot.

"It's Suzie here with the first guest "family" segment of the tournament. I have one of the remaining players Mike Fealtman, his sister Tammy who works here at the casino, and their parents. They have an announcement of their own. Michael has accepted a partial baseball scholarship to St. John's University in Queens, New York. Hearty congratulations, Michael," Suzie said to him.

"Thanks," Michael replied. "We're very happy to get this finalized and I hope to make enough here to round out what I'll need to go to St. John's."

As the interview was going on Clint walked by and slid up next to Suzie.

"Hey, Mikey," Clint said, "I just heard you're going to St. John's. That's great. Not as good as North Carolina, but it'll do."

Fealtman didn't say anything but you could tell he was having a hard time holding back.

"I have a little announcement of my own," Clint continued. "I've decided to go to Carnegie Mellon and called North Carolina to tell them I wouldn't be accepting their offer of a baseball scholarship there. Too bad you didn't wait. You were their second choice weren't you, Mikey? Wouldn't want to go back on your word now Mikey boy, would you?"

Fealtman's sister started toward Clint but Fealtman stopped her before she had a chance to do something stupid.

"Later Mikey, Tammy," Clint said with a huge grin on his face. "Gotta run Suzie," Clint said as he turned and walked off camera.

The entire Fealtman family looked devastated.

Without another word to the Fealtman's, Suzie flashed her best P.R. smile and signed off with a, "That's all for now."

Harry now knew the identity of the other star pitcher Max and his buddies had been talking about. He's the one Clint had been essentially screwing royally by holding out on accepting or rejecting the scholarship offer. Harry had watched Clint stab him in the back on camera and twist the knife but good—with a smile.

Chapter 32

Play got very tight. Tension was mounting. Ten more players went bust before the dinner break, but it seemed the last five who would join them and go home empty handed didn't want to go. At ten minutes to eight it was down to one more to go before the "cashees" would be declared. An ALL IN was heard and the whole room stopped play to watch.

A squiggly looking kid with a small stack shoved in all his chips when the flop showed AKJ of diamonds. The big stack at the table, a tallish kid with a buzz cut, called immediately. The Turn and River were two small spot cards, one club and the other a spade.

Small stack smiled and placed his 10 and 8 of diamonds on the table showing his 10 high diamond flush. He had flopped his flush.

The tall kid shook his head and turned over the Q and 4 of diamonds producing the nut flush. Big stack won, squiggly took a hike and the 350 cashees were now set.

The room exploded at that point. There was more high fiving and hugging going on than Harry had seen in a long time. Simultaneously, BrianK stepped to the podium and asked for some quiet. At his side was his new traveling buddy, Clint.

"Quiet down now everyone," BrianK started. I would like to congratulate the three hundred fifty players still in the tournament at this moment. You will all cash."

Loud cheers filled the room.

"I would also like to thank every other player who participated in the tournament and wish them well in their continued play at pokcolmon.com," BrianK continued.

As BrianK began applauding the entire group, the entire room stood and applauded along with him. Clint could be seen on the screen taking the podium.

"Guys and gals," he started "congrats to all of you who will be adding to your scholarship accounts; and to those that didn't quite make it, keep on trucking, man. Tomorrow morning at nine sharp we will continue play and get us a winner. And don't forget,

'May the cards light up your lives.'"

May the cards light up your lives. May the cards light up your lives. If Harry heard Clint say 'May the cards light up your lives' one more time he thought he might just puke.

The players dispersed for the night with thoughts of tomorrow's play and mounds of scholarship money dancing in their heads. At least some of them did. Others had thoughts of what might have been if they had played a certain hand differently, or if one card had turned another way. In other words, thoughts of winners and losers.

Harry decided to hit the sack with high hopes thoughts of cards would darken his mind and he could get some serious shut-eye, pronto-quick like a bunny.

Chapter 33

The following morning, well rested with a coffee cup in hand, Harry fired up his laptop to watch the final day of the tournament. A group of 350 kids would be deciding their college scholarship futures based on the play of what had heretofore been considered a big people's game.

Fast and furious with reckless abandon was the best way Harry could describe the action that ensued. The blinds started out high and escalated faster than shit through a goose. Antes were five thousand a player. ALL INS abounded with the remaining small stacks trying to get back in it in a real hurry. Alas, most hit the bricks, but they hit em with fatter scholarship accounts than when they had arrived four or five days earlier.

Just prior to the lunch break, play concentrated on a table with some loose play and serious stacks of chips. BobbyBoy was still the chip leader by a comfortable margin and raised the pot a million pre-flop. He was probably just trying to steal the pot. After the next two players folded, a re-raise to two million brought plenty of attention from the surrounding tables. The fact a girl had re-raised the tournament chip leader was big doings.

The fact she had on a pink tank top that said Million Dollar Chickie on the front was cool in Harry's mind. The rack that sat behind Million Dollar Chickie caught his attention as well.

Two folds followed to the big blind who promptly went ALL IN with his last six million chips. BobbyBoy called as did Chickie.

The flop was AK of clubs and 7 of diamonds.

Bobby Boy checked to see what MD Chickie would do. She looked at her hole cards once more and bet one million. Without hesitating, BobbyBoy called.

The Turn card was the A of spades.

Bobby Boy looked at his hole cards, counted out some chips, waited a minute, changed his mind and checked.

MDC checked as well.

The River card was the 10 of clubs.

Bobby Boy checked.

Chickie pushed all of her remaining chips into the middle of the table and said loud enough for half the room to hear—ALL IN.

BobbyBoy asked the dealer for a count and was told he would need to call four hundred twenty thousand more.

He called.

By now play had stopped around the room again and the remaining players were watching the action intently. A large number of chips would change hands with the outcome of this one poker hand.

Million Dollar Chickie stood and turned over her cards – she showed a pair of A's giving her a powerhouse of a hand—four A's.

The female contingency in the room exploded.

BobbyBoy looked at the pair of A's Chickie had lain down on the table as if they were a pair of moldy dog turds. Next he looked around the room at the celebrating going on, pushed back his chair and stood. He then turned over his cards to show the QJ of clubs giving him a straight flush. In fact, it was a Royal Straight Flush.

A hush fell over the room. Million Dollar Chickie looked down and saw the cards BobbyBoy had placed on the table giving him the winning hand. "I'll be a son of a bitch," was all she said.

Clint appeared out of nowhere and put his arm around Million Dollar Chickie's shoulder to offer condolences on behalf of himself, BrianK and all of the pokcolmon family.

Chickie looked at Clint, said, "Fuck you, Clint," and promptly left the room.

Chapter 34

By six that evening the final table was set. Nine players were left with BobbyBoy having accumulated more than twenty million chips. Richie from the Isle of Mann had just under seven million and BobbyGirl's stack was at five million even. The other six players at the final table were sucking wind compared to the three leaders.

Play began and it was clear a good portion of the players were dog tired. Four hands later the final table was down to six and another player dropped on the next hand. Nothing spectacular— ALL IN's, lose the hand, and head on home with a fattened scholarship account.

BobbyBoy had won the two largest of the ALL IN's adding to his commanding lead. Richie remained in second place and BobbyGirl closed the gap on Richie slightly.

The next hand was a doosie!

The only other girl left at the table, who had on a New York Yankee cap, went ALL IN and was immediately called by the player to her left with the same number of chips left—helicopter beanie cap and all. Richie thought about calling and looked like he was trying real hard to convince himself he should, but eventually he folded. That left the Bobby's.

BobbyGirl was next and she spent very little time considering the situation or her position—ALL IN was her call.

BobbyBoy smiled and said, "No thanks," and tossed in his cards.

Not surprising at all, Clint appeared across the table from the camera and he was now positioned prominently in view.

Three players went to the flop with Richie and BobbyBoy out of the hand. They were left to observe the outcome.

The other girl at the table (YankeeGirl to Harry) who had gone ALL IN showed a pair of 6's, helicopter boy had KQ of hearts. BobbyGirl laid down the AK of diamonds.

Question: if AK is Big Slick, then would that make AJ Little Slick?

The flop came down J of clubs and 7 and 6 of diamonds giving YankeeGirl a set (three of a kind) of 6's and BobbyGirl a flush draw.

BobbyGirl and copter boy were in trouble.

The Turn card was the 2 of hearts—no help to anyone.

Helicopter boy could now fire up his engine and fly off into the sunset—stick a fork in him cuz he was done.

The dealer tapped the table, buried a card, and turned over the River.

The 5 of diamonds.

BobbyGirl had made her flush.

YankeeGirl was toast.

BobbyGirl screamed.

BobbyBoy smiled.

Clint smiled, and although you couldn't hear what he was saying over the screaming and cheering that was going on everywhere, you could see him mouthing the words into the camera—May the cards light up your lives.

Harry didn't smile, but he did hope the wiz he was about to take would light up his life.

Chapter 35

Sans a life enlightening experience, Harry took up his position in front of his laptop to watch the finals of what he was now calling the MTCLUYL tournament.

BobbyBoy was in command. He had more than double the number of chips of either Richie from the Isle of Mann or BobbyGirl. From his play it was clear he was determined to use it to his advantage and bully his last two competitors on the way to the championship.

His main target was BobbyGirl. Any hand she played, BobbyBoy raised her unmercifully. If Richie folded pre-flop, BobbyBoy raised enough to put BobbyGirl ALL IN on every hand. To her credit, she held her ground, folded her cards biding her time.

On the fifth hand, Richie must have been dealt a load and determined it was his time. He pushed in his chips and declared, "I'm ALL IN for my tournament life."

BobbyBoy said, "Okay, Richie, I'll play. I call."

BobbyGirl folded as quickly as she could.

Richie turned over his cards to show AK of spades. He was betting the last of his chips on the big one—Big Slick as an Ace and a King together were also known by in poker circles. But you already knew that by now, didn't you.

BobbyBoy winced when he saw Richie's cards. He turned his over to show the AQ of hearts.

BobbyBoy was dominated.

The dealer buried a card and turned over the flop—10 of spades, 4 of hearts and 2 of clubs. A rainbow of no help to either Richie or BobbyBoy.

Richie had three cards to a spade flush and BobbyBoy three cards to a heart flush. Richie still dominated BobbyBoy.

The Turn card was the 7 of spades.

Richie now had four spades to a flush and still dominated BobbyBoy's AQ with his AK—Big Slick. An A, a K or any spade and he won. Only a Q could beat him and send him to the sidelines to watch the final two players battle it out.

The dealer tapped the table, buried a card and turned over the

River.

Q of diamonds.

BobbyBoy had a pair of Q's and won the hand.

When the Q hit the table, he jumped in the air and pumped his fist, a "Yeah, man," punctuating his leap.

Richie was shown staring at the cards on the table and shaking his head.

"That's poker," he said as he shook BobbyGirl's hand. She gave him a hug and kiss on the cheek. At least he got something out of the hand.

Richie and BobbyBoy shook hands and Richie went off to watch the finals chatting with the ever present Clint along the way.

Harry was sure Clint was explaining to Richie how the cards had truly lit up his life.

The Bobby's would do battle for the championship.

~ * ~

After a short break, they returned to the table to finish play—mano a girlo. Before they started, BrianK took the podium and again thanked every participant for joining pokcolmon for its inaugural "Under 18 World Championship of Poker" tournament event. He thanked the parents for supporting their kids and all the friends that had come to cheer on their favorite competitors. He promised everyone this was just the beginning of great things to come, and then he yelled, "Let's Play Poker!"

BobbyBoy dominated BobbyGirl more than three to one in chips as they began play. With blinds of one million and two million plus antes of one hundred thousand each hand, BobbyGirl needed a big win and quick.

On the first hand, she took her shot.

"Let's give it a go. I'm ALL IN, BobbyBoy," she said.

"I'm sure you have me, but we came to play, so let's play. I call," BobbyBoy answered.

BobbyGirl turned over her cards—a pair of K's hit the felt.

"Nice," BobbyBoy said as he laid his cards on the table. The crowd could see on the overhead screens BobbyGirl's pair of K's had his QJ of hearts covered.

BrianK, Clint, Suzie and the rest of the pokcolmon.com entourage encircled the table to ensure maximum exposure should the tournament end with this hand.

The dealer turned over the flop to show the K of hearts, 4 of diamonds and 7 of hearts.

The crowd erupted at the sight of BobbyGirl's set of K's. Harry noticed it was mostly the female contingency that did the erupting led by BobbyGirl herself. The little jump and twirl she did was impressive.

BobbyBoy stayed quiet and looked at his flush draw.

The dealer waited for the room to quiet down, tapped the table, buried a card and showed the Turn card.

9 of spades—no help to either Bobby.

One more no-help card and BobbyGirl would double up and get right back into the tournament. BobbyBoy needed a heart, any heart other than the 9 or 4 of hearts. Either of those would pair the board and give BobbyGirl a full house.

"A blank, gimme a blank," BobbyGirl shouted.

The dealer tapped the table, buried a card and turned over the River card.

The other side of the house erupted when the dealer showed the 8 of hearts giving BobbyBoy his flush. He had won the first ever "Under 18 World Championship of Poker" tournament.

After a full minute of "Oh, Yeahs" and fist pumping gyrations, BobbyBoy went over and gave BobbyGirl a big hug. They congratulated each other and held their clasped hands high.

The crowd roared their appreciation.

BrianK was at the podium starting the tournament ending festivities, but Harry had no interest. He turned off the DVD player and started his normal process—what did I learn and how can I use it.

Chapter 36

Harry had spent the better part of an hour going over what he had seen and heard on the "Under 18 World Championship of Poker" tournament DVD. It turns out it was co-produced by an affiliate of the pokcolmon.com organization. When he was done he realized he didn't have much.

What did he need to find out to determine if there is actually something to this? Information. Jaxy.

Having formed a classic Harry Mickey Shorts QAS, he dialed the phone to get it moving.

"Jaxy, my man, it's Harry. You be down?" Harry asked him.

"Like a pillow full of feathers," Jaxy responded.

How the hell was he always so fast was what Harry always asked himself when he talked to Jaxy.

"What can I do you for, dude?" Jaxy continued.

"Some solid intel that's not for the common man," Harry told him.

"You know where to go, you know where to wander and you know where to stop," Jaxy answered.

Harry had no idea what the hell Jaxy was talking about.

Harry laid out the information he was looking for, what he didn't know, and what he wanted to know.

Jaxy, being Jaxy, understood both.

"Buckets of bucks behind this scenario dig, you dig?" Jaxy asked.

Harry deciphered, then said, "I dig, my man, I dig. But, unfortunately this time it's on me, something I'm looking into for Max, so tread lightly so's I can eat this month."

"I'll twinkle toe my way through the tulips and do a solid for my brother Maxy. This one be on the hacienda," Jaxy said. "You, you'll owe the Dudes a heavy next time down the sixty-six, H-a-r-r-y," Jaxy dragged out.

The 66 had Harry confused until he figured out 66 meant Route 66, or down the road. Understanding Jaxy got to be more trying every time Harry talked to him.

"Cool," Harry said.

"Cooler than an Eskimo's ass on the outhouse throne," Jaxy answered and he was gone.

~ * ~

With his intel machine on the case, Harry headed up to EBIL's office to see what was up with his favorite ex-brother in law and his delectable assistant. Entering the office, Harry stopped dead in his tracks.

Sherry was standing there talking to Mel. While doing so, she was locked arm-in-arm with an Adonis look-a-like, or wannabe.

Harry quickly tried to retrace his steps and beat a hasty retreat, but he wasn't quick enough.

"Harry, come on in," Mel boomed.

Sherry turned to see Harry re-entering the office.

"Hi, Harry," she smiled.

"Hi, Sher. Didn't expect to see you here," Harry stammered.

Mel sat there silently laughing his ass off.

"Hey, sis, aren't you going to introduce your friend to Harry?" Mel said.

Sherry turned to look at Mel. Her face said that's enough you instigating bastard. Her mouth said, "Of course I am. Harry this is Brad; Brad, Harry."

"Pleasure," Brad said flashing enough white to blind a blind man.

"Glad to meet you, Brad," Harry returned.

"Well, we better be off," Sherry said. "See you, Mel. Later, Harry," Sherry said as she and Adonis moved past him.

Once they were gone, Mel proceeded to make like he was busy with work totally ignoring the fact that Harry was still in the office.

"So?" Harry said.

No response from Mel.

Harry waited a minute, and then he repeated, "So?"

"Okay, since you're helping Max, I'll talk. Brad is a present I gave Sherry. Got his services in a deal I did last week with a guy who needed an apartment fast and cheap. He runs a Personal Training company and Brad's one of the personal trainers. Ten sessions free of charge and I gave it to Sherry."

"And?" Harry pressed.

"Oh, alright. Only because of Max and since I already got my jollies by seeing your face ten minutes ago. Word is Brad the hulk's got a shwance the size of a Redwood and wields his sword any chance he gets. But," Mel continued by pausing for what seemed like forever to Harry, "he's gayer than a three dollar bill."

Mel's laugh boomed throughout the office.

"Asshole," Harry said over his shoulder as he left the office.

Chapter 37

Harry had Googled Clinton Rensford and found out he lived in Pennsylvania not too far from Mechanicsburg. You will recall one of Harry's previous adventures dropped him into that burg for a rather interesting case, plus extras. Very interesting extras they were, Harry Mickey Shorts style.

Since the high school playoffs were underway in Clintonland, Harry decided to do a bit of snooping while also getting to enjoy some baseball as an added bonus. On Friday morning, he fired up his vintage Datsun B210 HoneyBee (circa 1975) and hit the road to catch some high school baseball. The Mustang Mach I was a bit too noticeable Harry decided.

With a cooler fully loaded with liquid refreshments, a Subway 12-incher plus a bag of cheddar chips for nourishment, the Allman Brothers providing the musical company, he was off.

The field was typical for high school baseball fields these days. It was better than some of the minor league fields Harry played on when he made his much too short foray into professional baseball. As it turned out, Clint's team was playing the local rival high school with both Clint and Fealtman scheduled to pitch. The locals in the stands proved to be very vocal and sentiment sided with the underdogs finally succeeding in bumping off the Clint led bullies this year.

Harry had brought enough aluminum encased liquid refreshments so he could share with his fellow fans. Should they get to talking while they shared a brewski or two, all the better. Sharing and talking didn't seem to be a problem with the four guys sitting right in front of Harry. The conversation reverted from baseball in general, to Clint and his team of bullies, and finally to Clint himself and his "friendly" rivalry with Fealtman.

"Clint can plain assed bring it," the guy they called Shorty said. "Fella with one of them guns had Clint at ninrty-four miles per hour he said."

"That's bullshit," a Fealtman fan answered.

"He showed me," Shorty replied.

"Fealtman can throw just as much heat and his bender rolls

off the table," the F-fan told Harry.

Top of the third and no score yet. Clint had allowed a bloop single and struck out four. Fealtman was perfect with three strikeouts through the first two innings.

"Come on boys, this is our year," came a voice from behind Harry.

"Yeah, we gonna do it to them, boys," Shorty agreed.

The game continued and Harry settled in to watch the action. The Subway tasted great and he shared his chips along with his brews. Through five there was still no score and both Clint and Fealtman were in control of the game.

Clint was the lead-off hitter in the top of the sixth. The first pitch was a fastball just low and outside followed by a curve ball that really looked like it fell off the table. With the count one ball and one strike, Fealtman wound up and fired a high hard one that knocked Clint on his ass.

Clint jumped up and yelled at Fealtman.

Fealtman smiled.

Both benches were on their feet and it looked like Harry was in for a real old fashioned donnybrook of a fight. Before anything got started, both coaches jumped out of their dugouts and yelled at their players to get back into the dugout and sit down. The umpire pointed fingers, issued warnings, and then he yelled loud and clear for all to hear, "Let's play baseball."

Since it was a playoff game with the winner playing the next game for the right to go on to the state championship tournament, Harry was fairly sure calmer heads would prevail. They did. Fealtman had gotten his point across and he and Clint actually smiled at each other before another pitch was thrown.

Play continued and there was still no score as they went to the bottom of the seventh—the last inning in high school baseball. Tensions were strung out tight with a chance to play for the right to compete for states still on the line. With one out and a man on first, Fealtman came to bat. Clint looked in for the sign from the catcher, got it and went into his stretch. Before he could throw a pitch, Fealtman dove backwards like he had been buzzed up and in by a Clint speedball.

The place went crazy.

The umpire called time and Clint lobbed the ball toward the plate like it was slow pitch softball. The uproar continued.

With order now restored, Clint delivered the first pitch to Fealtman and he laced a line drive over the second baseman's head into the gap in right center. The runner on first took off with the crack of the bat and sped around second heading for third. The third base coach was waving him around all the way yelling for him to "Go, Go, Go…"

The relay throw from the second baseman got to the plate at the same time as the runner. In a slam bang play, the umpire yelled "SAFE" and Fealtman had driven in the winning run to give his team the victory over the hated Clinton led bullies.

The fans from both teams yelled long and loud. But, as the players from both teams lined up for the congratulatory handshakes, the fans stood and applauded two teams who had played one hell of a baseball game. As he walked back to the bench, Fealtman fist pumped the air that would have made Tiger proud. For once, he had won. He'd gotten the best of Clinton Rensford.

Chapter 38

Harry hung around after the game waiting to see what Clint was going to do. There didn't seem to be a school bus, so the kids must have gotten to the game on their own.

Fifteen minutes of saying goodbye to his new found friends and sucking on a last cool one, Harry found himself watching Clint hook up with what Harry assumed was his parents. He moseyed on over to console the loser boy.

"Great game," Harry said to Clint as he stepped into their space.

Clint looked at Harry with that "who are you" look. His parents did the same.

"Do we know you?" said the guy Harry took for Clint's father.

The turned up collar on his Izod golf shirt, tailored shorts and Gucci loafers sans socks spoke of his status when it came to the wealth category.

"Actually, no you don't," Harry replied.

Everyone looked at each other waiting for Harry to continue. He didn't.

"Let's go," Clint finally said.

Harry smiled his killer smile and said, "I'm Johnny Blanchard. No relation to the Yankee. Glad to meet you Clint. You're Clint's parents I presume?"

Clint looked at his father who looked back at Clint.

"What is it we can do for you," Clint's father said stepping between Harry and his wife and son.

"It's actually what I can do for you," Harry started. "I work for a Major League Baseball affiliate as a roving advisor assessing talent for them countrywide. Well, worldwide actually. I was here today to watch Clint in action and I had hoped to get a few minutes of his, and also perhaps your time, to chat."

Harry's statement produced quizzical looks all around from the Rensford family.

"Clint will be attending Carnegie Mellon in the fall," Clint's father said.

"We're well aware of that," Harry replied. "We like to build a complete file on all the talent we consider to be of major league quality whatever their immediate plans might be."

"Major league quality?" Clint repeated with obvious interest.

"I'll handle this, Clint," his father said as he turned his attention back to Harry.

"What is it you want, Mr. Blanchard?"

Harry did a quick assessment of his options and winged it. Nothing ventured, nothing gained he thought to himself.

"I just wanted to introduce myself and let Clint know he is on our radar screen. Carnegie Mellon is an excellent institution and will provide Clint with a top notch education. Accepting North Carolina's scholarship offer would have pointed Clint in a different direction, but everyone must make the decision that's best for them.

"Plus," Harry continued, "the poker scholarship money will be put to good use at Carnegie Mellon."

"Poker scholarship money? How do you know about that?" Clint's father asked. He was obviously taken aback by Harry's knowledge of the existence of that fund.

"Mr. Rensford, we make it our business to know as much as we can about the individuals we are interested in," Harry replied.

The quizzical looks among the Rensfords returned.

Harry thought he'd take a flyer and see what kind of reaction he could get.

"The pokcolmon.com group and BrianK have been good to, and for, Clint. His continued association with them isn't a concern for us at all. The medical situation at the tournament had us a bit worried, but BrianK and his people were right there to do whatever was necessary to ensure Clint was well cared for," Harry said.

"College is expensive, and even with your considerable financial wherewithal, two hundred thousand is nothing to sneeze at," Harry continued.

With a stern voice and obvious agitation, Clint's father said, "Mr. Blanchard, we're done here. My family's wherewithal and Clint's "association" as you call it with the PCM group are of no concern to you and whoever you work for. Don't bother Clint or my family again or I'll take measures to ensure you don't."

As the Rensfords hurried away, Harry called to their backs.

"Thanks for your time, Clint. And yours, Mr. Rensford."

Harry had hit a nerve with his pokcolmon comment and he couldn't help but wonder why. That would need some serious follow up.

Chapter 39

Saturday morning came and Harry arrived at his kid's door precisely at nine o'clock sharp as he always did. Their Saturdays together started with Harry picking them up at nine and heading over to IHOP on Northern Boulevard for a veritable breakfast feast.

Today was no different than their preceding Saturdays together.

Before Harry could get out of the flaming red Hummer he had rented for this particular Saturday's adventure, Max and Briande came bounding down the steps and hopped in the car. To say they were anxious to get the day started would have been a major understatement.

"Nice wheels, poppyson," Max said as he got settled in the back. He deferred to his older sister Briande and gave her the front seat.

"Very nice, daddy," Briande said demurely.

"Hints?" Harry tried.

"IHOP," Max offered.

"Anything else?" from Harry.

"All in due time," Briande replied with a smile.

This must be a good one Harry thought to himself.

Once they had stuffed their faces and stretched their stomachs to the point of bursting, Harry pointed the Hummer for the George Washington Bridge as instructed. Dave Mason took them part of the way followed by U2's Joshua Tree. Briande would get her choice on the ride home.

One hour and two minutes later they arrived at their destination. To Harry's surprise, Ms. Timmons, Trundle's number one assistant was waiting for them at the entrance to what looked like an entertainment park.

Harry rolled down the window to greet Timmons.

"Ms. Timmons," Harry greeted her.

"Harry," she replied.

Jumping into the back seat of the Hummer, she said, "Max, Briande, how are you both today?"

"We are dynamite," Max said with just a tad too much excitement.

Briande seconded Max's sentiment with a bit more reserve.

Harry gave a, "Good, I guess," in reply.

"Park this monstrosity in the lot over on the right," Timmons instructed.

Harry obeyed as instructed.

Once everyone had exited the monstrosity, Harry asked, "What is this place?"

"May I, Max?" Timmons asked.

"Be my guest," Max replied.

"This park is part of Trundle Entertainment Enterprises," Timmons began. "There are a number of like and kind amusement parks around the country that Mr. Trundle commissioned to cater to the specific needs of the local communities and regional interests. Max and Briande did some research and found it on the company website. They thought you might like what we have to offer and called me to help them set up the day."

"What is it that is offered at this particular site that might interest me?" Harry asked.

"I have some business to take care of," Ms. Timmons said. "Max and Briande will take over from here," she finished as she walked off.

Harry enjoyed watching Ms. Timmons walk off until Briande cleared her throat thus spoiling his fun.

"Let's go big guy," Max said. "We have a lot to do and we only have all day to do it."

"This way," Briande told Harry as she led him towards the open gates in front of them.

Once inside, Harry saw a picture of a grand prix racing car on a huge sign just inside the entrance. Just below the sign was a replica of the same car. They were greeted by a man in overalls with a patch on his left breast indicating his name was Wes.

"You two must be Max and Briande. I'm Wes," he confirmed. "And you would be Harry I take it?" extending his hand toward Harry.

"Harry Shorts," Harry replied shaking Wes' hand.

"Great. If you'll are ready, let's have some fun."

Chapter 40

"Holy smokes," was what came out of Harry's mouth when they rounded the corner to the right of the grand prix racing car sign.

"Isn't it cool, daddy?" Briande said.

"Cool? Cool doesn't even begin to describe this place," Harry replied.

They were looking out at a one mile grand prix racing style track that snaked in all directions in front of them. There were overpasses and small tunnels, banked turns and hairpin turns. Cool really didn't begin to describe it.

To the right was a line-up of grand prix replica cars suitable for amateur racers like Harry and his brood. Stenciled on the side of the first three cars in big, bold letters, they could see Max on the blue car, Briande on the pink one, and Poppyson on the red one.

"This here is Blue," Wes said as a wiry guy approached them.

You guessed it—he was dressed in blue from head to toe.

"He's gonna give you the low down on how to run these beauties through the track and how not to kill yourselves while doing it. And do me a favor, don't kill yourselves. Mr. Trundle hears about that kind of thing he'll have my hide for sure."

Everyone laughed.

"Hi'ya, folks. Let's go inside and I'll give you the lecture on how to navigate the track. Then we can come on back outside and I'll demonstrate how you start up one of these machines and how you can have the most fun with em. Plus, I'll tell you again not to get hurt so Wes here doesn't have to deal with Mr. Trundle. We like Wes and aim to keep him for a spell longer."

"What do you think, poppyson?" Max asked.

"Way cooler than cool," Harry replied.

"We agree," Briande concurred.

Blue took them into the building behind the cars. There they found a wall size rendering of the track with multi-colored electrical lighting to illustrate different sections of the layout. Blue explained to them what speeds to use in each of the intervals around the track and where to "step on it" to get maximum lap times. Next he took them over to a car in the middle of the room to demonstrate how to shift gears and work the break and gas pedals separately, and in tandem, all-the-while up-shifting and downshifting.

Close to an hour after they had arrived at the park, Blue said, "Questions?"

Quiet as a mouse.

"No. Then let's go out onto the track and have some fun."

Max was the first to actually venture out onto the race track. The electric board on the infield in the middle of the course had been turned on. Each of their names was listed on the board. Blue had explained that their lap times would be displayed on the board along with the cumulative time for the three laps they would run.

Blue made sure Max was ready and then told him, "Remember, Max, these aren't go karts. Take two or three practice laps and then come back into the pit. We'll make sure you're set, then you can head back out for your timed laps. And Max, have fun big guy."

The smile on Max's face left little doubt fun was about to be had.

Harry and Briande watched Max fire up his racer and roll out onto the track. By the time he went by after his first lap he had the car moving at a fair clip. The second pass was what Harry would have called "hauling ass." As Max brought his car into the pits, you could see the exhilaration on his face.

Harry and Briande went over to him when his car came to rest.

"Was it fun?" Briande asked.

"Fun? Man, it was a blast," Max shouted. "Let me at that track. I'm gonna burn it up," he continued.

Blue stepped up to make sure Max was set for his timed run. When he was satisfied Max wouldn't kill himself trying to break the land speed record, he sent him back out onto the track.

Max took one lap around the track to get up to speed and hit the starting line flying. He handled all the turns and curves with care and gunned it on the straight-aways. When he had completed his three laps, his combined time was three minutes and fifty-five seconds with the last lap the fastest at one minute and ten seconds.

Harry high-fived Max when he got out of the car.

Max beamed.

Briande was next to go and took her car onto the track like she had been racing them her whole life. Her practice laps were smooth as silk and fairly quick for the first time out.

Blue got her ready and sent her on her way for her timed laps. Harry watched her carefully and swore she was at home in that car. Her three-lap time was five seconds behind Max's. Harry was fairly sure she dogged the last lap to make sure she didn't come in under Max's time. He knew Briande and she wouldn't deflate Max for some stupid car time.

Harry went next and had the time of his life. The car flew when he gunned it and turned on a dime in the corners. On the last turn of his third lap he wobbled and limped across the finish line ten seconds behind Briande's combined time.

Max was the grand prix champ, but both Harry and Briande knew.

Chapter 41

The day just kept on getting better. After a great lunch on a balcony overlooking the entire park, Ms. Timmons joined them for dessert. The four of them took golf carts to a back piece of the park. There they (without Ms. Timmons) donned life jackets and traversed the white water rafting river that wound around the whole park. Their guide took them over small falls and chose the roughest channel for the last quarter-mile bringing them back to where they started.

Coming up the bank after they exited the raft, they were met by Ms. Timmons who was standing next to a small minibus.

"Have fun, guys?" she asked.

Briande couldn't help herself and blurted out, "It was great!"

Harry and Max agreed with Briande with only slightly less exuberance.

"Alright then, let's get in the bus and head on over to the tower," Timmons told them.

"Tower? What tower?" Harry asked hesitantly.

"Come on daddy," Briande told him. "You're gonna love this."

Harry looked at Ms. Timmons who shrugged her shoulders in an "I don't know" gesture.

"Okay, let's go," Harry finally agreed.

The tower, much to Harry's dismay, proved to be a one hundred fifty foot tower with a platform on top. As soon as Harry saw it he knew what it was and knew this might be going just a tad too far.

"Bungee jumping?" Harry exclaimed. "Haven't we already done enough today trying to end our lives?"

It was Briande and not Max who said, "Come on, daddy. You only live once and you haven't gone bungee jumping yet."

"I didn't know it was required," Harry replied.

Ms. Timmons shrugged her shoulders.

Harry had always wanted to try bungee jumping, so he was actually excited at the opportunity to try it. He wouldn't let the kids know that, though.

"Okay, here's the deal," Harry said. "I go on up that tower and do this under one condition. Ms. Timmons joins us."

"Oh no you don't," Timmons said immediately. "I'm just here to facilitate. You're not getting me to climb that thing and then jump off of it. No way, no how," she continued.

"Fine, then I'm not either," Harry said.

"Ms. Timmons," the kids pleaded in unison.

"Harry," Timmons pleaded her own case.

"You and me or no can do," Harry insisted.

Realizing she couldn't disappoint Max and Briande, Timmons reluctantly agreed. Mr. Trundle would have been proud of her.

The four of them climbed the tower and prepared for their jump. Jumping in twosomes, Max would go first with Briande, then Harry and Ms. Timmons would follow.

Maybe.

Tethered and ready to go, the kids yelled Geronimo and leapt off the platform. Harry could see them descend, hit the low point and then rebound high into the air screaming all the way. Multiple bounces later, they were raised back up to the platform.

Giggling like school kids, which they were, Max and Briande hugged Harry and told him to get Ms. Timmons and get the show on the road.

Getting Ms. Timmons sounded good to Harry. The "show on the road" part had less appeal.

With the bungee cords securely in place, Harry and Timmons were ready.

"Have fun," Harry told her.

"I'll get you for this," Timmons told Harry and she jumped with a trailing OOOOOHHHHH SSSSSHHHHHIIIIIITTTTT that could be heard all the way down and back up again.

Harry laughed and jumped.

~ * ~

Sitting on a blanket laid out on the grass inside the outdoor concert amphitheater, the four of them laughed and agreed they had a blast bungee jumping—even Ms. Timmons.

As dusk fell, the headliners took the stage for the concert that would round out the kids' Saturday with their dad. It had been one of their best.

A small crowd of two hundred of Mr. Randle Trundle's hand

selected guests were scattered about on blankets of their own.

Harry nearly shit himself when The Boss himself took the stage.

Chapter 42

Online poker sites took a recent hit as the government tried to ride roughshod over the industry. One of the biggest sites had been shut down and all of them were changing their modus operandi to try and stay out of harm's way.

Harry signed up for one of them and deposited a modest amount to get online and play. If he was to fully understand what and how things went on in this alien world he figured he better get the inside poop up front and personal.

May cost him a few dollars, but research was sometimes painful. The bikinied babe that graced the site entry page eased a bit of Harry's pain.

A rainy Saturday afternoon seemed like the perfect time to do some research. He logged on and selected a Sit-N-Go $5 No Limit Holdem two table tournament that was scheduled to start in twenty minutes. Cooler of beer at his side, he was ready to do battle with his fellow contestants.

The tournament started and he was seated at his table. When the cards where dealt he hit an Ace and was on the button as the dealer. Being a novice Harry decided he'd bide his time and get a feel for how these tournaments went.

Each player got $1500 in chips to play with. Harry hoped this wasn't one of those sites where players talked on the phone to each other as they played. He'd read about the practice during his online researching, but a $5 Sit-N-Go didn't seem like it would be worth it.

For the first twenty minutes of play, Harry contributed the small and big blinds when required, folded his hands and watched play. He was biding his time. A few players seemed to raise with the often stated "reckless abandon," while others played mortal lock hands only. The fact he had shit cards contributed to his inaction.

A bit of impatience combined with a pair of K's brought Harry into play. The player to his right (RedDog) raised the $50 big blind to $100 and Harry re-raised to $200. Not exactly tiptoeing into play, but not bulldozering in either. Two players called plus the original raiser.

The flop was QJ of diamonds and 7 of spades.

Harry had the K of diamonds.

RedDog bet $200 and Harry called. Maybe he should have re-raised again but, not knowing exactly what his hand called for, he just called the $200.

The other two players folded leaving two players in the hand.

The Turn card was the 10 of diamonds giving Harry a pair of K's with four diamonds to the K—an open ended straight flush draw.

RedDog checked. Harry paused, looked at his pair of K's, and then checked as well. Sounded good at the time.

The River card was a red 9, but not diamonds. It was the 9 of hearts giving Harry a straight to the K.

RedDog checked again giving Harry the feeling he had top hand with his straight to the K.

Harry bet $300.

Without a seconds hesitation RedDog went ALL IN.

"Oh shit," escaped from Harry's mouth.

Had he been suckered in by RedDog? Sure. Run for the hills and fold.

A classic QAS that gave Harry a no-brainer solution.

But what could RedDog have? With no pairs on the board, he could have a pair down and have trips. Harry had learned trips didn't mean multiple vacations. It meant three of a kind. If that was the case, Harry's straight would win the hand.

Or, he could have an eight for a lower straight than Harry's. Or, worse still, he could be holding AK and have a straight to the A. Harry would go down in flames if that was the case.

But, he hadn't bet like he had the high straight. He had checked. Twice—before and then again after the River. Maybe he was trying to bluff Harry out of the pot.

Harry realized a pro would know what to do. A good amateur probably would know what to do. Him, in this case he was a dumb shit without a clue what to do.

The clock was winding down and he had to decide.

He called the ALL IN for all his remaining chips.

RedDog's hole cards appeared showing Big Slick (AK) giving him an A high straight. Harry's hand said MUCK and the little pop-up screen informed Harry he had finished in eighteen place.

His first tournament and Harry had finished dead last.

He was out $5 and hadn't learned a whole lot. He did have some fun and would be better prepared the next time he played online. After all, he still had just south of $95 in his till.

Chapter 43

The next week dragged case wise. The Web Dudes hadn't produced anything useful yet and Harry had nothing on the agenda to investigate. He did some needed work in and around his apartment and hit the links for a game of golf with Mel's buddy, Shack. Mel was too busy trying to keep his head above water to join them.

He didn't sell any houses and would have felt better chasing the little white ball around the course. Plus, the beers on the course and in the clubhouse after would have helped brighten up his mood.

Thursday afternoon was a total washout with enough rain to clear all the bird shit off his deck railings. You put up a bird feeder, you get bird shit. It wasn't an absolute washout, though.

Around about five that afternoon, his neighbor Sandy stopped by with a plate of Chicken Cordon Bleu. Turns out that wasn't all she brought. When she took off her rain coat, she had on an orange string bikini and nothing else.

"It's new, Harry," Sandy told him. "I wanted a man's opinion before I wore it out to the Hamptons this weekend."

Harry had her turn around to get a look from all sides.

"You like it?" Sandy asked.

"I like it a lot," Harry told her. "It seems to fit you quite nicely and shows off your better features."

Sandy smiled.

"But," Harry continued, "you don't want to take any chances that you might get some of that Chicken Cordon Bleu on it before you get to show it off this weekend."

"What would you suggest?" Sandy asked.

"I suggest you take it off right away just to play it safe," Harry replied.

Sandy agreed with Harry. As she removed the bikini she told him, "I'll play, Harry, but safe isn't what I had in mind."

The bikini hit the carpet and play began in earnest.

~ * ~

As planned, Harry picked up Max and his buddy Robby after school on Friday. They then got Robby's dad at the Manhasset railroad station and headed south. The Regional pokcolmon.com tournament Max had told him about was scheduled for this weekend beginning Friday evening. The fact it was just a stone's throw away from Mechanicsburg, PA, and that very special lady from his recent past, was an added benefit in Harry's mind. Finagling a visit might not come to be, but the possibility existed. After all, what more could a lowly P.I. wish for.

Plus, there was Tom, his buddy and prior mentor, who lived there as well.

The ride south went smooth. They pulled into the Marriott Residence Inn parking lot at a few minutes before seven and they were checked in and back in the car in twenty minutes.

Max and Robby were excited to be going to their first live tournament. Even though they couldn't participate, they knew Clint was a possible participant, or at the least, he might be there in person for them to meet. Kids never change when it comes to something new and exciting in their tunnel-vision view of the world.

Harry doubted Clint would be there since he had received the top-up from BrianK during the Championship Tournament.

Wonders never cease—Harry was dead wrong.

~ * ~

Just as soon as Harry had parked the car in the lot outside the tournament venue, Max and Robby bolted from the car and streaked for the entrance. It was a few minutes before eight— tournament starting time.

Harry and Robby's dad exited the car and took their own sweet time as they strolled on over to the door. Robby's dad, who had introduced himself to Harry when they first met as Robert, not Bob, opened the door.

Harry's first thought upon entering was, "Put a tent over this circus and gimme some popcorn." The size of the venue was the first thing that caught Harry's attention—it was much larger than it looked from the outside. That was of course secondary to the sheer madness that was going on before him. These were only kids Harry had to remind himself, but there were so many of them all trying to act like they were twenty years older than their actual ages. After all, they were POKER PLAYERS today!

Kids were all over the place, in every outfit you could imagine, one more outrageous than the next. Harry immediately zeroed in on BobbyGirl's ensemble which was not to be missed. Fire engine red leotard top with the mid-drift cut out in a diamond shape exposing a belly-button ring they screamed "I'm made of diamonds." Her jeans were cut so low on her hips there was no way she could have gotten away with them without having shaved her nether region. Since her leotarded upper body advertised a no bra, big boobs, silver dollar nipple view not normally found on immature members of the opposite sex, Harry was sure a tidy shave job had been performed out of necessity.

Not that he was looking, but P.I.'s need to be observant.

The crowd of boys around her seemed to be being equally as observant.

Harry had pity for any male player that found himself at her table. Concentration on the game at hand would be nearly impossible.

Chapter 44

Tearing himself away from the vision that was BobbyGirl and her temporary entourage, Harry found Max and Robby seated front and center in the "Peanuts Gallery." It was set up to mimic a high school gym with a fold down seating section that jutted out of the wall. It was jammed with kids of all sizes and shapes all of them equally as jazzed up over what was about to take place in front of them. Above the section they were seated in was a large banner screaming "Peanuts Gallery" as if those in attendance didn't already know who had stormed that section of the venue's seating.

"Peanuts" was another name for the kids that couldn't play yet.

Robert was front and center at the makeshift bar set up for the parents, family and friends who were there to hopefully watch the youngsters add to their college accounts.

No reason not to be friendly, so Harry joined him.

"Beer, Harry?" Robert asked.

"One for now will do," Harry answered.

Robert thought about that, smiled like he got it, and ordered Harry a beer—just one.

"Thanks," Harry said when Robert handed him an Amstel Light.

At least it was cold.

Before he could say anything else, BrianK took to the podium to start the evening's activities.

The drone of noise lowered to a murmur as all eyes were on BrianK.

"Well, well, well," BrianK started along with a big smile. "It does my heart good to see all of you here for the East Regional pokcolmon.com tournament. We had four hundred twenty-seven players registered and all but two have signed in and are here to-night."

Applause from the crowd coupled with a few whistles and a whoop or two. Nary a holler though—just whoops. Robert nearly dropped his Amstel Light trying to join the crowd.

"I'm not going to keep you long," BrianK stated. "There are plenty of hands to play and money toward your college scholarships to be won. So let's get this thing started. Just before we do, I wanted you all to hear a word from one of you—Clint Rensford."

Plenty of whoops and hollers could be heard as Clint took to the podium.

Waving his arms to quiet the crowd, Clint said, "Once again it's a true pleasure to be here with BrianK and his team to cheer all of you on and join them in helping each of you increase your scholarship accounts. You know what I'm gonna say, but I'll say it anyway—Enjoy your game and May the cards light up your lives."

Cheers went up as BrianK took the mike and said, "Let's play cards."

~ * ~

The first night of play was set to last a maximum of either three hours, or one hundred players going bust, whichever came first.

Three hours of Amstel Lights was more than one human being could, or should, be required to tolerate. Harry drifted away from the bar as play began.

The view as seen through a private investigators eyes is much different than the view seen by mere mortals. Harry's view as we have come to learn is weirder still.

First and foremost in Harry's viewfinder was BobbyGirl and her eighteen year old leotarded body. It was barely thirty minutes into the evening and her chip count was already climbing. The play at her table seemed normal to Harry, or as normal as Harry could figure with his limited knowledge base with which to work from. The only odd thing was BobbyGirl's uncanny ability to win all the big pots. The boys at the table were obviously ogling her very ogleable frontal headlights, but they weren't folding away pots. BobbyGirl had the winning hand in every pot Harry saw her play through the River.

Coincidence or plain dumb luck?—maybe.

Coincidence or plain dumb luck six hands in a row?—still maybe. But surely worth watching in Harry's mind along with those very ogleable aforementioned frontal headlights.

Harry may be getting older, but he ain't dead yet.

Chapter 45

Exactly three hours from the starting time of eight sharp, play ended at eleven on the dot. A total of fifty-nine players had busted out and headed home. BobbyGirl had personally sent eleven of them on their way. The ten boys she bankrupted would have plenty to dream about tonight.

Soon after play ended, Harry rounded up Max, Robby and Robert and headed for the exit. As they made their way toward the exit door, Clint crossed their path.

Max and Robby couldn't help themselves.

"Clint," Max started, "Can we get an autograph on today's program?"

Finding the obvious pair of "Peanuts" in his path, Clint stopped and broke into a broad smile.

"Not a problem at all," Clint replied as he took the program from Max with Robby impatiently waiting his turn. "You guys enjoy the action tonight?" Clint continued.

"Yeah, it was cool," Robby replied.

"Would have been great to see you in action," Max added.

Clint thought on that for a second and then he said, "I'd have loved to be in there mixing it up with the rest of the guys, and gals. But, I have my max money and enjoy watching the rest of the players fill up their accounts just as much. BrianK and his pokcolmon.com team are doing great things for us kids—don't you guys forget that, Peanuts."

Harry mused on what he had just observed—autographs provided, company line spoken, day's work accomplished.

Harry also observed Clint walking through a door at the opposite end of the room into the pokcolmon.com lounge area his arm hugging BobbyGirl tight to his side.

When they got back to the Marriott, Harry said, "Enough excitement for one day, guys?"

"It was way cool," Robby said.

"And meeting Clint was more than way cool," Max added.

Harry looked at Robert who had made the acquaintance of one too many Amstel Lights, and said, "How does eight sound for tomorrow? We can get some breakfast and maybe take a quick tour around before we head over to the venue."

Robert nodded and led Robby into his room without saying a word.

"Eight it is then, I guess," Harry told Max. "Let's hit the sack and get plenty of rest for tomorrow, okay, kiddo?"

"You got it, poppyson. And thanks," Max said.

~ * ~

While Max went out like a light, Harry sat up for a while and reprocessed the day's events in his mind. There was Max and Robby acting like kids in a candy store with a fist full of pennies in their hands. Robert and his Amstel buddies might have been nothing more than boredom, or maybe there was more to it. Not Harry's problem.

Clint, BrianK and the pokcolmon.com team cozy as bed bugs in a ten year old mattress.

BobbyGirl...well, just BobbyGirl.

Clint and BobbyGirl joined at the hip.

BobbyGirl winning every hand Harry saw her play.

The case, or lack thereof.

His hefty retainer, or lack thereof.

Enjoy your game and may the cards light up your lives.

All of them were individual thoughts running through Harry's mind. No rhyme or reason connecting any dots, just thoughts.

One more thought, though.

BobbyGirl, the diamond cutout, the jeans, the dreams....

Chapter 46

At eight sharp the following morning Harry knocked on Robert and Robby's door. Max was already in the car eager to get the day started.

Robert answered looking slightly worse for wear.

Robby bounded out, said good morning to Harry, and jumped in the back seat with Max.

"You good to go, Robert?" Harry asked.

"Give me five minutes and I'll be right with you. That good with you, Harry?" Robert asked.

"Right as rain, Robert," Harry answered. "You want a quick beer to kick start your day? I have some in the room," Harry continued.

Robert blanched and closed the door.

"Guess not," Harry said to nobody who might be listening.

Perhaps ten minutes later, Robert came out and got in the front passenger seat.

"All set?" Harry asked.

Robert just stared ahead without answering.

Harry didn't think Robert's Amstel posse would be joining him any time today or night.

"Ready boys?" Harry asked Max and Robby.

"You bet, big guy," Max replied. "Let's blow this popsicle stand and get the day moving."

Harry started the car and rolled out of the parking lot. With nary an IHOP in site, Harry settled on a diner that looked like it could slop some pretty good mush on their plates. Standard greasy food and mediocre coffee that would warm any road warrior's heart.

When their food arrived, Harry saw he had hit the proverbial nail right smackeroo on the ole' headski.

"Not hungry there, Robert?" Harry asked with a slight smile.

"Coffee will be fine for this morning," Robert responded.

"These eggs are the best I've ever tasted," Robby beamed. "Slopping up the yokes with the toast, and the bacon, and the home fries," he continued to boast of its greatness.

"Good choice, poppyson," Max agreed.

Robert took another look at what Robby was eating and excused himself from the table...in a real hurry. By the time Robert returned, Harry and the boys had finished eating and Harry was taking care of the check.

"You gonna make it there, Robert? You look a little piqued around the gills," Harry said.

"I'm fine, Harry," Robert replied. "Are we ready to go?"

"You bet," Harry replied.

To add insult to injury and break a few stones, Harry added, "I hear they have great roller coasters over at Hershey Park. You game for a few thrills, Robert?"

Looking like just the thought of riding a roller coaster might make him barf, Robert just walked away.

"Guess that's a no, hey poppyson," Max said.

"You got that right, kiddo," Harry replied.

"Let's head out that way anyway. I wanna get a look at Hershey Park and the Giant Center where the local hockey team plays. I think they're called the Hershey Bears and have a pretty good team every year. The place they played in before the Giant Center was built is still standing and it's the oldest hockey arena in the country. Be neat to see." Harry said.

"Cool," Max said. "I brought mom's digital camera along with me and we can snap some shots if you want. She even knows how to get pictures out of this thing, too."

"No shit," Harry replied.

"I shit you not," Max agreed.

Robby looked at Max and said, "You can say stuff like that in front of your dad?"

"Yeah, poppyson's cool as long as my moms isn't around. If she caught me saying stuff like that she'd kick my ass," Max told him.

"I guess some dads are just cooler than others," Robby said as he turned and headed over to find out why his father was bent over behind the car.

Chapter 47

While Robert napped in the front seat, Harry and the boys managed to get inside both the Giant Center and the old Hershey Arena. Harry loved the old park and thought that's the way all hockey rinks should be built. Nostalgia hung from every rafter and spoke to you as you circled the arena. They don't make em like that anymore Harry thought to himself; and what a shame they don't he added to himself as well.

Harry almost always listened to himself.

After a quick breeze by Hershey Park, they headed back over to the venue where the tournament was being held. Play was to start at 11:00 am and the boys wanted to get primo seats in the "Peanuts Gallery."

BrianK and Clint were stationed just inside the building on opposite sides of the main entrance. Meet and greet was another way of proving the pokcolmon.com organization cared about their family. The high five Max and Robby got from their idol Clint made their day.

"Hi, I'm Harry Shorts," Harry said as he shook BrianK's hand. "I think what you're doing here is great and I'd love to talk to you about it some if you have a minute later on."

"Sure, Harry," BrianK said in reply. "Talk to one of the gals and they'll set it up," he continued as he walked past Harry to greet the next person entering the building.

Fat chance is what he was actually telling Harry in his most pleasant pokcolmon.com organizational tone.

"Sure, thanks, I'll do that," Harry replied to BrianK's back realizing it would never come to pass.

The boys had already moved over to the Peanuts Gallery and wedged themselves into second row center seats. As an added bonus, they looked thrilled Clint was sitting right next to Max. Harry could tell from looking at their faces, to be in the company of the top account player was a true privilege in their eyes. Harry, he couldn't give two rat's asses.

As play was gearing up to get started, Harry saw one of the pokcolmon.com "gals" as BrianK called them walking in his direction. No reason not to take a shot, so he did.

"Excuse me," Harry started, "BrianK suggested I speak to a member of his staff to set up a few minutes for me to speak with him later on today. Would you be able to help me with something like that?"

Seemingly put out she had to even stop and dignify Harry's question with an answer, the "gal" gave Harry a look that people get on their face when they realize they just stepped in dog shit, and said, "Yeah, like that'll happen."

She then turned and walked away.

Harry's previous realization it would never come to pass came to pass.

"Thanks so very much, sweet cheeks," Harry said to her back.

The slightest hesitation in her step told Harry she heard him and wanted to retaliate, verbally or otherwise, but chose to keep on walking instead.

"Sweet cheeks indeed," Harry said quietly as he turned to the person behind the make-shift bar and ordered a bottle of the local favorite—Yuengling. It was after twelve somewhere in the world.

Harry spotted Robert coming in his direction. He held the bottle up as an invitation for one, but Robert turned and walked back where he had come from.

"Hair of the dog," Harry yelled to his back.

Robert kept on walking.

"I'll have one with you, Mr. Shorts," Harry heard from behind his back.

"Great," Harry said, "and I'll even buy, whoever the hell you are."

"The name's Frenchie," the man said as he extended his hand to Harry.

"No need to say I'm Mr. Harry Mickey Shorts since you already know I'm Mr. Harry Mickey Shorts. Or at least Mr. Shorts," Harry replied as he shook Frenchie's hand.

"No, probably not, Harry. How can I help you?" Frenchie asked Harry.

"Lemme be sociable and I'll buy you a cool one. Maybe then you can tell me who you are and what you might be able to do for me," Harry answered.

Chapter 48

Handing the man who called himself Frenchie the best choice available, a long neck Yuengling, Harry said in his best French accent, "So, who are you, M'sieur Frenchie?"

"Frenchie will be fine," he replied with a small grin. "I work for the organization," he told Harry.

"THE ORGANIZATION!" Harry quizzed with a raised eyebrow.

Frenchie frowned over Harry's question for a few seconds, then understood.

"No, Harry, I work for the pokcolmon.com group," Frenchie corrected.

"Oh," Harry replied.

Sips of long necks ensued.

After the appropriate waiting-him-out-time, Harry said, "And what do you do for the organization?"

The appropriate emphasis on "organization" could be heard very clearly in Harry's question.

"This and that," Frenchie replied.

"This and that?" Harry repeated as a question.

"Yeah," Frenchie repeated again, "this and that."

"More this than that?" Harry quizzed.

Frenchie smiled knowing Harry was playing with him.

"Depends on what's required, this or that," he finally answered.

"And I'm getting this because I'm not getting that?" Harry asked.

"The best you're going to get is this, Harry. If we are speaking of the same "that," and I believe we are, then "that" isn't going to happen."

"No "that" today?" Harry asked.

"Most likely," Frenchie said, "no "that" ever."

"Worth our time "thising" it any longer?" Harry asked.

"I have all day and all night, but "this" is as good as you're gonna get, Harry," Frenchie indicated with a tip of his long neck.

"Be sure and thank BrianK for allowing me to take up your

time with all of this "this,"'" Harry said as he turned and walked away.

~ * ~

Robert was leaning against a wall watching the beginning of play. Harry could see the boys were doing the same in the Cintified air of the Peanuts Gallery.

Harry sauntered over to Robert.

"Anything interesting going on," Harry tried.

Harry still wasn't sure how much of this poker thing Robert grasped but, considering where they were, it was a good way to break the ice.

"Lots of cards being dealt. Lots of betting going on," Robert said without turning his head.

Pretty observant for a guy standing in a room where a poker tournament was going on Harry thought.

"Any interesting cards? Any interesting betting?" Harry tried.

Robert did not respond.

Harry watched Robert's eyes as they scanned the room moving from table to table. He looked like he was actually paying attention to every detail, at every table, throughout the entire room. But, at regular intervals, his eyes averted back to the table where BobbyGirl was playing.

Harry assumed he was interested in what was going on at that particular table for some reason, or he liked the BobbyBalloons.

Harry didn't mind them either.

"Robert?" Harry said to get his attention.

Coming out of his trance, Robert turned toward Harry.

"Yes, Harry," he said.

"I asked if there were any interesting cards or any interesting betting."

"Yes and no," Robert replied. "Let's take a walk, Harry."

Robert headed for the door and Harry followed. When they were outside, Robert turned to Harry and said, "Harry, I work for a special group and I'm here on official business. I'm trusting you with that fact because I believe I can. Don't disappoint me."

"Special Group?" Harry asked.

"Special Group, Harry," Robert confirmed.

"So, what are you after? Or who?" Harry asked.

"Harry, I'm going back inside and do what I was doing before. You do your thing, but do it alone. Let me do my thing, alone. When I can, if I can, I'll tell you more. But not before, so don't ask," Robert finished as he walked past Harry back into the tournament venue.

"I'll be damned," Harry said to Robert's back.

Chapter 49

A "Special Group" is what he said. Robert was with a Special Group. An honest to god fucking Special Group. An honest to god, hung over man that works for a Special fucking Group at that.

Question was—what in the holy name of hell was a Special Group supposed to mean?

Harry prided himself on being able to dope out who people were and spot a particular type of person. Robert didn't fit that category. Harry had failed to spot it. Either he was getting soft, or Robert was damn good at what he does. Harry was hoping it was the latter.

Re-entering the building, Harry spotted Robert standing in the identical spot he was at before they went outside. His eyes were scanning the room as he sipped on a long neck. He was back in the saddle.

Harry grabbed another long neck and positioned himself across the room from Robert. He had an identical view of the room from the opposite side. What Robert looked at, Harry looked at. When Robert sipped his long neck, Harry sipped his. When Robert farted, Harry farted.

Well, at least Harry farted. Luckily it was quiet, and it wasn't SBD.

Harry spotted an ALL IN call at BobbyGirl's table and she called. Looking up, Harry saw Robert intently watching that table's action as well.

The River was a small spot card—a two. That gave Bobby-Girl a small straight beating the ALL IN kid's two pair. BobbyGirl had busted another player's dreams of victory and scholarship riches.

When Harry looked up, Robert was gone.

After that last hand a break was called. Harry wandered over to the Peanuts Gallery to see if the boys needed anything.

"Hungry?" Harry asked Max and Robby.

"Yeah," Max said.

"Yeah," Robby eloquently agreed.

"Come on, let's get something to eat and you can tell me what's going on at the tables."

"Cool," the boys said in unison.

They made their way to the concession stand and loaded up on burgers, fries and cokes. Well, the boys had cokes. Harry availed himself of another long neck. They found a table in the back of the room and settled in.

"So, what's been going on?" Harry asked the boys.

"Clint says the kids that should be doing good are doing good," Robby started.

"Yeah, a few surprises Clint didn't expect, but in general it's going as Clint would have expected," Max chimed in.

"That's nice," Harry said.

The boys looked at Harry expecting him to continue.

Harry sat quietly and ate his burger and fries, drank his beer.

"That's nice. That all you going to say?" Max asked him.

Harry looked at the boys, then said, "No sense in talking to you two. If I want to know what's going on I'll ask Clint directly since you two only seem to parrot what he says. If you don't have an independent thought between you, why waste my time."

"We were just saying…" Max started before Harry cut him off.

"No, you weren't saying anything. Both of you told me what Clint said, not what you saw and thought. You want to try again?"

Max cocked his head in thought, got it, and then nodded.

"Yeah, you're right as usual, poppyson."

Robert sat down just as Max was about to tell his side of what was happening. Robby got up immediately and walked to the head.

Chapter 50

Sprinkling some salt and pepper on his fries, Robert asked, "What are you guys talking about?"

Robert didn't seem to even see Robby walk away, or didn't care.

Harry answered, "I was asking the boys what's been going on during today's play."

"And?" Robert added.

"And," Harry said, "you sat down and Robby got up and walked away."

Robert added a piece of lettuce from his plate to his burger and an extra shot of ketchup as well. He took a bite of his burger without saying another word to Harry or Max.

Max looked at his dad as if to say, "What's up with this dude?"

"It may be none of our business, but just so we know what's going down, did you and Robby have some kind of disagreement?" Harry asked Robert.

After finishing the food in his mouth, Robert wiped his lips with his napkin and replied, "Nothing there, Harry. Let it go."

Harry gave Max a look. Max promptly got up from the table to go in search of his friend Robby.

Harry watched Robert take another bite of his burger, chew his food, and wipe his lips as he had done before.

Being the curious type, Harry said, "What the fuck's wrong with you?"

Before Robert could answer, Harry's cell phone rang. It was Jaxy.

"I gotta take this," Harry told Robert. "We can discuss what just happened later, but this ain't done."

Robert didn't say a word in reply.

"Jaxy, my man, got some scoodle to ya doodle?" Harry said into his cell phone.

"Harry, mon compadre, my doodle been scoodlin every which way including tight," Jaxy replied. "Mostly scoodtoodily-tight," he finished.

"Tight be where it's at," Harry added.

"You got dat, Scat," Jaxy finished.

"Info down?" Harry asked.

"Down and around, like Strangers in the Night done found their way to Hotel CalifornicatinIfreakinA," Jaxy answered.

"Spill," Harry said.

Jaxy spilled.

When he was done, Harry smiled.

"You da man as always, Jaxy," Harry told him.

"Yeah, da man with the moolah in the can—ya dig me?"

"First thing, Jaxy. Payment in full shall find its way to the usual account with your very generous Max discount taken into consideration. And thanks, I needed this shot of know-something," Harry told him.

"Sometimes knowin' somthin's like knowin' nothing, only now ya know it," Jaxy said as he disconnected.

Harry had no idea what the hell Jaxy just said, but it sounded deep.

~ * ~

When Harry got back to the table, Robert was gone. Max and Robby were nowhere in sight. The sounds from the inner room led Harry to believe the tournament was about to start up again. With nothing better to do, Harry reentered the tournament room.

Chapter 51

Robert was across the room holding up the same wall just as he had done before they went off to fill their collective bellies. Scanning the rest of the room, Harry saw Max and Robby back in the Peanut Gallery taking in the action. Clint was nowhere to be found.

As he did before, Harry watched what Robert watched. A funny feeling that Harry couldn't quite put his finger on that Robert was more than advertised made Harry look at him in a different light. He wasn't a dad that came along for the ride because his son wanted to go and watch a poker tournament. His interest level surpassed the casual observation point. He was watching and retaining what he saw.

BobbyGirl was what he saw the most. Robert's interest moved from table to table throughout the entire room. But, when he centered in and concentrated his attention for any length of time, BobbyGirl was front and center every time. As we have discussed previously, front" being the primary operative word with BobbyGirl.

Harry didn't know why, but Robert didn't strike him as a tits kind of guy. They were great tits, young ones, and there was no denying they were great tits, but not Robert's cup of tea. No rhyme or reason to his theory. Harry just had a feeling and his "feelings" were almost always right some of the time.

Play continued for the next three hours. Some kids' dreams of college riches were dashed while other's grew with larger and larger stacks. BobbyGirl's stack grew biggest and fastest of all.

Robert witnessed every bit of it.

Harry did too.

~ * ~

As play was winding up for the night, Harry felt a hand in his back gentling moving him toward the door. Without looking back, Harry knew whose hand it was.

"We going anywhere in particular, Mr. Frenchie?" Harry asked over his shoulder.

"A chat outside. That is if you don't mind?" Frenchie responded while applying the same gentle pressure to Harry's back.

"Let's chat then," Harry replied as they exited the building.

When they were far enough away from anyone one else currently standing outside the front door, Harry turned toward Frenchie.

"So, chat," he said.

"I've been watching you for a good part of the day," Frenchie started, "and you seem to be paying significant attention to the play."

"So?" Harry countered.

"So, more attention than your casual dad here with his kid," Frenchie said.

"So?" Harry repeated.

"So, BrianK asked me to let you know we observed you observing. The other guy, too," Frenchie told Harry.

"Well, that does my heart good to know you observed. And?" Harry finished.

"And, have a nice night," Frenchie said as he turned and walked back toward the front door. Before he went back inside, Frenchie stopped and turned toward Harry.

Harry waited.

"Don't observe too close for too long if you know what's good for you," Frenchie threw at Harry.

Before Harry could respond Frenchie was through the main door and back inside the building.

When Harry got back inside, Frenchie was nowhere to be found. Harry found Robert and the two boys waiting for him.

"You alright?" Robert asked Harry.

"Right as rain," Harry replied with a smile.

Turning toward the boys, Harry asked, "You guys wanna do something or just head back to the hotel?"

"We're kinda whipped," Max replied. "If we are gonna get here early tomorrow to get choice seats for the final day of play, maybe we should just head back to the hotel. You and Robby's dad can hang in the hotel if you want."

"Sounds like a plan," Harry said. "Let's vamoose."

They did.

As they were leaving, Harry caught sight of Frenchie and BrianK watching them from across the room.

Chapter 52

"What'd the guy want?" Robert asked Harry once they were seated in the chairs outside the door to Harry's room. The boys were in bed and both Harry and Robert had beers in hand just as you might expect.

"What guy?" Harry replied.

Robert sipped his beer.

Harry waited, sipped his own.

"The guy that gently guided you through the front door and out of the hall," Robert said nonchalantly.

"Oh, that guy," Harry replied. "You saw him?"

"Then and the first time you spoke to him," Robert told Harry.

"Hmph," was all Harry said in reply.

"Seemed to want to talk to you in private this time," Robert said. "Rather insistent it seemed to me from afar."

"How afar?" Harry asked.

"Not very," Robert replied.

"Why?" Harry asked.

Robert seemed to be thinking about that question and before he responded, "I didn't like the looks of your first talk with him. I didn't like the look of how he escorted you out of the building. I didn't like his looks, period."

To repeat his previous response to something Robert said, Harry said in reply, "Hmph."

"And," Robert continued, "there was another guy waiting in the wings should you have resisted the invitation for a chat outside with the first unknown guy."

"For you to see all that, I'd say you weren't very afar at all," Harry replied.

Harry thought he saw an almost imperceptible nod from Robert.

"So, at the risk of repeating myself, what'd the guy want?" Robert asked Harry again.

"The guy, Frenchie, suggested I, 'Don't observe too close for too long if you know what's good for you' before he walked back inside. He also mentioned he saw me observing too close and the "other guy" too," Harry told Robert.

"The other guy being me I presume?" Robert stated as a question.

"I would assume you presume correctly," Harry agreed.

"Unfortunate for Frenchie," Robert said with conviction.

Harry looked at Robert with an unspoken question in his eyes.

No answer was forthcoming.

Robert finished his beer and got up. Before Harry could offer him another, Robert said, "I'm turning in, Harry. Same time tomorrow morning for breakfast?"

"That'll work," Harry answered. "Have a good night."

"You too, Harry," Robert said as he walked off to his room.

~ * ~

Since it was still early by Harry time, he took out his cell phone and hit one of the speed dial numbers on his phone. It rang five times before someone answered.

"Yeah," was all Harry heard.

"That all you got to say you old bastard?" Harry said.

"Yeah," was the only reply.

"I'm in town, Tom. A few cool ones?" Harry asked.

"Sorry, Harry. I'm looking into something out near Pittsburgh. I won't be back till middle of the week. How long you in town for?"

"Be gone tomorrow," Harry told him. "Next time?"

"Yeah," was all Tom said before he disconnected.

Tom was one of Harry's oldest and best friends who happened to have taught Harry the business. Next time would have to do.

With no place else to go without the distinct possibility of getting his ass in trouble, which he surely didn't need right now, Harry turned in for the night.

Chapter 53

Harry found Robert in the hotel lobby early the next morning when he went over to get a cup of coffee to jump start his day.

"You're up early," Robert said when he turned and saw Harry.

"Need my coffee if I'm going to be at my observant best today," Harry replied with a smile.

A tip of his half empty coffee cup to Harry confirmed Robert was thinking along the same lines.

"See you at eight?" Harry said.

"We'll be ready," Robert agreed.

~ * ~

Harry and Max had their gear loaded in the trunk of Harry's car when Robert and Robby emerged from their room. Their shared laughter led Harry to believe fences had been mended overnight and all was right with their world.

"Hungry, guys?" Harry asked as they loaded the additional bags into the car's trunk.

"As compared to yesterday, quite," Robert answered.

"Can we go to the same place as yesterday?" Robby asked.

"Yeah," Max agreed.

"You like that place?" Harry asked Robby.

A bit shyly, Robby said, "I'd never been to a real diner before yesterday. It was kinda fun."

"Then the diner it shall be," Harry told Robby.

"Okay with you, Robert?" Harry asked.

"If it's where Robby wants to go, and everyone else is good with it, then so am I," he said.

"Max?" Harry inquired.

"I'm seeing two eggs over easy, bacon, white toast and OJ in my immediate future," Max replied. "That answer your question?"

"The diner it shall be. Strap in kiddoes, we got eats to get," Harry said as he started up the car and their day.

"I'll even pay," Robby's dad said.

"I was counting on it," Harry chimed in.

They all laughed.

~ * ~

The waitress told them it was a pleasure seeing them enjoy their food "with such gusto." She also said she couldn't believe how much food they had consumed and thanked Robert for the generous tip.

"It was my pleasure," Robert assured her.

"Shall we head on over to the hall?" Harry asked the group.

"Yeah," Max said. "I can't wait to see one of the guys nail BobbyGirl and put her in her place.

"Yeah, me too," Robby agreed.

Robert looked up and gave Harry a look.

Harry knew what that look meant.

The boys would be waiting a long time if they thought Bob-byGirl was going to get hers today. Harry was fairly sure Robert would agree with that assessment. Harry wasn't as sure Robert would agree with the 'bad' Harry's assessment that nailing Bob-byGirl would provide quite a good time.

~ * ~

The hall was filling up quickly when they got there. Five tables, forty-five players, individual accounts to be filled. Some would go home with a big financial leg up on the next four years of their lives. Others would be happy, but not content, with what could have been. The rest would add to their accounts but they would be have-nots in the bonanza category.

The boys scurried over to the Peanuts Gallery to grab prime seats for proper viewing of the day's final play.

Robert grabbed Harry's elbow as they entered the hall.

"You see the truck?" he asked Harry.

"The big black pick-up following us since we left the diner?" Harry answered.

"That's the one," Robert confirmed.

"Been on our tail since last night," Harry continued.

"Another time?" Robert asked.

"Yeah, not now, not with the boys here," Harry told him. "Let's go watch the poor boys try and burst some balloons."

Chapter 54

The morning's play would have been described by some as being nothing short of frantic. After the first hour of play, forty-five players had been whittled down to thirty-one. Her reigning highness of the tables had personally dispatched five of them.

Robert had taken up his normal spot across the room from Harry's normal spot. Both vantage points allowed full view of the remaining tables.

Frenchie was nowhere to be found.

On the other hand, BrianK was everywhere to be found. He and Clint worked the room offering encouragement to the departing contestants and cheering on the remaining ones. While BrianK was non-contestant specific, Clint did everything short of slobbering all over BobbyGirl.

Just before the morning break the room quieted as play heightened at one of the tables. Of the eight players at the table, two moved ALL IN pre-flop and five players total had declared ALL IN after the flop.

The exposed hands combined with the flop showed straight, flush and full house possibilities. The K and Q of hearts plus 10 of diamonds had prompted the flurry of ALL INS. The other three players at the table sat watching knowing their positions would improve by sitting and doing nothing.

From Harry's take, the favorite of the five had the A and 2 of hearts drawing to the nut flush. The player to his left had J and 4 of diamonds drawing to a straight and needing runner runner diamonds for a flush. Trip K's was high hand for now looking for the board to pair for a full house. The lone girl in the five-some of ALL INS had what would usually be a monster hand with trip Q's, but she was looking all but dead now.

The dealer buried a card and the Turn card was the 9 of diamonds.

The kid with the straight draw pumped his fist and yelled "Yo Baby" while pointing to his posse in the Peanuts Gallery. His boys were going absolutely nuts. He now had his straight and a flush draw as well.

The heart flush and trip K kids looked dejected.

Harry looked over and saw Max and Robby jumping around with the rest of the nuts in the Peanuts Gallery. He did remind himself they were only kids watching kids playing for a ton of money.

Once the room had quieted down, the dealer tapped the table, buried a card and turned over the River card.

It was the 3 of hearts.

"YES! OH YAYYA BABY! YOU BETTER BELIEVE IT!" came the cry from the kid with the nut flush and the winner of the hand. He was jumping up and down swinging his arms in the air like he wanted to take off. The kid who thought he was going to win the hand with the straight just stood there looking at the 3 in utter disbelief. The room went wild around him.

Harry looked over at BobbyGirl. She had a big smile on her face knowing her lead was still plenty safe and four more losers had been all but vanquished from the game. Less players meant she was closer to winning the whole thing.

Not surprising at all, Clint was standing right behind her.

BrianK was at the podium trying to get some semblance of order back into the room. After tapping the mike to no avail, he whistled into the mike and everyone looked up to see what was going on.

"Alright, alright, calm down now," BrianK started. "Everybody quiet down."

Slowly the room quieted.

"That is what this is all about," BrianK said. "Congratulations to Teddy for a big win and the other four of you shouldn't be hanging your heads. You played great and will be leaving with a nice addition to your accounts."

A smattering of applause could be heard around the room.

"Come on, now. Everyone put your hands together for all the players, those that are still competing plus those that have already gone home. You all have played your hearts out up to this point. Everyone here is a winner," he told the room.

When the applause stopped, BrianK said, "Alright then, let's take a break for lunch and then we can see who's going to win this thing."

Cheers erupted and everyone moved out to get some lunch and prepare for the afternoon run to a champion. Harry got Max and Robby, and together with Robert, they headed out for food and drinks. As they headed for the door, Harry saw BobbyGirl going through the doorway into the "No Entrance" area with Clint right behind her.

Chapter 55

The local Appleby's was their choice for lunch. They had decent food, quick service, and half-way decent beers on tap.

You need more?

To make sure they got out quick enough to be back before the afternoon session started, they ordered before getting down to discussing what went down in the morning session.

Max and Robby ordered burgers, fries and cokes. Robert had the Chicken Caesar salad and water, and Harry went for a bacon cheeseburger with a Killian's chaser. No fries for Harry—there would be plenty to steal from Max and Robby's plates.

Once the orders were placed and the waitress was gone, Harry said, "So, what did you guys think of this morning's action?"

Max and Robby both started jabbering away at the same time so you couldn't understand what either one was saying.

"Hey, slow down you two. One at a time," Harry told them.

"Let Max go first," Robert told Robby.

Robby nodded and Max took the floor.

"It was cool," he started. "There was hand after hand that moved kid's stacks up and down all morning. For a while kids were getting bounced so fast it looked like we'd be done this morning. That last hand was awesome, man."

"Yeah, it was really neat," Robby chimed in.

"When the nine hit, the kids right behind us went ballistic for their dude. We were sure his straight was going to take the hand. You could see the girl with the set of queens was done for. She looked like it was over already, and it was. No way she catches the case queen there."

"No way, man," Robby agreed. "She was toast."

"Then the heart hits and the place exploded. Glenn's a cool kid. We chat with him online all the time. He's cool with the Peanuts," Max told Harry and Robert.

Robby was nodding the whole time.

"Who's your favorite now?" Harry asked.

Max and Robby looked at each other before Max spoke up.

"BobbyGirl's pretty tough to beat. She seems to get the card she needs every time she's in a big hand. I like Glenn, but she's gonna be tough to beat with the stack she has," Max said.

Harry, the bad dad, wondered which stack Max was talking about.

"Yeah, it's like she can't lose the big hands," Robby agreed. "But I'd rather see Glenn knock her down and win it all."

The food arrived and there was a flurry of activity with ketchup, salt and napkins flying all around the table. Harry protected his Killian's at all cost.

"Let's eat, boys," Robert said. "We want to get back in plenty of time to see the finals."

When they were all done Harry paid the tab and they piled into the car to head back to the venue. Max and Robby were hyped up to see Glenn take home the crown for all the Peanuts.

~ * ~

Max and Robby ran for the Peanuts Gallery when they got back to the hall. The place was already a beehive of activity and you could tell the excitement level had ratcheted up a notch or two.

Two tables and eighteen players were left. BobbyGirl was the chip leader by a wide margin with almost twice as many chips as her closest rival. Glenn was in third as play began.

Robert was about to move over to his position on the other side of the room when Harry caught his arm.

"You didn't say anything about this morning's action," Harry said to him.

"Something in particular you're looking for me to say, Harry?" Robert asked.

"Nah, just observation is all," Harry answered him.

"Well, I'd say it was an interesting morning of play. I'd also say Max is a very observant kid, wouldn't you, Harry?"

Thinking about that for the shortest of seconds, Harry said, "Yeah, I'd agree with you, Robert. Very observant indeed."

As Robert walked away, Harry could hear the scratch of the microphone as someone was about to address the group.

"With everyone at their seats, the dealers can now begin play for this afternoon. Let's all have a great time and how about a big cheer for our final eighteen players," Clint said to the group.

When the noise subsided, Clint said, "Let's begin play, and

May the cards light up your lives."

He didn't know why, but Harry had the strange feeling before long he would be the one lighting up Clint's life.

Chapter 56

Harry watched: one, two, three, four, five players dropped in the first half hour of play. The low stacks were now gone and when Glenn bounced two players by catching a 4 for a full house, play was down to the final table. It had only taken a little over an hour to move from two tables to one.

BobbyGirl still led the chip count parade but Glenn had closed the gap some. When they were settled at the final table, Glenn was seated to BobbyGirl's right. Either Glenn would have the advantage by virtue of having the ability to move first and force BobbyGirl's hand, or BobbyGirl would have the advantage of seeing Glenn's action before having to make a move. She could go over the top of Glenn and make him play defensively.

Or, one of the other players would clean both of their clocks and steal the tournament.

Only time would tell.

Blinds were five thousand, ten thousand and antes were a double thou. There is a set betting method among the professionals who play the game, or any knowledgeable poker player for that matter. Multiples of the big blind normally dictate the betting patterns. That sounds good, but the kids bet whatever they want, whenever they want, however they want. Wild action normally ensues.

Harry didn't know exactly how many chips were in the game at the final table. If there were 425 players to start, and each started with 10,000 chips, then there should be just over 4.2 million chips in play. As Harry was eyeing up BobbyGirl's stack (of chips), an electronic scoreboard came on listing the chip counts of the players at the final table. BobbyGirl had 1.7 million of the 4.2 million chips in play at the table. Glenn, the next player on the board, held 840,000 chips. Low man, or boy in this case, had a stack of 145,000 chips.

Advantage BobbyGirl.

The final table at the East Regional pokcolmon.com tournament was about to begin. The pot was right at 33,000 chips. The first player folded and the next player limped in by calling the 10K big blind. Next to play was the small stack and he wasted no time in determining his fate. ALL IN was his call; loud and clear for everyone in the hall to hear. He pushed in his stack of 143K chips and stood to watch the rest of the table's action.

His boys from the Peanut Gallery let out with a modest cheer on his behalf. A last hurrah as you will. Max wasn't among them.

Two folds brought the action to Glenn. A call of 143K in chips would risk roughly 17% of his remaining chips into a pot with 186K in chips. He checked his hole cards again and called.

BobbyGirl smiled. She turned toward Glenn ignoring the rest of the players at the table and said, "ALL IN," in a voice that dared him to call.

Glenn smiled back.

The small blind to the left of BobbyGirl folded, but the kid in the big blind with a stack just shy of 300k pushed in all his chips and called.

Everyone was on their feet now.

Once the 10K limper folded, play moved to Glenn. Still looking directly at BobbyGirl with a big smile on his face, he pushed his cards into the middle of the table. He folded.

The girls in the Peanut Gallery went wild and the place was a nut house with cheers of 'BobbyGirl, BobbyGirl' starting up. She hadn't won anything yet, but the female population in attendance was clearly behind her.

When the noise level subsided, the dealer called the pot right and asked for the ALL IN players to lay down their cards.

The original ALL IN player turned over a pair of J's at the same time the big blind was showing his AK of spades. BobbyGirl hesitated long enough to show her down cards last. Finally she flipped her cards over to show a pair of 9's.

That prompted a minor uproar from the room that quickly died down.

The dealer buried a card and prepared to turn over the flop. When he did the cards showed the 7 and 4 of spades plus the 2 of hearts. The tall blond kid in the big blind pumped his fist after seeing his spade flush draw materialize. Small stack and BobbyGirl missed the flop entirely.

Missing the flop didn't seem to faze BobbyGirl one bit. She continued to smile her million dollar smile especially when she looked over in Glenn's direction.

The dealer buried the required card and turned over the next card—it was the 9 of hearts giving BobbyGirl trip 9's. Blond boy's shoulders slumped noticeably when he saw the 9 hit the felt. He would need a spade or his tourney was over. Small stack was dead unless a J appeared. Luckily he had the J of spades, so that was in his favor.

The undercurrent of noise was there and ready to explode. As if out of nowhere, Clint appeared right behind BobbyGirl and put his hand on her shoulder to give her a good luck squeeze.

"Gimme a spade. Gimme a spade," blondie yelled almost pleading.

The dealer drew out the break between cards to heighten the anticipation to the point of explosion. Finally he tapped the table, buried a card and turned over the River card.

The 2 of spades.

When he saw the spade, blondie jumped, what seemed to Harry, at least two feet in the air. It wasn't until he landed that he realized the deuce that gave him his flush also paired the 2 on the board giving BobbyGirl a full house. Hand to BobbyGirl, tournament over for blondie and small stack.

When Harry looked over, BobbyGirl was being mobbed by her girl gang. Clint was gone.

Chapter 57

There was such pandemonium it took five minutes to regain control of the room. For the first time since their little chat, Harry saw Frenchie who was assisting with moving the fans back into the Peanut Gallery. BrianK and Clint were also active in restoring order within the hall.

Looking up at the electronic scoreboard, Harry saw the current chip count totals:

BobbyGirl	2,325,000
Glenn	695,000
Paolo Barroni	415,000
Tommy B.	310,000
Ze-ro	265,000
Damian	150,000
Angelo	90,000

From Harry's viewpoint, BobbyGirl was laying a freakin kick-a-booty on the boys who were left in play. An old fashioned, low-down, kick-a-my-freakin-booty.

His next thought was who the hell is Paolo Barroni? Could he be attached to the Italian contingent that has been yelling something unintelligible all day? It was all in Italian Harry now guessed. And lastly, what the fuck is a Ze-ro with a dash in the middle?

These were all questions that would have to wait. A cool one to refresh himself wouldn't. Robert met him at the makeshift bar.

"Thoughts?" Robert asked.

"One," Harry started after he sipped his long neck. "In the midst of the donnybrook that just broke out during a poker tournament, why were you staring so intently at the dealer?"

Robert took a pull on his Amstel Light and looked at Harry.

"Just curious," he finally answered Harry.

"What do you mean curious?" Harry asked.

"Just 'curious,'" he replied again.

"Okay," Harry repeated, "just 'curious' will do for now. Not forever, but for now. And you still didn't answer my question."

Harry grabbed another long neck and walked away.

Harry on his wall, Robert safely back at his, play resumed.

~ * ~

Angelo and Damian departed in the next three hands, their ALL INS resulting in an increase to Glenn's chip stack. BobbyGirl was biding her time with what everyone could only assume were no useful cards to even think about playing. Play continued, and with Glenn on the button, the shit hit the ALL IN fan.

Ze-ro and Tommy were short stacked and both went ALL IN to shorten their misery. Glenn made it 350K to play and Bob-byGirl quickly called. Paolo thought about it, looked at his hole cards, thought about it some more and eventually pushed ALL IN. Without a second's hesitation Glenn called. BobbyGirl calmly said, "I'm ALL IN."

It was tournament decision time for Glenn. Pot committed, he had no choice but to call BobbyGirl's ALL IN.

BrianK, Clint and the entire pokcolmon.com contingency quickly surrounded the outside edge of the playing area. Once they moved to accommodate the Peanut Gallery, play got serious.

When the cards were turned over, Ze-ro and Tommy had nothing hands with unsuited QJ and a suited J9 of diamonds respectively. Glen was next to show and turned over the 7 6 of hearts. The Peanuts Gallery went nuts with Glenn showing a mighty pair of nuts of his own going ALL IN with only a suited 7 6. When BobbyGirl dropped a pair of Ladies on the table, her girltingency shrieked their brains out. Paolo, showing last, smiled as he placed his two Cowboys on the table.

Italian filled the room.

Ready to get the show on the road, the dealer laid down the flop exposing the A of hearts, 8 of diamonds and J of clubs.

Ze-ro and Tommy had paired their J's but still trailed Paolo as well as BobbyGirl for that matter. Paolo, BobbyGirl and Glenn caught a whole lotta nada from the flop. Glenn was going to need some runners to get back in this hand or take a trip to adiosville.

The dealer buried a card and showed Fourth Street. It was the 5 of hearts giving Glenn an open ended straight draw and flush draw. Nobody else improved.

"Give me the runner runner," Glenn yelled. "One time with the runner runner," he continued.

The Peanuts Gallery started a chant of "runner runner—

runner runner—runner runner."

When Harry looked over at Robert, he was leaning against the wall intently staring at the dealer.

The dealer tapped the table, paused, buried a card and then laid the River card on the table.

Q of clubs.

Glenn came up empty. BobbyGirl's trip Q's beat Paolo's lonely Cowboys to take the pot—end of ballgame. The female contingency shrieked and started their own chant of "BobbyGirl, BobbyGirl, BobbyGirl…" as they mobbed the tournament champion.

Chapter 58

Harry and Robert were standing off to the side of the front door waiting for Max and Robby. The boys were roaming the room congratulating the final table players and saying goodbye to their buddies.

Harry could see Robby looking over in Clint's direction. While both he and Max would have loved to get in a few last words with their hero, Clint was posing with BobbyGirl and Glenn for the photographer. Clint had his arm wrapped around BobbyGirl's shoulder, but not Glenn's.

Max and Robby finally made it over to Harry and Robert.

"That was unbelievable," Robby blurted out as soon as he got within arm's length of his dad. "Did you see it?" he asked him with obvious anticipation.

"Yeah, it was great," Robert told Robby. "It was really exciting," he said trying to make it sound like he meant it.

Harry knew he didn't mean it.

"I thought Glenn was going to take her," Max said. "We all thought he was…" he trailed off.

Harry patted Max on the head and said, "Let's get out of here. We saw a great tournament and it's time to reward ourselves with some of the best Hershey ice cream this area has to offer."

"Their chocolate chip any good?" Robby asked.

"The best," Harry answered.

"Then let's do it," Max told the group.

Just before he walked out, Harry turned to look over his shoulder. Feeling it, knowing he was there, Harry saw Frenchie watch them leaving from across the room.

Harry smiles at him and mouthed the words, "Another time."

~ * ~

The boys went to sleep almost immediately as they got started on their way home. Harry drove and Robert was quiet for the first half-hour of the ride. His eyes were closed, but Harry had the feeling he wasn't asleep.

Eyes still closed, he finally said, "Thoughts?"

"About what, the economic conditions in Poland?" Harry replied. "They suck. Soap suds are up five cents a box."

Robert opened his eyes and looked at Harry.

"You think you're pretty funny, don't you, Harry?" Robert said.

"I have my moments," Harry replied.

"Yeah, you do," Robert concurred. "So, your thoughts?"

"If you mean the tournament, I have a few. If you mean the extracurricular activities surrounding the tournament, I have a few. If you mean you drinking Amstel Light, I have one."

"The latter?" Robert said.

"Pisswater," Harry replied.

"And your long necks are consumed by the fine beer connoisseurs of the world?" Robert retorted.

"Not the choice of as you say 'fine beer connoisseurs,' but not pisswater either," Harry answered.

"I'll let that one slide for now. The middle?" Robert said.

"Frenchie sent me a message that I got loud and clear. Don't mean shit, but I got it. I was working in the shadows, but now BrianK knows I'm around and I guess you can take that as either good, or bad. The truck bothers me some, but not now. It ain't behind us, but the old expression 'I know where you live' probably applies."

"Ah, agreed," Robert agreed, "at least as it applies to you."

"Not you?" Harry asked.

"I don't live where you think I live, Harry. Robby's mom doesn't even know where I live," Robert told Harry.

Harry turned toward Robert but his eyes were still closed.

"In case I forget, remind me to find out where you live," Harry told Robert.

"You can try…" Robert let trail off.

"You'd be surprised, my man, you'd be surprised," Harry replied to the sound of Robert snoring.

Chapter 59

Traffic wasn't as bad as Harry thought it might be and they made great time. With everyone else snoozing, Harry listened to some tunes and replayed the weekend.

"The first?" Harry heard as they approached the Northern Boulevard exit on the Cross Island Parkway.

"Not to worry, I got the driving. No need for you to offer to share the driving on the way home," Harry threw in Robert's still closed eyes direction.

"Don't worry yourself; I didn't, and I won't," Robert replied. "The first?"

"If I owned a house, I'd have bet the house on BobbyGirl," Harry answered without having to think about it.

"Reason?" Robert asked.

"Clint and BobbyGirl make quite an adorable couple. King and Queen of the Under Eighteen Poker World according to BrianK."

"That's very astute, Harry. And the rest of the tournament players that were there for the event. You didn't give them much chance?"

"Sure, they had a chance. They had a chance to increase their bank accounts to the tune of second place, or somewhere south of that. It just looked like it was meant to be from the get go. Champion BobbyGirl rides off into the sunset with Clint and her moocho fortified bank account."

"An interesting scenario you have painted, Harry. Very interesting indeed," Robert commented. He didn't say anything else.

~ * ~

Max woke up just as Harry turned the corner onto Linden Street and pulled up in front of his house.

"Here you go, big guy. Be sure and tell your moms I took great care of you this weekend," Harry told Max.

"Got it, bigger guy. I'll be sure and tell her we only drank light beer and hit the sack before midnight," Max joked.

"I'll kick your butt you tell her that," Harry laughed.

"See ya," Max said to Robby's dad as he and Robby jumped out of the car. "It was nice to see you again. I had a great time."

"Thanks," Robby said to Harry.

"See ya, Dad," he said to his dad.

Once they were gone, Harry said, "Where to Robert?"

"The Manhasset train station will be fine, Harry."

"You sure? I can drop you somewhere if you need."

"The train station will be fine, Harry. I can manage from there."

Harry dropped Robert at the station and they said they would get together again soon. Neither believed it, or meant it, but it was the thing to say.

~ * ~

Harry drove on to his apartment and grabbed a beer from the fridge before he hit the message button on his machine. The answering machine said there were three messages waiting. The first two were crap, but the third proved interesting.

"Another time, Shorts, definitely another time."

Unless Harry was totally mistaken, the French Man had paid Harry a phone visit since he had seen him last. Frenchie knew where he lived and he wanted Harry to know he did. So did BrianK.

"Another time for sure, Frenchie. You can count on it," Harry said out loud to himself.

Chapter 60

Bright and early the following morning, Harry was up at ebil's office making notes in the case file on the computer. He wasn't sure what Robby's last name was, so he called Max to find out.

When he dialed Max's number, Sherry came on the line.

"Hello," she said.

Why Harry was so surprised Sherry had answered the phone, and why she had said hello he didn't know. But, for some unknown reason, he was caught totally off guard.

"Hello," Sherry said again. "Is there anyone there?"

Regaining his wits, Harry answered, "It's me, Sher."

"Harry, it's good to hear from you," Sherry told him. "To what do I owe the honor of this call?"

"I was actually looking for Max," Harry told her.

"Well, that's disappointing, Harry. Here I thought you were actually calling me," Sherry responded. She sounded duly disappointed

"You know I love talking to you, Sherry. I just wanted to ask Max something."

"Well, you just missed him, Harry. He needed to get something from one of his friends and left early for school. Are you sure I can't give you what you need, or want, Harry?" Sherry asked.

That familiar stirring stirred.

"I believe you could as you always do, Sherry," Harry answered. "Don't you have plans for today?"

"Not until after lunch, Harry. I was just making myself some breakfast and I would enjoy breakfast in bed if I had someone to share it with," she answered in what sounded like a purring sound to Harry. "I'm making waffles, Harry. You know what I like on my waffles, don't you, Harry?"

The stirring had escalated to a high speed whipping.

"Might that be an invitation I just heard, Sher?" Harry asked.

A few seconds later, Sherry answered, "Sorry, Harry, I needed both hands to get my shorts and top off."

Whip something too long and it gets very firm. Hard even.

"Leave the door open, Sher, I'm on my way," Harry told her.

~ * ~

They had to finish the last waffle without any whipped cream. A half-a-can of whipped cream can only go so far when you have six waffles and…well you know.

"That was good, Harry," Sherry said when they had finished the last bite of waffle.

"The waffles?" Harry asked.

"Them, too," Sherry answered.

Harry leaned over to look at the bed side clock. Sherry was on her side leaning on an elbow not making it easy for Harry to see the clock.

"You in a hurry, Harry?" Sherry asked him. "You sure weren't in any hurry a little while ago."

"You said you had all morning and mornings are a terrible thing to waste," Harry told her.

Sherry smiled.

"Speaking of a terrible thing to waste," Sherry said as she ran two fingers over the plate which contained the remains of the syrup they had used on their waffles. She carefully dabbed the syrup on both of her nipples.

"Sweet," was all Harry said.

When they had spent all the time they could afford in bed, Sherry asked Harry, "Do you want to shower first or do you want to rest here while I go first?"

It was Harry's turn to smile.

"I hear tell, along with mornings, water is also a terrible thing to waste," Harry responded.

"Harry, you never cease to amaze me," Sherry said. "But we don't have much time. It's eleven now and Max will be home for lunch at twelve on the dot. He always is—just like clockwork."

"That won't be a problem, Sherry. You know that when I have to I can be quicker than most human beings," Harry said.

"I hope not," Sherry answered as she got out of bed and headed for the shower.

"Maybe not this time," Harry agreed to her back and, from Harry's vantage point, a beautiful back it was.

The water was a perfect temperature. Their bodies melded with the pulse of the shower massage further accentuating the pleasure both of them experienced for what was probably only fifteen minutes but seemed like forever. When Sherry placed her palms on the shower wall and leaned back into Harry, he knew it was time to get quick. Not too quick, though. No, once they started moving together, too quick definitely would not do at all.

Chapter 61

Harry was rounding the corner when he spotted Max coming down the block from school. It wasn't noon yet, but even so, he hadn't gotten out of Sherry's house with much time to spare. Seeing Max reminded him he didn't get Robby's last name while he was with Sherry. He decided being otherwise occupied for the entire time was probably the reason. He also decided that was cool with him.

On occasion, being otherwise occupied with Sherry was better than cool.

He drove back to the office to finish what he had started first thing that morning. The office was still empty giving him some peace and quiet to get his work done uninterrupted by Ebil chatter. He wouldn't have minded Bunny chatter, or at least looking at Bunny. She wasn't there either.

He didn't have Robby's last name, but he could cope. There was plenty he needed to add to the file to keep him busy for the rest of the day.

Robert Somebody, or Robby Somebody's dad, was one thing. Who he was, what he was, and where he was needed answering. Harry wondered if Robby and his dad actually shared the same last name. That could complicate the matter some, but it wasn't insurmountable.

As soon as Harry talked to Max, he would provide the first clue to the puzzle. If Robby's mom had remarried, she'd probably have a different last name now. If she had indeed remarried and Max didn't know Robby's previous last name, it might be necessary to enlist Max in a bit of sleuthing. That is if Robby had taken his mom's new last name. This got more complicated the more Harry thought about it. He stopped thinking about it.

Harry's mind wandered: what if Robby's mom hadn't gotten remarried. What if she was wandering around in that big house of hers all day long, loneliness consuming her every waking hour? She needed consolation, compassion, a shoulder to cry on. Someone to talk to, to share her joys and her sorrows, her ups and her downs. Someone to provide her multiple ups and downs while banging her silly in every room of that big house of hers.

Yeah, she was probably remarried and he wasn't needed. But, one never knew and it was worth confirming.

Returning his attention to the computer, Harry started working on the notes from the weekend. Frenchie was an interesting addition to the case. Did his presence escalate the BrianK organization uncertainty, or solidify Harry's prior suppositions. How far would they go to keep things in check and who in BrianK's world would Harry have to look out for? What was the real relationship between Clint and BobbyGirl and was she now part of the pokcolmon family? If the answer was yes, why? Maybe the actual answer was why not.

There were definitely several HMS QAS's in there somewhere. Harry was about to try and flush them out when the phone rang.

"Shorts," Harry said into the phone.

"Putz, it's Mel. Your ex called me because she couldn't reach you. She needs you to call her right away."

"I've been here in the office. Why didn't she try me here?" Harry replied.

"Fuck do I know, Harry. She tried your apartment. When you didn't answer she called me. I'm at a closing and don't have time for this "find Harry" crap. Call her," he said as he hung up.

Harry had seen Max heading home so it shouldn't be anything to do with Max. Briande always ate lunch at school. If there was a problem there Sherry would be able to handle it herself. She always did.

What was it?

Harry called her.

"Sherry, its Harry. Mel called and said you were looking for me?"

"Harry, you better come back over here right away."

Knowing that voice, Harry said, "I'm on my way."

Chapter 62

Sherry opened the door before Harry had even gotten to the front porch. She didn't look good.

"What's wrong, kiddo?" Harry asked her.

"Dad," Harry heard from inside the house.

Harry stepped into the house and asked Max, "You alright, bud?"

"I'm fine, pops," Max told him.

"Then what's up?" Harry asked.

Sherry answered.

"I just got a call from Robby's mother. She was a little shaky on details, but it seems Robby's dad got jumped and beat up last night. She didn't know his condition, only that he was in a hospital in New York and being evaluated," Sherry told Harry.

"What hospital? How bad?" Harry asked.

"She didn't know, Harry. Even though they don't live together, she sounded pretty shaken up."

"They divorced? She remarried and have someone to stay with her? He remarried? Where's he live?" Harry rattled off.

"I'm sorry, Harry, I don't know her that well. Max and Robby are friends, but she and I don't run in the same circles in town. I've only met her a few times," Sherry told Harry.

Harry looked at Max for some help.

"Robby doesn't talk about his dad much," Max said. "This weekend was the first time I met him. He's never been at their house when I was there. And no, Robby's mom isn't remarried. At least I don't think so. Well, no guy lives there for sure. I've seen one particular guy that has been around on the weekends, but when I stayed over at Robby's he was never there."

Sherry had started to cry.

"What are you crying for?" Harry asked her.

"It could have been you, Harry. It could be you lying in some hospital all beat to shit," she told him. "I'm scared, Harry."

"Come on, mom," Max said.

Harry gave Max a look that said stay out of this for now.

"First of all, Sherry, I barely know Robert. He got attacked in

New York and I'm here in Manhasset. It probably was a random burglary attempt, or a case of mistaken identity. It has nothing to do with me, Sherry," Harry tried to assure her.

"You don't know that, Harry. You just met the guy and he immediately gets his ass kicked," Sherry said.

"We don't know he got his ass kicked," Harry started. "And, the fact I just met the guy has nothing to do with what happened to him."

At least Harry hoped it didn't.

"I'll track down where he is and find out how he is and what happened. We'll have forgotten about this before you know it," Harry tried to reassure Sherry.

"I better go see Robby's mother. I want to make sure she's alright and doesn't have to wait this out by herself. Max is coming with me for the afternoon. I already called the school."

"That's cool, Sherry. You help your mom, okay Max? I'll call as soon as I know anything at all," Harry said to both of them.

"Thanks, Harry. I didn't know what to do, who to call, how to help. I was so worried," Sherry said as she started to cry again.

"It'll be fine, mom. Dad will take care of it, won't you?" Max asked Harry.

"I'm all over it, Max. I'll call you later."

Harry kissed Sherry on the cheek and slapped Max in the back of his head to show him he approved of how he was handling the situation.

Max understood.

Harry left and went back to the office. He was going to need his brown suit, cuz somebody had done turned on the fan.

~ * ~

After three calls, Harry hit paydirt.

"Thanks, Marty. Now you're sure from what you know he's not in any danger?" Harry asked.

Harry listened intently.

"Thanks again, Marty. And thank the New York Police force for me. I'll head over there right now."

Chapter 63

As has been discussed before, hospitals are not Harry's favorite places on earth. Very little good has happened to Harry when hospitals were involved save the birth of his kids—which he missed. That is not to say others rejoice at the thought of visiting hospitals, but Harry just plain don't like them.

Harry found the room and pushed open the door. He found the occupant asleep in the only bed in the room making it a private room in a New York City Hospital. That for the uninformed in the group ain't so easy, or cheap.

Harry stood next to the side of Robert's bed and dripped single droplets of water onto his forehead. The annoyance eventually woke Robert up.

"What are you doing, Harry? And why are you doing it, Harry?" Robert said without opening his eyes.

Harry dripped another droplet onto Robert's forehead.

"If you aren't going to answer me as to why you are doing it, Harry, would you at least cease doing it?"

"Sure, Robert," Harry told him. "Of course that assumes your name is Robert, Robert. Also, if your name is Robert, Robert what?"

Robert opened his eyes and looked at Harry.

"Are you always this much of a pain in the ass, Harry?"

"Not always," Harry answered. "Most of the time, but not always."

"I thought as much," Robert responded.

"So, what the fuck happened, Robert Something?" Harry asked.

"I believe the correct term is 'blunt force trauma' to the back of the head," Robert told Harry.

"Did you happen to see him, or them, that perpetrated this 'blunt force trauma' to the back of your head?" Harry asked him.

"No, Harry, I didn't. I was going in through the back and I was out cold before I even knew what hit me. He, or they, were good, very good," Robert said.

"Back of where?" Harry tried.

"Of where I live, Harry," Robert replied vaguely.

"Any idea who it might have been? You have anyone gunning for you?" Harry asked.

"Well, I know I wasn't followed, so it couldn't be someone connected to the weekend. That is unless they are in a category I choose not to put them in at this time. Other than that possibility, there always could be, Harry," Robert replied.

"Could be, as in could be multiples of other candidates?" Harry asked.

"How's the weather outside, Harry?" Robert answered.

"Getting chillier, like it just got in here," Harry said.

"Clever as always, aren't you, Harry?" Robert said as he closed his eyes.

Before Harry could respond, the sound of light snoring indicated to Harry talk time was over. Robert would stay a mystery for now.

The nurse walked into the room and told Harry visiting hours were over. By the look on her face, Harry figured it was time to hit the road.

A quick stop at the nurse's station produced the anticipated "we aren't at liberty to divulge..." speech that sent Harry on his way knowing nothing more than when he entered. He didn't even get Robert's last name, unless his last name was Lee. Robert E. Lee to be precise since that was what was on his chart. Harry had peeked.

~ * ~

As Harry was leaving the parking lot, a big black pick-up truck pulled into the lane a few cars lengths behind him. Harry made a right turn two blocks up and the truck made the same turn. A left two blocks later produced the same results.

"No shit," Harry said to himself out loud.

At the next corner, the light turned red and Harry had to stop at the light. The truck pulled up right next to him just as the light changed and sped past him. Harry didn't have a chance to see who was driving. The truck made a quick left and was gone. Harry chose not to follow.

Coincidence? Harry hoped so, but didn't know for sure. If it wasn't, he had the feeling he and they were in deep shit.

Chapter 64

The poker bug is ever vigilant, always looking for a pocket, or pockets to jump into. Harry didn't notice it, or feel it as it happened, but the poker bug must have jumped into his pocket because he suddenly had the urge to play poker.

"Tank, it's Harry Shorts," Harry said into the phone.

Momentary silence on the other end was followed by, "Oh, yeah, Mel's guy. What's up, Harry?"

"I'm looking for a game, Tank. Nothing too big, and surely not with guys that are gonna clean my clock before I even get started. If you have a beginner's game...I think you saw that's about my level."

"Yeah, I can do that, my man. Wednesday at ten, same place as last time. You be able to find it?" Tank asked.

"Yeah, I can find it," Harry told him. "What's the buy in?" Harry asked.

"Flat game so's nobody can lose too much scratch. Buy in is five hundred, and when you tapped, you be gone. Ain't no re-buys in my games." Tank told him.

"I'll be there. Thanks," Harry told Tank.

"Wednesday," Tank said as he disconnected. "And next time go through Mel like I 'tole you before."

~ * ~

Harry called Sherry to let her know he had found Robert and he was alive and fairly stable.

"Yeah, I found him after a few calls to some guys I know in the city. He's in a hospital being kept for observation as far as I can tell. They don't give much information to non-family members," Harry told her.

"How do you know that much, Harry?" Sherry asked him.

"I read his chart," Harry told her.

"Smart thinking, Harry."

"Thanks, Sher."

"Max good?" Harry asked.

"Yeah, he's fine. Robby had him over and they came back

here for diner so Robby's mom could go see Robert. She was contacted later in the day and she went right into the city to see him."

"You find out anything about them?" Harry asked.

"No, not from Robby's mom, ah, I mean Nancy. That's her name. You?"

"Nothing useful to speak of. Robert said little and evaded any questions I threw at him. He's an odd one," Harry told Sherry.

"Look who's talking, Harry."

"You didn't think I was too odd yesterday morning, Sherry my dear," Harry chided.

"That depends on your definition of odd, Harry. Some people might find what you can do with a can of whipped cream somewhat out of the ordinary, Harry my dear," she threw back at him.

"You complaining?" he asked.

After a second, she said, "No, Harry, I'm not complaining one bit. And, if I wasn't on the way out, I'd love to not complain right now about your use of the new can I have in the fridge."

"Pity," Harry said.

"It's not going anywhere, Harry," she said.

"That's good to know, Sherry. See ya soon?" Harry asked.

"I'd like that, Harry. I'm late and gotta go. Bye, Harry."

"Bye," Harry said to a dial tone.

Another rain check and one Harry knew from experience would brighten up anyone's rainy day, especially his.

~ * ~

The information Jaxy had provided while Harry was down in Pennsylvania still needed some processing. Harry had it stored in his mind since it wasn't something that would sit well in his file documentation. At least not yet, not until Harry could confirm some pieces and put other pieces together with it. If they summed up right, Harry would have solved a big piece of the puzzle.

Mind you, the puzzle keeps on getting jumbled every time something unexpected happens. Frenchie jumbled things a bit. Robert jumbled them some more. Robert getting the "blunt force trauma" treatment put a crimp in Harry's mental picture and added a few previously unforeseen pieces to the puzzle. End result—he felt like he was trying to put a puzzle together with too many pieces in some places, not enough in others.

Chapter 65

Wednesday night came and Harry wasn't feeling it. He didn't know what he was supposed to be feeling but, whatever it was, he didn't have it. He had played poker for years in home games with buds that drank some beers and played some cards. He had played in a few poker room games in other parts of the country during his walk-about days, mainly for small stakes in pip squeak smoke filled poker dens. He had the feeling Tank's joint wasn't pip squeak territory.

At a few minutes after ten, Harry knocked on the door of the house he had visited the last time he saw Tank. Having "second thoughts time" was now gone.

"Yeah," said the guy who opened the door.

For want of anything better to say, Harry said, "I'm Harry Shorts. Tank said to come by at ten."

"Yeah," the guy said again as he closed the door.

Harry waited.

Two minutes later the door opened and Tank told Harry to come inside.

"The game's getting started in the room top of the stairs down the hall to the left. Jersey's at the door and knows your coming. Good luck, Shorts," Tank said.

Tank put out his hand and Harry placed five one hundred dollar bills in it. Tank smiled, turned and walked away.

When Harry got to the room top of the stairs down the hall to the left, Jersey met him at the door. At least Harry assumed the large man was Jersey.

"You Shorts?" the guy asked.

"You Jersey?" Harry asked back.

"You a funny guy?" the guy responded.

"Sometimes," Harry answered.

"You Shorts?" the guy repeated.

Figuring his funny guy time was up, Harry told the guy he assumed was Jersey, "Yeah, I'm Shorts."

"Good, go ahead in," Jersey instructed.

"Thanks, Jersey," Harry told him.

Entering the room, Harry was struck by the blankness. The room contained a poker table and eight chairs situated around the table. The walls were painted white-wash white over bare wood floors. Nothing else was on the walls, or the floors, or anywhere else for that matter. Just a poker table and eight chairs situated around the table. A "home" it wasn't by any stretch of the imagination—even Harry's.

"If you're Shorts, sit down and let's play poker," one of the guys said in Harry's direction.

Harry sat in the only empty chair and found a stack of chips sitting on the table in front of him.

"Name's Lindy," said the guy that directed Harry to sit. "Green chips are twenty-five, blue chips are ten and the whites are five. It's a five-ten No Limit Holdem game. I assume you know how to play. You have a question, you ask me. That clear enough?" he finished.

"Crystal, and it's Harry," Harry replied.

"Game starts at ten and we always start on time, so we already dealt for dealer. You're big blind first hand," Lindy said.

Take that new kid.

Nobody else volunteered a name, so Harry put his ten dollars in the pot and play began.

~ * ~

The first half-hour of play was sit back, wait and see time for Harry. He wanted to get a feel for how the game went and the guys he was playing with. As they got into the game the other players loosened up and Harry got to learn most of their names. One player said nothing and nobody said much to him either. He put his chips in the pot when required and folded without a word.

When Lindy chided Harry for playing too slow because Harry didn't realize it was his turn to bet, the other players jumped on his ass, too. The new kid had been accepted.

Sitting on the button, Harry drew a diamond suited Big Slick down and decided to get involved. He raised to three times the big blind to test the waters. Three times the big blind had been the standard mid-raise up to this point.

Folds around to Lindy who called as did the quiet guy. They played three handed to the flop.

The flop was A of clubs and 3 4 of diamonds.

Two checks to Harry. With a pair of aces and a diamond flush draw, Harry's first thought was to go up big, but he decided to try a slow play and also checked.

The Turn card was the Q of hearts.

Lindy checked and the quiet man bet fifty. Harry had the feeling the quiet one had paired his Q and he was being tested for weakness. He didn't want to take any chances, so he raised a hundred. Lindy folded. After two looks at his hole cards, quite man folded as well.

"Good fold Marcel," Harry said to the quiet one.

The guys at the table looked at Harry, realized what he had said and to who, and they practically fell on the floor laughing.

Chapter 66

"That's a good one. First time I've heard it. Name's John, but I go by JT. May have to change it to Marcel now," JT said. He smiled as he said it.

"Glad to meet ya, JT," Harry said.

"Good, can we play cards now?" JT asked.

"Yeah, deal the cards, will ya," Lindy agreed.

They dealt and they played.

Harry held his own and was up about two hundred when they took a break at midnight.

"What time does the game usually break up?" Harry asked Lindy while they were waiting to use the pissatoruium.

"We go until we're down to four handed," Lindy answered. "We tried with four a few times, but it didn't work out too great. So, we pack it in when the forth guy busts out."

"Could take a few hours, could take all night?" Harry asked.

"Yeah, that's right, Harry. We've been done by midnight a few times, and played till dawn a few times, too. Usually we're out of here by about three or so," Lindy said.

"What's Tank get?" Harry asked.

"Bigger games he gets ten percent. Small games like ours, he takes five. We decided, we being the regulars that is, the big winner fronts Tank's share. If the two guys on top come out close to even, they split it. That way the losers don't pay part of the house money, and the winners can afford to front for the table," Lindy told Harry.

"Work out pretty even over time?" Harry asked.

Lindy thought for a minute, then he said, "Yeah, probably does, Harry. But it's only two hundred bucks with a full table and hasn't been a problem yet."

"Cool," Harry said.

~ * ~

It was just after one when the first player went out. Lindy caught a four on the River for a straight beating the guy's two pair ALL IN. The guy was low stack and had nothing to lose. By 1:45, a guy named Tony was the next player to go. He was ALL IN with trip J's against JT's flush draw going to the River. When the River showed up as a club, JT had his flush and Tony was saying his "See ya next week" to the table.

They were down to six and Harry was just short of doubled up at 950 in chips. His conservative play with an occasional push hand thrown in had served him well. Lindy was the big stack at the table with probably a bit over fifteen hundred. JT's neat stacks added up to a thou even leaving the three small stacks to fill out the six players at the table.

Harry had the feeling it would be a short night if one of the short stacks didn't double up. He was determined not to let any of them double up at his expense if he could help it.

The hand was dealt and Jerry dumped his last one hundred forty chips in the pot blind. Two folds to JT who called. Two more folds and Jerry and JT went heads up to the Flop.

JT threw his cards on the table showing QJ of spades. Jerry turned over his first card—4 of clubs—then his second which was the 9 of hearts. Not much to write home about.

The flop was K 6 of diamonds and deuce of clubs. No discernable help for either player.

The turn was the 7 of spades. Ditto on the discernable help leaving Jerry hoping for a 4 or a 9 or he was gone.

The River was an A and the game was down to five players.

They played for another fifteen minutes before the small stack tossed in his chips and Lindy called. When Lindy showed a pair of K's to the other player's bubkiss, it was all over but the crying. The flop produced another K and Lindy was golden with the small stack drawing dead.

Harry finished 435 bucks ahead in his first game of serious poker and felt like a million bucks. He tossed 35 bucks into the "pay Tank" fund telling Lindy and JT he thought he should donate since it was his first game and he had come out on top. They appreciated the gesture and told Harry he was welcome any time in their game.

"Thanks," Harry told them and he split.

Tank was waiting by the front door when Harry got downstairs.

"Enjoy yourself, Harry?" Tank asked.

"Yeah, Tank, it was a blast," Harry replied.

"Hear tell you fit in, so you come back whenever you get the urge again, Harry. Tell Mel Tank said you be alright," Tank told Harry.

"I will, Tank. And thanks," Harry told him as he left.

Chapter 67

At eight the following morning, after managing just a few hours of sleep by the time he had hit the sack, Harry answered the phone that just happened to be ringing right beside his ear.

"Gimme a break, will ya," Harry said before he put the phone back in its cradle.

No sooner had he turned over to try and go back to sleep when the phone rang again.

"You're not gonna give me a break, are ya?" Harry said into the phone.

"Nope," was all he heard in return.

"Excuse my franchaisy, but who the fuck is this?" Harry asked.

"It is I, Rowbear," Robert said in his best French accent.

"Your French sucks," Harry told him. "What do you want?"

"Get up and get in here, Harry. My head's back on straight and we need to talk," Robert told Harry.

"Was it on crooked?" Harry said.

Thinking that was a good one, Harry laughed out loud.

"It is I, Rowbear," Robert repeated in his best French accent.

"Okay, maybe it wasn't that funny. A little, maybe?" Harry tried.

"Um, maybe, but just a little," Robert agreed. "Now, are you coming?"

"Actually, no I'm not. Not at the moment at least. If I had a tall blond with big tits and a great ass, and..."

Robert cut Harry off, "Enough already, Harry, I get the picture."

"If you can picture her, maybe I should leave you to it and you can call me back later?" Harry joked.

"Can't you ever be serious for one minute?" Robert asked in obvious frustration over Harry's verbal antics.

Skipping the obvious one liner Robert had teed up for him, Harry said, "Of course I can...fifty nine, fifty-eight, fifty-seven," and he started laughing hysterically.

"Get your ass down here," Robert told Harry as he hung up.

~ * ~

It was almost noon by the time Harry made it downtown to Robert's hospital room. Feeling light and carefree, he amused himself by driving his Datsun HoneyBee with the Honeybee painted on the side.

Don't ever forget, Harry does amuse easily.

Pushing open the door to Robert's hospital room, Harry walked inside. A guy standing on the other side of Robert's bed looked up at Harry as he entered and stopped talking immediately. He walked around the bed and left the room without saying another word to Robert, or to Harry for that matter.

"Good seeing you," Harry said to the guy's back as he walked past Harry.

"Harry, must you always…" Robert started. He didn't finish his thought.

"Not always," Harry answered.

Robert shook his head.

"You summoned, I'm here," Harry said.

Robert shook his head again.

"If it were I," Harry started, "a guy that got 'blunt force traumaed' upside my head, I wouldn't shake my head so."

Harry smiled.

Robert didn't. Harry could see in his eyes he was dying to, but he didn't. Guys with 'Special Groups' have excellent self-control.

"Since I wasn't coming as you so graciously inquired, and you insisted so, I figured I'd come. Well, maybe not come, but I'd come."

"Enough. Shut the hell up, Harry, before I take out my gun and shoot you in self- defense," Robert told him.

"Shutting up, boss," Harry replied. He took his fingers and made a zipping motion across his lips.

Robert started to shake his head again before he stopped himself abruptly.

Harry nodded his head approvingly and made another zipping motion across his lips.

"Maybe I should just shoot myself and put myself out of my own misery," Robert said.

"Please don't," Harry told him, "at least not yet. I'm having too much fun."

This time Robert laughed and Harry laughed with him.

Chapter 68

Harry sat in the corner reading a copy of Readers' Digest from October 2006. He had already done the P.I. thing and memorized the room and everything in it. Hospital rooms are all the same and there wasn't anything different about this one other than the guy in it who Harry didn't really know at all. If he had it pegged right, he probably never would.

When the nurse finished with Robert and left, Harry went back over and sat in a chair he had pulled up next to Robert's bed.

"So, all bullshit aside, why'd you want me to come down here?" Harry asked.

"As much as I have enjoyed the quality time we have spent together," Robert started, "as with all good things, it must come to an end. But, first, a few facts you should know. One, I work for the Government, Harry. That's as far as I can go with an explanation, but you're a smart guy, I'm sure you can dope it out. Second, I need to rest up a bit after the conk on my head and then I've been reassigned to another "issue" that needs my particular expertise. Third, the pokcolmon group needs further looking into and I believe you will do that. Here's a number you can call if you need my help."

Harry took the card from Robert and looked at it. Printed on the card was a phone number and nothing else.

"You can call that number, day or night, any time you need, Harry. If I don't immediately answer, I or someone that works with me will be back to you in less than two minutes no matter what time of the day or night."

Harry nodded and put it in his pocket.

"And fourth, you be very careful, Harry. If we're right, you have stepped into something here and it could lead to a slippery slope that you don't want to travel. I can't promise anything but, if you find yourself in dire straits, the code word is "comeback," as in 'He's making a big comeback.' "

"Comeback," Harry repeated.

"Yeah, comeback," Robert confirmed. "Use it in a sentence, on the phone or in conversation with someone, or scream it from the rooftops, but use it if you need my help. Again, no promises, but if we can help, we will," Robert finished.

"We?' Harry asked.

"Yeah, "we," Harry. We have our ways and I'll leave it at that if you don't mind."

Harry thought for a time, nodded, then said, "Sure, Robert. It's been a blast and I got a strange feeling me and you and the rest of the "we" might cross paths again sometime in the future."

"Later, Harry," Robert said as he held out his hand.

"Yeah, later," Harry said as he shook Robert's hand

Harry got up and left Robert's room without looking back.

When Harry had gotten half way down the hall, he stopped at the nurses' station and waited for the nurse who was sitting there to get off the phone.

"Can I help you?" she said when she was finished with her call.

"Yes, ma'am," Harry said as he flashed her his badge. It was his P.I. badge but, when flashed quickly, it looks as official as any other badge.

"I've just come from seeing Robert in Room 214. He's asleep," Harry whispered, "and I'll need to call him later to confer on an official matter. I will be traveling for the next six hours and I forgot to ask him what name we have him listed under. Don't say it out loud, but can you either show it to me on a chart or write it on a piece of paper that I can then easily destroy. Security reasons; you understand we can't be too careful."

The nurse looked at Harry as if he had three heads and had just asked her to get naked and satisfy the entire New York Giants offensive line at halftime of Sunday's game.

Regaining her composure, she looked up and down the corridor, and when she was satisfied the coast was clear, she wrote something on a piece of note paper. She folded it in half, and handed it to Harry.

Harry unfolded the paper and looked at the name the nurse had written. He smiled when he saw the name SHORTS, refolded the paper and put into his mouth. He turned and started walking down the corridor away from the nurses' station. When he was far enough down the hall, Harry removed the piece of paper from his mouth and made a "Pithlaw" sound as he half spit, half gagged in an attempt to get the perfume taste out of his mouth.

Robert Shorts—what a true wise ass.

Mental note #1 by Harry Mickey Shorts to Harry Mickey Shorts for future use: nice note paper from a very gullible nurse with a cute face, nice smile and adequate breasts. Store it for a rainy day in case rain checks already held in reserve are not available for use.

Mental note #2 by Harry Mickey Shorts to Harry Mickey Shorts: Robert is a G-Man.

Mental note #3 by Harry Mickey Shorts to Harry Mickey Shorts: watch Harry's back for him

Chapter 69

"Well, well, if it isn't Harry Mickey Shorts," Ms. Timmons said into the phone when she heard Harry's voice on the other end.

"In the flesh," Harry responded. "Well, since you can't see me, you can't see my flesh. That is if you even wanted to see my flesh, which you haven't up to this point."

"I get the point, Harry. How can I help you, in a work related way," Ms. Timmons qualified.

"I need a geek," Harry told her. "An IT geek that can do stuff on the web that most mere mortals can't do. You have one of those?"

"Is it legal, Harry?" Timmons asked.

"What we would do together?" Harry teased.

"Shorts," she replied gruffly. "Is what you want the IT geek, ah professional, is it legal what you want him to do?"

"Well…" Harry trailed off.

"That's great, Shorts. How am I supposed to deal with you?" she said.

Being good, Harry said, "You don't, Ms. Timmons. Just gimme the geek and I'll do the rest. You don't have to know squat about what happens from there."

"Somebody will call," she said and she was gone as usual.

~ * ~

Harry was chilling in his living room, sucking down a few Labatts, listening to the Beatle's White Album (vintage vinyl of course) when the phone rang. Mellowed out, he thought about letting the machine get it.

Something said pick up the phone. He did.

"Shorts," he said.

In a rapid fire form of what sounded like English, Harry heard what he thought the person say, "ThisisAlbertWannerman. Ms.TimmonssaidIshouldcallyourightawayso (small breath) Im-callingyourightawaylikeshetoldmeto."

"Huh?" Harry said into the phone.

"ThisisAlbertWannerman. Ms.Timmonssaid…" the person started saying again.

Harry yelled, "YO, COOL IT!" into the phone.

There was the sound of several quick breaths and then quiet on the other end.

"Talk slowly, very slowly" Harry told the caller. "Say your name, take a breath, where you're from, take a breath, say who told you to call me, take a breath, and then stop talking."

Harry could almost hear him thinking over the phone.

"This is Albert Wannerman…from Trundle Industries…Ms. Timmons said I should call you right away…I," and he stopped.

"That was excellent, Albert. Well done," Harry told him. "Now, if Ms. Timmons asked you to call me, does that mean you work in the IT department at Trundle Industries?"

"Yeah, ah, I mean yes," Albert Wannerman told Harry. "I'm a geek."

Interesting he should call himself that Harry thought to himself; but, he is actually a computer geek Harry reminded himself.

"Thank you for calling me, Albert. Do you like to be called Albert, Al, or something else?" Harry asked him.

"My friends call me Square Peg, but you can call me Al, I guess," Al told Harry.

"Square Peg?" Harry queried.

"Ah, yes, Square Peg," Al confirmed. "They always said I kept trying to put a square peg in a round hole in everything I did, so I became Square Peg to some friends. One of my email addresses is squarepeg."

He has friends. That's a good start Harry decided. Then he realized he said "one of my email addresses is squarepeg" and Harry wondered how many he had.

Harry took a long tug on his Labatt for fortification, then he said, "Al, I'll call you Al if you don't mind. Did Ms. Timmons tell you why she wanted you to call me?"

"No," Al said. "Ms.TimmonssaidIshouldcallyourightawaysoIcalledyourightaway."

"Al, you have to talk slow and take breaths in between all those words if I'm going to understand what the hell you're saying. You got that, Al?" Harry told him.

"Sure, Mr. Shorts," Square Peg said. "I got that."

"It's Harry, Al, call me Harry."

"Okay, Harry," he replied.

Harry realized the next question he was about to ask Al was probably a waste of both time and breath, but he had to ask.

"You play poker, Al?" Harry asked him.

"Play poker, me, that's a funny one, Harry. I didn't realize you would be so funny, Harry. Play poker, me, no, that's funny. But I studied it," Al said.

"Studied it?" Harry the comedian asked Al the computer geek.

"Yes, studied it," Al said. "The mathematical permutations, probabilities, card sequence variables, odds and things like that," Al told Harry.

He had to ask, so Harry said, "Why, Al?"

"Well, for fun, Harry," Al replied.

"Al, hold on a minute, I'm gonna need another beer for this," Harry told Al.

Chapter 70

"You still there, Al?" Harry asked when he got back on the line.

"Well, sure I'm here, Harry. You told me to hold a minute didn't you?" Al replied.

What's with the "good puppy" bullshit Harry wondered. Oh, yeah, IT geek he remembered.

"Here's the deal, Al. I need someone to look at an online poker site and help me "navigate" through it. Maybe get under the covers and manipulate things a bit," Harry told Al.

"Harry," Al started, "can you define navigate, under the covers, manipulate things a bit for me? Maybe expound on your meaning. Indicate your intentions. Explain what you…"

"I heard you, Al," Harry interrupted. "Why don't we meet and I can do all of the above for you."

"Meet? Al said in a surprised voice.

"Yeah, meet, as in we both show up at the same place at the same time. Together. That a problem, Al?" Harry asked.

"Ah, no, Harry. It's not exactly a problem," Al replied.

"Huh?" Harry said. "What do you mean 'not exactly a problem'?" Harry asked.

"Well, we, I mean, I don't usually go out and meet with people. We, I mean, I'm used to being in my cubicle doing work. All the time. Inside. Not outside. Meeting people, without my system, ah, computer, no," Al bumbled out.

"Well, exceptions happen, Al. You drink?" Harry asked Al.

"Of course, Harry. All beings must consume liquids on a regular basis to continue to exist," Al replied.

A deep breath, a quick 10987654321, and Harry was ready to continue.

"Alcohol, Al, I mean alcohol. When's the last time you had a load on?" Harry asked him.

"Alcohol? You mean drink alcohol, Harry? Me?" Al asked. "And to answer your other question, I did laundry two nights ago."

"Laundry," Harry repeated, "what the hell does laundry have

to do with anything?"

"You asked when was the last time I had a load on. I did a load of laundry two nights ago, Harry. I don't know why you want to know, Harry, but you asked me," Al told him.

All Harry could do was laugh.

"Plain and simple question, Al. Do you drink alcohol? Yes or no?" Harry asked him.

"Alcohol, me? Yes. Harry, I do. But it makes me do crazy things when I do," Al told Harry.

"Trust me, Al, crazy is good. Sometimes crazy is the best thing," Harry told him. "Where do you live?"

"Live?" Al asked in return.

"Yeah, live. You do leave the building and go home, don't you, Al?" Harry asked.

"Oh, yeah, Harry. Queens...I live in Queens," Al told Harry.

"Where?" Harry asked.

"Queens, Harry. I just told you, I live in Queens," Al said.

"Yes, Al, I heard you. What I'm trying to ascertain is where in Queens do you live?"

"Oh, I get it, Harry. Where in Queens. I live in Little Neck."

"That's great, Al. Do you know where Patrick's Pub is?" Harry asked him.

"Yes, I've seen it. It always looked so lively from the outside," Al told Harry.

"Cool. Meet me there tonight at seven. Can you be there by seven?" Harry asked.

"Seven tonight?" Al repeated. "By seven o'clock tonight, on a work night?" Al asked.

"Yes, seven tonight. On a work night. I promise I will have you home in time to get plenty of sleep, Al," Harry told him. "Just be there. I'll be inside wearing a Yankees cap," he said and hung up the phone.

Harry thought, what the fuck have I gotten myself into this time.

Chapter 71

"Give it to me in plain English, will you. If I wanted to understand fucking accounting talk I would have been a fucking accountant," BrianK said.

"Sure, B. The current projection…I mean, at your current pace you will get to ten million dollars in less than eighteen months. Earliest time frame would be twelve months if you can increase your take by something in the range of twenty percent over that period," Josh told him.

BrianK looked at the papers in front of him and shook his head.

"I can't do much more in the states," BrianK told his long-time friend and financial advisor. "We're everywhere we can go and more publicity would only put us further into the public eye. That's public as in kids, parents and potentially some government agency that might want to know how we're doing what we're doing. Can't chance it," he said.

"What else is there?" Josh asked him.

"Foreign players aren't signing up at the same rate as the kids in the US. Their parents ask too many questions and we can't give them all the information they ask for. The legality issue rears its ugly head and we have to back off the kid. There's got to be a way to penetrate that market better than we do now. Got to be a way," BrianK said.

"I'll have our guy in the UK give us his plan by next week," BrianK heard from one of the other people sitting at the table.

"Yeah, you do that," BrianK said. "We need more foreign players to push the US kids to pile in the money. A lot more of the foreign kids to fork over their money. I can't hold this thing together forever."

~ * ~

Harry was sitting in Patrick's Pub at his favorite table talking to his favorite waitress.

"Here you go, Harry. One JFL for my favorite private dick," Dolly said as she put his drink in front of him.

"Thanks, Dolly," Harry said.

"You waiting for someone, Harry?" Dolly asked.

"Yeah, a guy named Al who also goes by the nickname Square Peg if you can believe it," Harry told her.

"Square Peg? That's a new one on me," she told Harry.

"You've heard the expression before, Dolly. Trying to put a square peg in a round hole. That's where it comes from he told me. Buddies used to say that about him and it stuck."

"Speaking of private dicks, pegs and round holes," Dolly said to Harry. "The construction dude I was seeing flew the coup, so they say."

"And?" Harry asked. "And who's they?"

"Forget 'they,' Harry. Call me, okay. Together we might be able to investigate how some of them might possibly fit together, so to say," Dolly told Harry with a big smile on her face.

"Square pegs don't fit in round holes very well, Dolly," Harry told her.

"You're right, Mr. Private Dick. But, long, hard, round ones do," she said. "At least it did before, Harry."

Dolly turned and walked away, slowly, giving Harry a good view of the swaying goods—so to speak.

"I'll call you," Harry said to the swaying goods, so to speak.

As he did, Al walked in the door. At least Harry assumed the guy that came in through the front door was Al.

Why you ask? Perhaps the long sleeved white dress shirt buttoned to the collar and nerd pack in his shirt breast pocket would be a starter. The deer in the headlights look could be another indication. And finally, when he put his hand on his forehead to shade his eyes from the light that wasn't there, Harry knew.

"Al, over here," Harry yelled to him.

A squint of the eyes, a nod of recognition from whence the, "Al, over here," came from, and Al headed for Harry's table.

"Al," Harry said as he extended his hand toward him.

"Yes, I am Al. Are you Harry?" Al said in perfect terrified robot speak.

"Yeah, I'm Harry."

They shook hands and Harry told Al to cop a squat. After he explained what that was, they sat.

As Dolly approached their table, Harry asked Al, "What do you want, Al?"

Looking very confused, Al said, "I don't know, Harry. It is you who asked to meet with me."

It took a second, but Harry got it.

"No, Al, what do you want to drink?"

"Oh, that," Al said. "I'll have what you're having, I think."

Harry told Dolly, "A JFL for my friend here, Dolly, and one more for me."

Harry thought there might be hope after all when Al snuck a peek at Dolly's swaying goods as she walked away from the table.

Chapter 72

When they had their drinks in front of them, Al looked at Harry and asked, "What's a JFL, Harry?"

"It's a beer drink, Al. You'll love it," he told him.

Harry picked up his glass and offered it to Al to clink in a toast. Al reached out to take it.

"No, Al, you pick up your glass and we tap glasses together. It's a kind of a toasting gesture people do. Then we drink."

Al picked up his glass, tapped his against Harry's, and then proceeded to drink down the entire sixteen ounces of his JFL.

Harry looked on in astonishment.

Putting down his glass, Al said, "That is a very refreshing beverage, Harry. Much better than Tang."

"Get the fuck outa here. You don't have any Tang. Tang's from a million years ago," Harry said.

Al looked perplexed.

"Sure we do, Harry. We, I mean me and the rest of the basement, we bought ten cases from a surplus website we get all of our drinks from," Al told Harry.

"And it's still good?" Harry asked.

"Well, I had thought it was the best thing I had ever tasted. That was before this thing you call a JFL," Al told Harry. "I think the JFL is much better."

It dawned on Harry at that moment that Al had said, "Me and the rest of the basement," but he decided to let that slide for now.

Harry waved for Dolly to bring Al another JFL and moved on to business.

"So, you ready for a little project work, Al?" Harry asked him.

"I think so," Al replied warily. "What kind of project work?" he asked.

"Fun project work. It's undercover, fun project work in fact," Harry told him.

"Undercover?" Al repeated, his eyes brightening at the thought.

As Al reached to pick up his glass, Harry said, "Talk first, drink second. I need you sober here, Al."

"Sure, Harry," Al agreed.

Harry handed Al a piece of paper with a website address, a logon ID and a password on it.

"I need you to log on to this site and figure out how it works. Do some kind of code busting thing you guys do and get under the covers. Find out how it works and how you can manipulate it any way we want. And, you can't let anyone know you're doing it. We're doing it. It's a poker site. Can you do that?" Harry asked.

Al got a faraway look in his eyes and didn't answer Harry right away. Harry was starting to get worried until Al said, "I don't know what we will find when we look at it, Harry, but the basement has never failed before."

Again with the basement Harry thought.

"That's good, Al. And what's with this 'basement' you keep mentioning?" Harry asked.

"The basement? Oh, the basement," Al said as recognition crossed his face. "We, that's me and the rest of our IT infiltration team, we call ourselves the 'basement' because we're in the basement of the Trundle Building. No windows, four walls, big room, lots of equipment and our own vending machines. The way we like it. Nobody bothers us, we don't have to talk to the others, and we get to do what we do, in private," Al said.

"The 'basement' it is then," Harry said. "If it doesn't matter to you, I'll just call you Al. So, can you do it?"

"Sure, Harry. We can do anything, or we have up to this point. I do the talking for the group, but we have some pretty crafty dudes, if you know what I mean. You don't think we can?" Al asked.

"Al, if you say you and your crafty basement dudes can do it, then I believe you can do it. Drink up," Harry told him.

Before he knew it, Al's glass was empty again and he was looking for the lady with the swaying goods.

Chapter 73

The following morning, Harry found himself sitting at the desk in the back of big Mel's office working on the PC. He had solidified his plans with Al and the basement boys. For now, he couldn't do anything but hurry up and wait for Al to get back to him.

He was currently updating his case file while pondering the questions that ran rampant throughout his brain. Questions like:

How big was the pokcolmon.com organization and who besides BrianK was raking in the big bucks?

Did the presence of Frenchie indicate multiple bad boys existed on the inside, or was he a one-off?

What was the legal loophole BrianK was using to make his operation a legitimate enterprise?

How big was "big bucks" and what was BrianK's take; how much went to the behind the scenes backers?

Why Clint; how Clint; when Clint; how long Clint; is he that good? Is he that good all on his own?

Was BobbyGirl now a part of the insiders, and why, etc.; is she that good? Is she that good all on her own?

Robert—all things Robert

And finally, while not necessarily an integral part of the case, there was Sherry—all things Sherry—and certain "things" that were Sherry more than other things

They were all good questions Harry had precious few answers for, except maybe for the certain "things" that were Sherry's. Of those, he had personal firsthand knowledge and could attest to their exquisite "thingness."

The ringing phone brought Harry out of his temporary Sherry dream state and back to reality.

"Hello," Harry said into the phone.

He listened, and then said, "Cool."

After listening some more, he said, "Cool. I'll see you at my place at nine tonight. And Al, thanks for getting on this so fast. Thank the basement boys for me, too."

As soon as Harry hung up the phone, it rang again.

It was Jaxy.

"How's it streaming, dude?" Harry asked him.

"Stream's flowing solid, my man. Got a line on the funds hidey-ho, Joe. Seen this Josh dude once before and he be righteously down, you dig? Squirrels it so's the nut fairy can't hardly do a sniff," Jaxy told Harry.

Harry thought he had deciphered what Jaxy had said and was fairly sure he understood. He pressed on.

"Can you tell what's there, and where?" Harry asked.

"From sea to shining sea, Jaxy can surely see," Jaxy answered.

"A .pdf to the usual box?" Harry asked.

"One .pdf PDQ," Jaxy confirmed.

"Cool," Harry responded. "Same back atcha. Moolah in the coolah."

"Nothin could be finnah, not even in Carolinah, in the mor-or-or-or-ning," Jaxy sang as he hung up.

Harry shook his head and smiled.

Chapter 74

At exactly nine on the dot that evening, two cool ones to the good, Harry met Al at the door to his apartment. Harry had a JFL in hand for Al as he entered.

"Neat-o," Al said as he accepted the drink from Harry.

Neat-o? Harry thought to himself.

"Come on in, Al. I'd show you the place, but it ain't much, and who gives a shit anyway," Harry said.

"That's okay, Harry," Al responded. "Thanks for the thought though."

Harry looked at Al slightly sideways.

"Grab a squat by the table," Harry told Al.

Al looked at Harry slightly sideways.

Noticing, Harry pointed and told him, "Sit down at the table over there, Al."

Al sat and took a healthy sip of his drink. The smile on his face indicated he enjoyed the first sip of his JFL.

"I have a laptop, but I see you brought your own," Harry said. "You would prefer to use yours?"

"Yes, Harry. I have the site pre-loaded with the work the boys and I have done on it down in the basement. It's ready to go as is," Al told Harry.

Harry could have sworn he barely blinked and Al's beer was gone.

"Another?" Harry asked pointing to Al's empty glass.

"Maybe one more," Al answered.

"I'll get the drinks while you set up your laptop," Harry told Al. "When I get back we can get down to it."

Al busied himself with his laptop and was prepared to "get down to it" when Harry came back with the refills.

"So, what'd you guys find when you looked at the pokcolmon site?" Harry asked him.

"We all decided we would have gone to college for free if this site was around when we were in high school. Not that we paid for college or graduate school anyway, but we definitely could have gone for free off this game," Al told Harry.

Deciding to pass on the logic behind that comment, Harry said, "And what exactly did you find when you looked at the site."

"It's well done on the surface. Nothing slick, but well done. We've looked at many sites over the last four years, but we didn't recognize any give away signs on who designed this one."

"Give away signs?" Harry asked.

"Yes, give away signs. It's kind of a code signature that allows somebody who knows what to look for to identify each major programmer out there," Al told Harry.

"So, what else did you find?" Harry asked.

"It took us almost a whole day but we were able to add some additional code to show all the hands that were being played."

"Wait a minute," Harry said. "How'd you get the code to be able to manipulate the hands?"

"Harry, you embarrass yourself with such nonsense," Al told Harry. "We have the two best hackers of the last ten years in the basement plus the best gamer to come along in, well, in forever, Harry. If it's out there, we can get it and we can manipulate it."

"Can you tell if they ever manipulated the code in the same way in the past?" Harry asked. "Maybe set it up so one player could see all the hands and the rest of the players couldn't. Set it up so he or she could win whenever they wanted to, or somebody wanted them to. Can you tell if that happened?"

"Interesting postulate, Harry, very interesting indeed. Give me a minute," Al replied.

If fingers can be described as flying, Al's fingers were flying over the keys. Harry had never thought that particular expression was worth two shits, but he had just changed his mind. The kid was burning up the keyboard.

Harry finished his beer and went to get another one. When he returned, Al said, "Yes."

"Yes, that's it, just yes? Not yes they can, or yes I believe it is possible, just yes?" Harry asked.

"Yes to all of those," Al replied.

"No shit," Harry answered.

Chapter 75

After explaining to Al what "no shit" meant, Harry sat down next to him to see what Al had seen.

"Show me," Harry said.

"Show you?" Al replied.

"Yeah, show me," Harry said again.

"Show you, ah, what?" Al asked.

"Show me how they manipulated the code so one player could see all the hands and the rest of the players couldn't. Show me what one player could see on the screen and the others couldn't. Show me," Harry said.

"Oh, show you," Al said as if he finally understood.

"Yeah, show me," Harry said again.

"Well, I can't really show you that, Harry," Al told him.

"What the fuck do you mean you can't really show me that?" Harry asked. "If you can't show me, then how do you know they did it? Or they could do it. Or it happened. Or you know it happened."

Somewhat flustered, Al said, "Look at this, Harry."

Fingers started flying and code started moving across the screen at light speed. The look on Al's face was part intense concentration and part Peter Pan is at your window and your fantasy has come true.

Unfortunately for Harry, it didn't mean didly squat to him.

"Al, dude, slow down," Harry said to him. "Codes nice and all, but pictures tell tales."

Al stopped and looked at Harry. He repeated, "Pictures tell tales?" as he continued to look at Harry.

"Yeah, pictures tell tales. As in, show me on the screen, Al. Code doesn't mean shit to me," Harry told him.

"Okay, Harry, let me fix that for you," Al told him.

A few flicks of the wrist and a dozen or so characters in what seemed to be organized in random fashion to Harry and the pokcolmon.com poker site appeared on the screen. There was a small box in the lower left hand corner that continued to show the code Al was producing with his magical fingers.

"That's the standard screen every player sees when they play on pokcolmon, Harry. If you set up the security parameters for a player thusly, you get this."

With a single keystroke, Al transformed the screen to show all the hole cards for all the players in the hand. Whoever had that security parameter set-up would be able to win any hand they wanted as long as they had the cards to do so. They also would know when to bluff and possibly what a bluff might do and to who.

"As you would say, Harry, no shit!" Al said.

"No shit is right, Al. Can you tell if they did this for any players who have played online through pokcolmon.com?" Harry asked him.

Al cocked his head to one side and thought for a second, then said, "We would have to scan the player profiles and security set-ups for every player that has had an ID on pokcolmon from the beginning. That would take some time, Harry. Yeah, we can do it, but it would take time."

"How much time?" Harry asked.

"I don't know, Harry. We have been able to circumvent the pokcolmon security scanners so far, but now you're asking for deep penetration into the bowels of their code. The basement will have to think tank the proper approach before we go in looking for what you want. You need it?" Al asked.

"If I'm asking you can assume I need it," Harry told him.

"Give us a day. I'll get back to you by tomorrow night with what you want. Is that okay, Harry?" Al asked.

"Al, that would be just honky-dory," Harry told him.

"Honky-dory. You're funny, Harry," Al told him.

"And you're about to get yourself another JFL, my man," Harry replied.

Chapter 76

Harry spent the following day busying himself with household-duty stuff. Two weeks of laundry had piled up to go with dishes that seemed to have multiplied in the sink. Getting the dishwasher fixed was probably going to have to hit the "priority" list sooner as opposed to later. Dusting and vacuuming the apartment remained in the "next time I get domestic" category—whenever that might occur.

With his chores completed and the majority of the morning pissed away doing so, he headed out to reward himself with lunch and a few cool ones down at the local watering hole. What, or perhaps it would be better to consider who Harry found there, caught Harry completely by surprise.

Entering the brewhouse in question, Harry found his beloved ex-wife sheltered away in a back booth with what could only be described as a hunk of a man. From his surfer blond hair, to the bulging biceps escaping his Plandome Country Club golf shirt, right down to his loafers/sans socks, Harry immediately hated every inch of him.

Jealousy? Could Harry actually be jealous of another guy having lunch with Sherry? His ex-wife. The ex part being the key there. Jealous? Harry. Of surfer boy with the Popeye arms?

Harry jealous?

Could the Pope be Catholic and also be Polish at the same time once in a blue moon?

Harry was turning to leave when Sherry caught sight of him and called out, "Harry, back here, Harry."

Well shit Harry thought to himself.

Harry turned and walked to the back of the bar to where Sherry sat with sans socks boy.

"Hey, Sherry, fancy meeting you here," Harry said for want of anything better to say.

"Hi, Harry," Sherry greeted him. Pointing to her companion, Sherry said, "Harry, this is Brett. Brett, meet Harry."

She didn't say anything else.

They shook hands.

"Nice to meet you, Harry," Brett said.

"You too, Brett," Harry replied.

Being the crackerjack private investigator Harry fancied himself to be on occasion, he noticed their plates were empty and their glasses were almost empty as well. He deduced they must have come in for an early lunch or a late breakfast.

Seeing Harry survey the table, Sherry said, "We came in for a late breakfast after a lesson at the club. Brett is teaching me how to play golf."

Harry wondered if that was all he was teaching her.

"Oh, I didn't know you had taken up golf, Sher," Harry said.

"I don't know if you would say I was actually taking up golf, Harry. Mel got a set of golf lessons from a client and gave them to me. So, I'm using them."

Harry wondered if that was all she was using.

"Brett's been working with me and he's very good," Sherry continued with that smile Harry knew so well. It was the "sink ships" kind of smile.

Harry wondered if that was all Brett was good at and with whom. Harry had a tendency to get formal in his language in times of stress involving his ex-wife.

"I'm learning how to play the game and some of the terminology, too," Sherry said. "Brett has been showing me how best to position the balls, good shaft angle, the proper stroke and the importance of following through strong. If you repeat the stroke properly over and over again eventually you can get it to go long and hard."

Harry looked at her and would have liked to have said, "Are you shitting me?" but he said nothing.

"Brett says my technique is getting better each time we do it," Sherry said.

"She was stroking it real good this morning," Brett added.

"I was," Sherry agreed nodding her head, "and I really enjoyed doing it. I was sorry when it ended and I think Brett was, too. He said he wished we could have gone on longer."

With a big smile on his face, Brett nodded in agreement.

Harry continued to just stand there and try not to look astonished at what he was hearing.

"Now that I'm using my hands better, Brett says next time we're going to work on how to get my body in the proper position. If you can work your body, you can really go after it like you want it. He's got me thinking about the right distance to spread my feet apart for good balance, back straight and bending slightly at the waist while sticking out my butt..."

Harry turned and walked out without saying a word.

Chapter 77

A cold shower was exactly what the doctor ordered. Or at least it was what Harry deemed absolutely necessary after listening to Sherry and Brett.

Harry was toweling off when the phone rang. He picked up the beer he had sitting on the corner of the sink and went to answer it. The beer had replaced the fifteen Advils Harry felt might remedy the ache in his head.

"Shorts," Harry said after he had hit the speaker button on the phone.

"Wannerman," was what Harry heard next.

"Al?' Harry asked.

"Harry," came the reply.

Harry sipped his beer.

"What are you doing, Al?" Harry asked.

"I'm calling you, Harry. We're on the phone," Al responded.

More beer for Harry.

"I know we are on the phone, Al. Why are you telling me only your name?" Harry asked him.

"Well, when you answered the phone you said your last name, so I thought I was supposed to say my last name. When you said my first name, I said your first name. It's a funny game, Harry. I don't know why you asked me what I was doing when I was clearly on the phone with you. I don't do anything else when I'm on the phone, Harry. Unless someone asks me to, that is, Harry. You didn't ask me to, so I wasn't doing anything but being on the phone with you."

End of remaining beer in bottle.

"I got it, Al. What have you got for me? And by the way, if it's about what I asked you to do, didn't you say you needed until tonight?" Harry asked.

"To answer your questions in order, I do have something for you, it is concerning what you asked me to do for you, and two of us would like to meet you at Patrick's Pub tonight. That's the tonight I said I needed until," Al said.

"Patrick's Pub at seven?" Harry asked.

"Patrick's Pub at seven would fit into our schedule for to-night perfectly," Al replied. "We'll be able to get back to the basement and help the rest of the team finish the rush project we need to present by noon tomorrow."

"You mean you'll be going back downtown to the office after we meet? To do more work? Like overnight?" Harry asked.

"I'm sorry, Harry, I don't understand your questions. Why wouldn't we be working overnight to finish a project we were asked to do? It's a rush project," Al answered.

"You work through the night regularly?" Harry continued.

"It's routine if we need to, Harry, and it's often routine. If I needed more than two hours of sleep a night I guess it could be-come a problem after a while."

"Take a nap and I'll see you at seven," Harry said.

As Harry hit the off button the phone rang immediately.

"Shorts," Harry answered.

"Why did you run away, Harry?"

"Who is this?" Harry said.

"Harry," Sherry answered.

"Can't be, I'm Harry."

"Was it something I said, Harry?" Sherry asked.

"Oh, I don't know, Sher. Think about what you said and see if there was anything that I could have misinterpreted," Harry told her.

Harry listened to the silence. He could see her replaying the conversation in her head.

"Sherry," Harry said.

"I'm thinking, Harry," she answered.

"While perhaps taken slightly out of context, try these, Sher: '...how best to position the balls, good shaft angle, the proper stroke...repeat the stroke properly over and over again eventually you can get it to go long and hard...she was stroking it real good this morning Brett said...right distance to spread my feet apart for good balance, back straight and bending slightly at the waist while sticking out my butt...'"

Continued silence, and then, "Taken out of context, I can see where you might get the wrong impression, Harry. And Brett is some specimen to go along with the possibly misinterpreted out of context dialogue," Sherry agreed.

"You think?" Harry added.

"Maybe if you came over you could help me perfect my stroke, Harry. Maybe even help me work on how to get my body in the proper position. Find out if you can work your body, you can really go after it like you want it," Sherry said.

"A quick lesson for the struggling trainee could possibly be arranged," Harry told Sherry.

"A lesson, Harry?" Sherry asked.

"Sure, Sherry," Harry said. "And by the way, will a stiff shaft do?"

"A stiff shaft will do quite nicely, Harry. I've been told working with a stiff shaft especially once you get your body in the proper position can let you really go after it like you want it," Sherry told him.

"Fore!" Harry yelled.

"At least, Harry, plan on four at least."

Chapter 78

Dolly had just placed Harry's Irish Whiskey neat in front of him when he saw Al and his basement compadre enter the pub. Harry thought a stiff drink might help him clear his head after his afternoon's activities. When the word stiff entered his thought process he winced and rearranged his body parts for more comfort.

Harry waved at Al.

When they reached the table, Al said, "Thanks for agreeing to meet us at this very fine place, Harry." Turning toward the guy with him, Al said, "This is Lars. Lars, say hello to Harry."

If Harry didn't know better he would have thought the time machine had got cranking and dropped a body from the past in front of him. A perfect specimen from Sweden, or Norway, or someplace over there from thirty years ago was standing right in front of him. All he needed was the pointy hat and he would have been absolutely perfect.

"Hello, Harry," Lars said as instructed as he reached over to shake Harry's hand. As he did, he bumped the table and Harry's Irish Whiskey neat slid to the end of the table and became an Irish Whiskey not-so-neat in Harry's lap.

Harry looked down at the growing wet spot covering the front of his pants.

Seeing what had occurred, Dolly rushed over and said, "Holy Shit." She immediately began rubbing the spot with the bar rag she was carrying. To Harry it seemed she did so with increasing vigor.

"If you continue to do that much longer we're going to have to go into the back room and finish the job in private," Harry told Dolly.

"Just trying to help, Harry," Dolly said with the biggest smile Harry had seen since, well, since that afternoon. Several times that afternoon in fact. Four times that afternoon to be precise.

Lars stood transfixed in a state of shock at that moment. He hadn't moved. Al on the other hand was busy watching the Dolly rubbing show wishing the drink had been spilled in his lap.

"Enough already. Sit, Al. Sit, Lars," Harry told them.

Al sat and he pulled Lars into the other seat next to his at the table.

Turning toward Lars, Harry said, "Forget it, Lars. It's just a pair of pants and my schwantz needed a drink anyway."

Lars looked slightly less than transfixed now and perhaps a bit confused.

"Okay basement guys, let's stop dicking around. Order a drink and then we can get down to you two telling me what you've got for me."

"I'll have one of those JFL's," Al told Dolly who was still smiling broadly.

"And what is deer in the headlights boy having?" Dolly asked.

"Give him the same, and one more for me. I'll try and drink this one," Harry told Dolly. "And stop smiling like you already got some."

Still smiling, Dolly went to get the drinks.

"So you guys have been dicking around in the program code area of the website I presume?" Harry asked.

Before Al could say anything, Lars answered, "I'm sorry, Harry, I just don't understand."

"You don't understand what?" Harry asked.

The perplexed look on Lar's face seemed to indicate he was contemplating the unsolvable problems of the world.

"Well, Lars?" Harry asked again.

Finally answering, Lars said, "I don't know what is dis "dicking around," Harry?"

Harry frowned, thought, then starting laughing out loud.

"Dicking around," Harry repeated.

"Yes, you keep saying dicking around," Lars said. "I don't know what is dis "dicking around" you keep saying, Harry?"

Al caught on and starting laughing out loud, too.

Lars wasn't laughing.

"Man, Lars, you're a kick," Harry said. "Dicking around is like messing around, fucking around. You get it—fucking around, dicking around?"

Lars still looked confused. Al leaned over and whispered in Lars' ear until he broke out in a big grin.

"Ah, I get it, Harry," Lars said. "Let's stop dicking around and get her done."

They all laughed at that one.

Chapter 79

"So, what do you have for me?" Harry asked them.

"Lars did a good bit of the work on this, Harry," Al started, "but I will speak for the basement. We 'got under the covers' as you have said before and we found what you wanted us to find. After looking at every player that has had or still has an ID and has played at least one hand at pokcolmon.com, we found two players that had the ability to see all the hole cards for all the players in the hands they were playing."

"Two players?" Harry asked.

Al looked at Lars. Lars nodded.

"Yes, two players is what Lars says he found," Al answered.

"How?" Harry asked Al.

"How?" Al repeated.

"Yes, how did Lars find that? Is it in the code he looked at? Did he find evidence in the actual code that two players were given the ability to see the hole cards of the competitors in the hands they were playing?"

Al looked at Lars and Lars again nodded to Al.

Before Al could say anything, Harry said, "Got it, Al. I'm sure I understand what Lars was trying to say. How long ago did it start and can they still do it? Also, did Lars identify how their ability to see the hole cards came about?" Harry asked.

"Came about?" Al asked.

"Yeah," Harry answered. "How did they get the ability to see the hole cards?"

Al looked at Lars.

Lars spoke.

"Harry, the code that allows pokcolmon to run is very sophisticated, that's the word I think I mean to say, and has good security. It takes guys like Al, and me, and the rest of the basement to do the breaking of the code like we did. Tricky code dis guy put into the code, but we can break dis tricky code. Not anybody can break dis tricky code and security he put in with it too."

"Uh, yeah," Harry replied warily.

"He means the code's good and the security was top notch,"

Al translated for Harry.

"That's what I thought he said, but..." Harry said.

"What else do you want to know, Harry?" Al asked.

"Again, how long ago did it start and can they still do it? And you said there were two players—do you know who they were, er, are?" Harry asked.

Lars was about to speak, but Al said, "Let me take this, Lars."

"The one started soon after the site got up and running from what we could see. He wasn't the first player to be assigned an ID, but he was the first player to rack up lots of winnings in his account. This term "rack up" is the right way to say it?" Al asked.

"Yes, that's the right term," Harry told Al.

"Good. This first one doesn't play anymore, so it really doesn't matter. For the records though, Harry, he still has the security patch to let him do it if he was to play again," Al said.

"Record," Harry corrected.

"Record what?" Al asked.

"You said 'for the records' and it is correctly stated 'for the record,'" Harry told them.

Al and Lars nodded at each other as they stored that one into their cavernous memory banks.

"Who?" Harry asked. He continued before Al could repeat his question of "who" by saying, "Who is this player?"

Al looked at Lars who said, "His name in the database files is listed as Clint. Clinton Rensford to say the whole name."

"Clint was helped to win online by BrianK or some member of his team?" Harry queried.

"Yes, that is the name I said. I don't know dis BrianK, or who put the patch there, but Clint is the name," Lars repeated for Harry.

"Clint Rensford," Harry repeated. "I want to make sure I understand. He could see all of the hole cards of all the players in the hands while he played online?"

"Yes," Lars said again. "Clint's profile has the security patch that overwrites the code to mask the hole cards before the hand is over in dis game they play—dis HoldHim Poker game."

"Holdem. I keep telling you it's No Limit Holdem Poker, Lars," Al told Lars.

"No shit," Harry said. "And the other player? Who is the other player that has this patch that allows him to see all of the hole cards of all the players in the hands while he plays online?"

Lars whispered something to Al and Al turned to respond to Harry's question for the basement.

"It's not a he, Harry. He's a she, or she's a she, or, ah, it's a she," Al stammered.

"A she?" Harry asked.

"Yes, a she," Al responded. "The other player with the special patch giving her the special power is the one called Bobby-Girl."

"No shit," Harry replied.

Chapter 80

Al and Lars had one more JFL while Harry made sure he had everything he needed and felt he could get out of them. If the ability to circumvent the game was there, and Harry felt all along it could be, Clint being the one didn't surprise Harry in the least. But a second player surprised him, and the name floored him.

Maybe it shouldn't have, but it did. BobbyGirl was a player in this thing and Harry had to figure out the reasons.

"BobbyGirl for sure?" Harry had asked Al and Lars.

"BobbyGirl is for sure the other one with dis patch," Lars had confirmed.

"When?" Harry had asked.

"Ah, when what?" Al quizzed.

"Yes, when did BobbyGirl's profile get the special patch to undo the security in the code?" Harry asked.

Lars and Al had put their heads together and semi-argued in whispered tones for a minute or longer. Finally Al said, "Lars knows but he doesn't know exactly."

"Lars knows but he doesn't know exactly?" Harry repeated.

"Ah, yeah, he knows but he doesn't remember the exact date the patch was installed in the code," Al said.

Harry nodded. Al and Lars watched him nod and had no idea at all why he was nodding.

Harry stopped nodding and said, "The exact date isn't important, Lars. Do you remember approximately when it was added, the patch I mean? Was it last month? Two months ago? Six months ago? Longer?"

Lars and Al again put their heads together and semi-argued in whispered tones for a minute or longer. Finally Al said, "Lars isn't definitely sure. He is very sorry he doesn't know the exact date because he should know the exact date and it is something the basement should always know and Lars knows that. But," Al continued, "he thinks it was Tuesday the seventh. That would make it almost three months ago."

"Whew!" Harry said.

"Whew? Al and Lars said together in question.

"Yeah, whew," Harry repeated. "I'm amazed he remembers the exact date the patch was installed, plus I thought you were never going to stop talking."

"Oh, whew," Lars said.

"Thanks for all your help, guys," Harry told them. "I owe you and the rest of the basement guys one, too".

"It was fun, Harry," Al replied before Lars leaned over and whispered something in Al's ear.

"And," Al continued, "Lars says he's sorry about the drink in your pants. He also says thanks for the JFL as you call it. He liked it, er, likes it, er, he did like it and still likes it, er…"

"Al, Lars, I get the picture," Harry told Al. "Now stop dicking around, finish your JFL's, and get the fuck out of here. I got some work to do."

At that very moment, Dolly appeared at their table minus her apron and tray. She looked like she was getting ready to leave.

Harry and Dolly exchanged the slightest of knowing nods, but not slight enough that Al and Lars didn't catch the exchange.

Al looked at Lars, Lars looked at Al, and then they both looked at Harry.

They finished their drinks and then Lars spoke first.

"Enjoy your work, Harry, and your dicking around."

With that Al and Lars got up and left.

Harry and Dolly were right behind them.

Chapter 81

Harry awoke the next morning feeling like a million bucks. It had been a long while since he had experienced that which was Dolly in her full glory and he now knew that had been an oversight on his part, and a very large mistake.

Dolly in her full glory was something to behold, and the beholding was just the beginning. What came next would have been well worth the price of admission. He knew he wouldn't be able to handle too much of Dolly, at least not on a regular basis. But small doses would definitely have to be added back into his social agenda.

The next thing that hit his brain's radar screen was the other revelation that had surprised him last night. Namely—BobbyGirl.

It seemed BobbyGirl was more of a player in this scheme, if it was a scheme, than he had anticipated up to this point. He had included her in the mix, but in the mix and part of the ingredients were two entirely different animals.

BobbyGirl = some kind of animal?

Harry quickly removed that train of thought from his social agenda line of vision that had been increased by one last night. A good "one" at that. A real good one. Oldies can sometimes come back to be one of the "goodiest" Harry reminded himself.

But why BobbyGirl? What would have motivated BrianK to muddy the waters and add another piece to the puzzle? A puzzle piece that couldn't be tossed away very easily at his whim. Another puzzle piece added to the inner circle when it was obvious he already had Clint sitting right smack dab in the middle of the puzzle, and inner circle.

"Why add BobbyGirl?" Harry asked himself out loud.

That light bulb Harry was famous for lit up above his head.

Guys and Dolls!

You start to max out on your "Guy" penetration and can't increase it significantly without an extensive marketing emphasis. That would put your little venture further into the public's eye. You need another avenue to increase playership. BobbyGirl had been added as a part of the scheme to garner the "Dolls" contingency out there.

Guys and Dolls!

Boys and girls!

Males and females?

Call it anything you want, but BrianK brought BobbyGirl into the fold to show the girls out there in cyber internet space that girls could compete with the boys and win big dollars toward their college dreams. Harry hated to do it, but he had to give the son of a bitch credit—it was a brilliant move. If one girl could play with the boys and win, they all could.

How?

Show her the hole cards of the other players she was playing against and let her clean up. Even if she was good on her own right, no sense in taking any chances when you have the power to manipulate the system—or in a word, cheat—and give her the means to trumpet 'GIRL POWER' all over the net.

Result—BrianK gets to shout "SHOW ME THE MONEY!"

Result—girls start signing up in droves to play so they can get in on the action and grab their piece of the college fund pie.

If BobbyGirl can do it, I can do it...

If BobbyGirl can beat the boys, I can beat the boys...

If BobbyGirl can be a winner, I want to be a winner too!

Result—BrianK gets to shout "GIMME THE MONEY!"

Result—BrianK doesn't have to shout "SHOW ME THE MONEY!"—the bastard already has their money.

End result—if his gut is right, Harry better hurry up and figure out what to do before a ton of kids get fucked over royally.

The SIXTY-FOUR THOUSAND DOLLAR QUESTION of course is how.

Chapter 82

Harry was sitting at the desk in the back of Mel's office. He was sitting in the dark. That's what sometimes happens when Harry sits at the desk in the back of Mel's office at two in the morning.

Harry couldn't sleep. The big money question had him temporarily stumped and he couldn't sleep. It sometimes happens when Harry gets stumped. Most times a half-dozen or so cool ones later and he's off to beddy-bye land dreaming of an appealing social agenda appointment he could make, and keep.

But not tonight. Not this stumper. Not with kids involved. Not when it was something Max asked him to do.

Max doesn't ask Harry for much; almost nothing actually. When he does, it's important. That makes this important. That's why he was sitting at the desk in the back of Mel's office in the dark.

Well, not actually, but let's just move on.

~ * ~

Sitting in the dark, Harry dialed the number and waited. Three rings later a computer generated voice said, "Leave a message."

At the beep, Harry said, "Bell bottom jeans are making a big comeback," and he recited his number.

Harry hung up the phone and waited. Two minutes to the second later his phone rang. When he picked it up he heard, "Are you okay, Harry?"

It wasn't Robert.

"Yes, I'm fine. I'd like to speak to Robert," Harry said.

After a five second lapse, Harry heard, "One hour, same number," and then he heard a dial tone.

Is there anyone that doesn't hang up on me before I think we're done talking?

With an hour to kill, Harry did what he did best. He got up and walked over to the small fridge Big Mel had in the very back of the office. He grabbed two bottles of yellow gold from the fridge and sat back down at the desk to review the case as he knew it so far.

Two bottles so he wouldn't have to get up in short order. Case thinking has a way of making a body extra thirsty. Harry methodically went over every step taken so far and every piece of "evidence" uncovered to date. When he was done he went over it all once again.

The second bottle had been gone for about ten minutes when it was time to make the call. Looking at the illuminated clock Harry kept in the bottom drawer of the desk told Harry it had been fifty-nine minutes from the end of his first call.

"Shorts," Harry said into the receiver.

"Are you good, Harry?"

This time it was Robert.

"Shouldn't you have said "Shorts" right back at me?" Harry said.

"Are you good, Harry?"

"I'm still fine, Robert. That is if I can still call you Robert," Harry said.

"Yes you may, Harry. What can I do?" Robert asked.

Not a, "What can I do to help," or maybe a, "What can I do for you, Harry," just "What can I do?"

"Can we meet?" Harry asked.

After a slight hesitation, the person Harry knew as Robert said, "That could be difficult at this time, Harry. When do you need to see me?"

Again, the "When" and not a "Why" caught Harry by surprise.

"I'm at a crossroad in the matter we have discussed and I need guidance and intel before I proceed," Harry told him.

"Can it wait?" was Robert's reply.

"It can wait, but I don't know for how long. Could be a year, could be a month, could be yesterday. I honestly don't know the answer to that question, but my guess is sooner as opposed to later would be best," Harry responded.

"I'll call you back. Sit tight," Harry heard and the phone went dead.

Chapter 83

Three sips into his next cool one, the phone rang.

"Shorts," Harry answered.

"Ten o'clock at Teterboro. Small six seater with call letters RHK30 on the side will be waiting at the east end of the terminal. Get in and don't ask any questions."

"What do I need?" Harry asked.

"Yourself."

Yep, you guessed it, the phone line went dead.

Harry had a fundamental weakness in his otherwise almost-but-not-quite-perfect being. It was his Datsun B210 HoneyBee. He would have driven the Mustang Mach but leaving that in the parking lot at Teterboro was tantamount to leaving a sign on it that said "Please Steal Me!" His HoneyBee had been with him a long time and he loved it to death. But, when placed up against his Mach, adios HoneyBee if one had to choose.

Harry got out of the car and walked in and through the terminal. He only had "Yourself" with him, so he walked out the east exit and onto the tarmac and spotted the small plane with RHK30 on the side.

"You Shorts?" the guy standing next to the plane asked.

"Yeah," Harry answered.

"Good, let's go," the guy said and jumped into the plane.

Walking up the ramp Harry noticed the windows in the back of the plane had been blacked out. When he got into the plane he saw the door to the front cockpit was closed. He guessed it would be locked and knocking on it would be a waste of time.

Harry walked up, sat in the first seat, and knocked on the door to the cockpit. As expected, there was no response.

A few minutes later the plane started taxiing and Harry said, "I'll have an Absolut Gimlet on the rocks and the peanuts," to the no one that was taking orders.

With nothing else to do, as he was often want to do, Harry ran through what he knew about the case. The answers Harry needed had started to come to him and the case was starting to come together. But, Harry still had too many questions.

How much did Robert, or whoever the fuck he was, know about BrianK?

How much did he know about his operation? pokcolmon.com?

Was this the case he was working on before he got called away and reassigned to another "issue" that needed his particular expertise?

Who's Frenchie?

What's with Clint?

Had BobbyGirl been dealt winning hands by a pro dealer at the tournament they had just been to? Could Robert have been watching the dealer so closely because he knew the dealer and sensed the fix was in for BobbyGirl?

If yes, how did he know?

If yes, why?

So many questions, only one man with answers. Or so Harry hoped.

~ * ~

Harry must have dozed for a bit and woke as the plane touched down with a bumpety-bump. Soon the plane came to a stop and the pilot came through the cockpit door and opened the exit door for Harry to deplane.

"After you, Shorts," the guy said to Harry.

"Thanks," Harry replied.

Harry jumped down and found himself staring at what looked like a farm house. When he looked to his left he saw a runway that split a corn field that seemed to go on forever on both sides. When he turned back around, Robert was standing on the front porch of the farmhouse.

Chapter 84

"How was your flight?" Robert asked.

"Great," Harry answered. "Need I ask where I am?"

"Don't bother," Robert replied.

"Didn't think so," Harry said.

Walking down the steps, Robert said, "Let's walk, Harry," as he turned and headed away from the plane and the runway.

Harry caught up to Robert and they walked over to a picnic table with benches situated under a huge oak tree.

"Let's sit, Harry. I'd offer you a cold beer but I don't have any at my disposal right now. I'll have to owe you one if you don't mind," Robert told Harry.

"That's no problem, Robert. This is my hour to lay off the stuff," Harry replied.

"Always the jokester, aren't you, Harry?"

"Always leave 'em laughing," Harry replied.

"You said the magic word and we are here for you, Harry. What is it you need?" Robert asked.

"Need I ask who 'we' are?" Harry asked.

"Move on, Harry. Now, what is it you need?" Robert repeated.

"So," Harry started. "I've been working the case and I've generated enough information through various sources to put some things together. As you would expect, I've got holes. Big holes. I think you can plug some of them. Can you? Will you?"

"Harry, I thought enough of you to put a hold on something I'm working on, something very important. I brought you here to help if I can, so ask your questions and I'll see what I can do to fill some of those holes."

"Okay, here goes:

"How much do you or your organization know about BrianK?

"How much do you know about his operation? pokcolmon.com?

"Just like me, were you working on this "case" before you got called away and reassigned to another "issue" that needed your particular expertise?

"Who's Frenchie?

"He conk you on the head? If not him, one of his guys?

"What's with Clint?

'Was BobbyGirl dealt winning hands by a pro dealer at the tournament we attended? Were you watching the dealer that closely because you knew the dealer and sensed the fix was in for BobbyGirl?

"If yes, how did you know?

"If yes, why?"

Harry realized he was leaning forward and he sat back.

Robert looked at Harry. Harry was sure he was assessing what and how much he would, or could, tell Harry.

Finally Robert said, "This could take a while, Harry. Let's go inside."

Robert got up and headed back to the farm house.

Harry followed.

When they got to the steps to the front porch, Harry said, "Holy shit. Where's the fucking plane? The plane's gone."

"Don't worry, Harry. Even if I tell you more than I should, I'll let you leave here alive."

Harry looked at Robert just as he broke up laughing.

"Asshole," Harry said and he laughed as well.

Chapter 85

The inside of the farm house was much different that Harry had envisioned while looking at it from the outside. Modern and tricked-out was what he saw coming through the front door.

"Wow," Harry said.

"Surprised you, Harry?" Robert said in reply.

"I believe 'wow' said it all," Harry replied. "What is this place?"

"It's a facility we use that's someplace off the beaten path. We have access to it when we need it," Robert answered.

"There's more computer hardware in this place than you'd find…than you'd find…well, than you'd find. Is that a satellite, radar something?" Harry asked.

"It's something, Harry. Now, no more questions and I won't have to not give you any more answers. Okay, Harry?" Robert said.

"Cool," Harry answered.

"Let's go in the back where we can talk in private," Robert said.

"Something tells me there ain't no 'private' in a place like this," Harry replied.

"Come on Harry, follow me," Robert said as he headed for a doorway into what Harry assumed was the back of the building—the private place.

The room Robert led Harry into was set up in simple conference room style. There was a rectangular table with ten chairs in the center of the room and a white board on the far wall. The only other furniture in the room was a small table with a Mr. Coffee and the fixings—powdered creamer and sugar packets.

When they each had a cup of coffee and were seated across from each other at the table, Robert spoke.

"I'm on a tight schedule doing something we aren't going to discuss, Harry. To the best of my ability, I will answer the questions you have posed and any others you may have. If I can't, I will tell you I can't. Don't ask it again. If you venture to someplace where I think you shouldn't, or I can't go, I will tell you. And, you can say anything you want in here, Harry. You're not being recorded. If that is agreeable to you, we can get started. Is that okay with you, Harry?" Robert stated matter of factly.

"I'm cool wit dat," Harry replied.

Robert shook his head, but he smiled at Harry.

"One at a time, I will repeat your question and give you the best answer I can. Here we go:

"How much do you or your organization know about BrianK?—We know a great deal about BrianK, his organization, his backers, etc.

"How much do you know about his operation? pokcolmon.com?—Some aspects of his operation are still being investigated and reports compiled, but suffice it to say we have a fairly comprehensive handle on BrianK and his operation. As far as pokcolmon.com goes, Harry, please don't have anyone screw around with their code any more if you would.

"Just like me, were you working on this 'case' before you got called away and reassigned to another 'issue' that needed your particular expertise?—I believe my answers to the previous questions will give you some idea of my involvement in the 'case' as you call it.

"Who's Frenchie?—Frenchie is a miscellaneous part here, Harry. He's a hired thug, but an expensive hired thug. He hasn't caused any major harm as of yet and will be dealt with and dispensed should he do so. For now, we're letting him play tough guy.

"He conk you on the head? If not him, one of his guys?—No, Harry, he didn't. As I said, he hasn't caused any major harm as of yet and would have been dispensed with should he have done so. Who did is none of your concern, Harry.

"What's with Clint?—Ah, Clint. As you know there is more than meets the initial eye with our boy Clint. You have a good handle on the outside view if you believe he is part of the operation, Harry. Dig deeper and you will find more, but don't ever believe BrianK will give away a piece of his shop to a kid. The answer Max is looking for is there for you to find, Harry. He may not like what you find, but it is there. Trust me on that, Harry.

"Was BobbyGirl dealt winning hands by a pro dealer at the tournament we went to? Were you watching the dealer that closely because you knew the dealer and sensed the fix was in for BobbyGirl?—Very intuitive, Harry. Good detective work on your part and poor visionary surveillance on my part. In your vernacular, Harry, she ain't that good.

If yes, how did you know?—I'll have to skip that one, Harry.

If yes, why?—Everyone loves a winner, Harry.

The door to the room opened and a man ducked his head onto the room. Without saying a word, Robert rose and left the room.

Chapter 86

Harry had gotten himself another cup of coffee and had just settled himself back down at the table when Robert came back into the room.

"You will have to leave in a few minutes, Harry," Robert told him. "Is there anything else I can help you with right now?"

"A few last questions if I may?" Harry asked.

"Just a few," Robert replied

"Did you know who I was before our kids hooked up on this?" Harry asked.

To Harry, Robert thought for what seemed like a longer time than necessary on that question. Finally he answered, "Let's just say your name was not unfamiliar to me or the people I work for."

"Is that good or bad?" Harry asked.

"Next question, Harry."

"If it wasn't Frenchie that conked you on the head, was the truck that was following me back to New York imaginary, or real?" Harry tried next.

Without hesitation Robert answered, "Real."

"No answer on the dealer at the tournament?" Harry tried again.

As he stood, Robert asked somewhat in dismissal, "Any more questions, Harry?"

"One last one," Harry said as he also stood. "Who the fuck are you?"

"It was a pleasure seeing you again, Harry," Robert said holding out his hand toward Harry. "The plane is waiting for you outside."

"As it was you, Robert," Harry replied, "I would hope we will have the opportunity to meet again sometime," Harry continued as he shook Robert's hand.

~ * ~

Harry didn't know what had happened to the people that were in the room when he got there or where they had gone, but they had vanished and the room was empty. Harry walked out the front door and into the waiting plane. The same plane that had brought him to wherever it was he had been brought to.

The pilot was seated in the cockpit as Harry settled into the same seat he had occupied during their first flight.

"Make yourself comfortable, Shorts," the pilot said through the open door. "The flight attendant will be along with your Absolute Gimlet on the Rocks and peanuts in a jiffy."

With that, the door closed and the plane began to taxi for the runway. A minute later they were in the air. Harry had a feeling it might take a while for the flight attendant to bring his drink and peanuts. A long while in fact.

~ * ~

Upon landing, the pilot opened the locked door to the cockpit and walked past Harry. He opened the hatch and deplaned without saying a word. Not knowing what else to do, Harry followed. When he hit the tarmac the pilot was nowhere to be found.

"Now that was one hell of a trip," Harry said to the only person he could see, himself, as he started off in search of his beloved HoneyBee. He would have to put his P.I. thinking cap on to process what he had learned and try and figure out how it fit with what he already knew about this case.

Fact or fiction, valuable or irrelevant, Robert had provided additional information that did, or did not, move him closer to unraveling the mysteries of pokcloman.com, Clint and BobbyGirl, or BrianK to name just a few.

Fact or fiction, valuable or irrelevant, two things Harry was certain of—he needed a drink to un-cloud his head and he needed some advice.

The drinks he could handle on his own quite nicely. The best advice he could ever ask for would come from, he hoped, one M. Randle Trundle.

Chapter 87

The dream kept coming back to haunt Harry over and over again. The ringing wouldn't stop no matter what he did. Ring, ring, ring like the world all around him was ringing for him to...to what? What did the world in his dreams want from him?

Turns out the world, or at least one person in the world, wanted Harry to answer the phone. Yeah, Harry's phone was ringing.

"Go away, man," Harry mumbled into the phone before he hung up on whoever was nagging his ass incessantly with the ring, ring, ring thing.

Two minutes of peace was all Harry got before it started again. Half-awake, Harry was slowly remembering the prior evening and how he had needed a drink to un-cloud his head. Problem was his head was now re-clouded with the mist of what was to be a nasty hangover from his un-clouding efforts of the night before, and early morning as well.

"Poppyson," was the next thing Harry heard when he answered the phone again.

"Max, my son," Harry mumbled.

"Tough night was it, poppyson?" Max asked.

"You are a smart boy, Max," Harry answered.

"Call you later," Max said.

"Thanks, my son," Harry replied.

Thirty seconds later Harry was sound asleep.

~ * ~

There it was again. Ring, ring, ring like the world all around him was ringing for him to...to what?

"Shit," Harry uttered as he opened his eyes and realized it was the phone again. It stopped.

The clock, if it was capable of speaking, would have said, "It's ten twenty-seven a.m., Harry."

When the phone rang again he picked it up. His senses were slowly returning.

"Shorts," he answered.

"Timmons," was her simple reply.

"On top," Harry said next.

Silence.

"On the bottom?" Harry said in the form of a question

"You left me a message to call you at three twenty-one a.m. this morning, Shorts. I'm calling you," Ms. Timmons replied.

"What took you so long?" Harry inquired.

"Shorts," she said.

"Timmons," Harry replied.

The phone went dead.

Harry could feel himself dozing off when the phone rang again.

"Are you capable of having an intelligent, adult conversation?" Timmons asked Harry.

Harry replied, "Yes, ma'am. Adult to adult, let us converse."

"What do you want, Harry?" Timmons asked.

"Any chance I can see Mr. Trundle?" Harry asked.

"There is always a chance, Harry," Timmons replied.

Harry could swear he heard her chuckle.

"Any chance I can see Mr. Trundle sometime soon?" Harry tried.

"The Schooners are in town tomorrow afternoon. The weather forecast is for sunshine and warm temperatures. I will leave you a pass at the will call window."

"Thanks, Ms. Timmons. I assume Mr. Trundle will be in attendance and I was wondering if I might see your smiling face as well."

"To quote a famous American, Harry, 'One never know, do one...'"

The phone line went dead.

Damn that Ms. Timmons.

Chapter 88

The sun was shining while the flag in center field fluttered under a soft breeze blowing from right field to left field. Harry was seated in seat #2 in the Bayport Schooners owner's box.

M. Randle Trundle always sat in seat #1 when he was attending a game.

In Harry's eyes, life was currently damn good.

The lovely chickeeda that slipped into seat #3 next to Harry was wearing yellow shorts, a matching yellow top and a floppy hat that covered a good part of her head and face. The quick glance Harry was able to sneak left him with a very favorable impression and a small stirring in an appropriate lower region of his body.

Harry was sipping his beer and almost spit out what he had in his mouth when the vision in yellow said, "Aren't you going to say hello, Shorts?"

Regaining his composure, Harry said, "Ms. Timmons?"

"There you are, Timmons. Here's your hot dog and beer," Trundle said as he sat down next to Harry.

Trundle was also dressed in shorts with a golf shirt instead of his usual business attire.

"Pass these to Ms. Timmons will you Harry," Trundle said.

Harry passed the hot dog and beer to Timmons and wondered what in holly hell was up.

"Is today a special occasion?" Harry asked.

"Why do you say that?" Trundle replied.

Timmons quietly ate her hot dog and sipped her beer.

"Yum, this is good," she purred in a way that made Harry's lower region gently begin to stir.

"Um, the shorts. The shirts. Where's the jacket and the, ah, you know what I mean," Harry stammered out.

"Company outing, Harry," Trundle beamed. "My entire senior staff is scattered around the lower sections of the park mixing in with the rest of the crowd. We packed everybody in a bus this morning and motored on out to the ballpark. That right, Timmons?"

"Right you are, sir. Bused 'em up and motored on out to the

old ballpark," Timmons replied with an 'I can talk street talk just like you, Shorts' reply.

"Bused 'em up?" Harry repeated.

"Yeah, we bused 'em on up and motored right on out here," Trundle repeated as well.

"Hey, Pete, give us three more dogs and have the beer guy scoot on over here, too," Trundle yelled to the hot dog vendor at the end of the row.

Three dogs and three beers later, Trundle, Timmons and Harry watched the Schooners take the field for the start of the game.

~ * ~

It was the middle of the third inning when Trundle said, "So, how can we help, Harry?"

Ms. Timmons turned to face Harry to give him her undivided attention. In her vision of yellowness, it was almost too much for Harry to handle.

Quickly regaining his composure as all trained P.I.'s are capable of doing, Harry started, "Well, it's the case I'm working on. I have the majority of it figured out, but I'm stuck on several pieces that play a critical role in the operation."

"Give me the Reader's Digest version of what you have and what's got you stumped," Trundle said.

Timmons continuing to look at Harry had the effect of additional stirring in the aforementioned guy region Harry treasured so.

"I'm over here, Harry," Trundle teased.

"Sorry, Randle," Harry said.

Harry proceeded to give Trundle and Timmons the Readers Digest version of what he had and what had him stumped to date. He was finishing with:

"While Robert didn't confirm it as fact, his response all but confirmed BobbyGirl had been dealt winning hands by a pro dealer at the tournament Robert and I had just been to together. Robert was watching that particular dealer that closely because he knew the dealer and he knew the fix was in for BobbyGirl.

The big thing that has me stymied is the whole Clint thing. He turns up unconscious on the morning of the biggest tournament in pokcolmon.com's history, hell Poker history for that matter, and BrianK practically anoints him his number one son after that."

"Interesting," Trundle says. "Let me think on it and let's talk after this half inning."

Chapter 89

The Schooners scored two runs in the bottom of the third to go up 4-1. They had been playing real well of late and it looked like today was going to be more of the same.

"I've been peripherally involved in your goings on during this case, just being nosy, Harry. I hear the basement boys helped out and I rewarded them with an extra difficult project to get their juices flowing. I'm sure you figured it out, but they are a weird bunch, Harry," Trundle said.

"Yeah, I doped that out real fast," Harry replied. "And by the way, how did you hear of the basement guys' assistance on my behalf? Did a little Yellow Canary go chirp, chirp in your ear perhaps?"

"How I came to find out isn't important, Harry. I became involved purely to amuse myself. You know I don't amuse easily, Harry, but with you being involved I figured it wouldn't take much," Trundle said. "While you work, I play!"

Harry looked at Ms. Timmons who had conveniently turned away to look at something on the other side of the stadium.

"Clint's an interesting kid," Trundle continued. "At my direction, my people did a little deep background look at him and uncovered a few interesting tidbits. One particularly interesting incident stood out. Clint was hit in the head by a pitch the summer between his sophomore and junior years and he feigned being unconscious on the field. He lay there on the field for more than two minutes not moving until a Doctor from an adjoining field came running over to see if he could help. It seems Clint 'woke up' just as the Doctor got there and made a miraculous recovery. He even finished the game and stuck out the side in the seventh inning on ten pitches."

"Feigned being unconscious," Harry repeated. "Did you say he feigned being unconscious when he really wasn't? How could you know that?"

"I know you have your Web Dudes as you call them and they are very good from what you have told me. I believe they are just that. But, my people aren't very good, Harry, they have been and will continue to the best in the world. Combine that with the breath of my available resources at their disposal and you have the best information source in the world. They 'find' what I need, Harry," Trundle said proudly.

"I looked myself and there wasn't any mention of that incident on the web. The Dudes didn't find it either," Harry stated confidently.

"As I said, my guys are that good. Here's what you or your Dudes couldn't find: the doctor filed an incident report with the hospital that he worked for; the umpire filed a report with the league office after the game; and, the coach filed a report with his league office a few days later."

"Really?" Harry said.

"Really," Trundle confirmed. "And do you know why, Harry?"

Harry was at a loss and looked it.

"Insurance, Harry. All three of them were covering their individual and collective fannies in case there was ever an insurance claim filed by Clint, his parents, or anyone else for that matter. You can never be too careful, Harry," Trundle finished.

"If that is true, and I trust it is, what does it have to do with Clint, and BrianK, and pokcolmon.com?" Harry asked.

Trundle looked past Harry and gestured toward Ms. Timmons who was now paying attention to their conversation again.

"When we got this bit of intelligence from our team, Ms. Timmons and I decided to hold on to it so as not to interfere with your investigation," Trundle said.

"We would have delivered the information and our speculations to you if you had come to us for help, or if you seemed like a bit of assistance was in the best interest of all involved," Ms. Timmons chimed in.

"Quite nice of you to decide what I needed and when I needed it," Harry said. "Speculations?"

The crack of the bat brought the crowd to its feet. Another home run by the Schooners made the score 7-1 which prompted Trundle to yell, "Beers for the whole section!"

Chapter 90

The crowd was now back in their seats including Harry, Trundle and Ms. Timmons. It had taken half an innings for the "beer guys" to beer up the entire section Trundle was sitting in.

Harry toasted Randle with a tip of his beer and then repeated, "Speculations?"

"Ms. Timmons," Trundle said with a nod in her direction.

"It is of course speculation, Harry. Some facts are definitely involved, but mostly speculation," Timmons started. "Let your imagination run wild, Harry, which we both know is not too hard for you. Suppose BrianK and Clint "cooked up" a scheme. Clint had all the money he needed for college in his account already, or he would very soon. What better way to generate tournament interest, and interest in pokcolmon.com as a whole, than the 'feigned unconscious' bit Clint had pulled off once before."

"Hold on," Harry interjected. "You're saying they faked the incident and Clint really wasn't found unconscious on the morning of the tournament?"

"Who found him?" Timmons asked.

"Um, I think it was BrianK and his people," Harry answered.

"And what was the diagnosis when Clint was taken to the hospital?" from Timmons.

"Ah, I'm not sure he went to the hospital. Did he?" Harry asked.

"There is no record of him being brought into any emergency room within twenty miles of the tournament site," Ms. Timmons stated. "No admittance records for any Clinton Rensford could be found, either."

Harry sat there and thought about what Ms. Timmons had just told him. Could she be right? Who knows? Ask questions and listen some more.

Yep, another Harry Mickey Shorts QAS just got laid on your persons

"But why? What would motivate Clint to do it when he was considered to be a lock to become the winner of the first 'Under Eighteen World Championship of Poker' tournament?" Harry asked.

"Once again, this is more speculation on our part, Harry. But look at what happens after he doesn't compete in the tournament. Maybe Clint gets offered a deal to promote the pokcolmon.com group and be designated something like a 'college fund delegate' or some such position while in college. He's also promised a piece of the action after college and he now has a source of income for the rest of his life," Timmons says.

"The kids would eat it up," Harry adds.

"Right," Trundle agrees.

"It's speculation, and a pretty good bit of speculation I give you," Harry says. "I had my suspicions from the first time Max and his boys spun the tale for me. But, from everything I saw when I started looking into the case, there was never any proof that there was anything shady going on."

"As you said, Harry, mere speculation," Timmons said.

"Pretty bright minds with a ton of resources to back up those bright minds and their speculations I would speculate," Harry said.

Trundle just raised an eyebrow in response to Harry's statement.

Ms. Timmons just continued to look so damn good in yellow.

"And there's no proof of any of this at all?" Harry said.

"Nope, none at all, Harry," Trundle confirmed.

"What next?" Harry asked.

"The game ends, the Schooners are victorious as it should be, and the Trundle Industries team gets back on the bus and goes back into the city," Trundle said after a sip of his beer.

"And Harry Mickey Shorts?" Harry asked.

"Well, Harry Mickey Shorts goes about his business and proves what are to this point mere speculations on our part. That's why you're the BTPI and get the big bucks," Trundle said with a laugh.

Timmons nodded her head and smiled at Trundle's statement. She looked damn good doing it. In yellow.

If they were right, how would he be able to tell Max?

Chapter 91

It was back to square one time again for Harry. He was sitting in front of his computer in the back of Big Mel's office reviewing the file and the case notes. He had been doing it for the past two hours.

The results so far were a big, fat nada. Zippo...squat...zilch.

The phone rang saving him from more torture of the same variety.

"Shorts here," Harry answered when he hit the speaker button.

"Max here," was the reply in return.

"Is that Max my favorite son?" Harry inquired.

"Your one and only son as well," Max replied.

"How you be, Max?" Harry asked.

"I'm good, poppyson."

"Mom tell you I returned your call the other day?" Harry asked him.

"Yeah, she did. I had to split to play some hoops up at the school. I figured I'd talk to you later. I guess it's later," Max said.

"I guess it is," Harry agreed.

"We good for next Saturday?" Max asked.

"Good as rain on an April morning," Harry replied.

"Unless you have a ball game that morning," Max corrected.

"In that you are correct, Max. Our normal time?" Harry asked.

"In that you are correct, pops. Our normal time it is," Max confirmed.

"I'm looking forward to it. Any hints for our Saturday-to-be that you'd care to share with your favorite dad?" Harry asked.

"Yeah, me and Bri decided it would be cool to..."

The dial tone told Harry that was all he'd be hearing on that topic for now. As always he'd have to wait until Saturday morning and be surprised just as he had been on every other special Saturday he had spent with his kids.

~ * ~

Unable to generate any more enthusiasm to pour through the same case file notes again, Harry decided to call it a day and head back to his apartment. He locked up, crossed Plandome Road, and headed up George Street to his apartment.

It was a black blur out of the corner of his eye that probably saved his ass to fight another day. He wasn't totally lost in space at that moment, but he also wasn't expecting to have to be on the lookout for marauding trucks barreling down at him at top speed. Excellent peripheral vision and quick reflexes saved his butt once again.

From his position sprawled out on the sidewalk, all he could see was a black truck speeding away down George Street.

Was it the same black truck? Hard to tell. Solution—Harry had no solution for this one. He'd just have to watch his ass more closely and hope he'd be as lucky next time, if there was a next time.

After a little time to wash the dirt from the scrape on his arm, a cool one and Dave Mason on the stereo to sooth his wounds, Harry was ready to figure out if he needed to make a call for the cavalry to come to his aid. It wasn't something he wanted to have to do, but going it alone might get dangerous if the bad guys were going to up the price of poker.

No, not yet.

No, Harry would have to fend for himself and think about the plan he had been formulating to go on the offensive before something bad happened to force his hand.

The black truck was a hand forcer in Harry's eyes. Taking the offensive would have to jump to the head of the class sooner rather than later. Sooner as in right about fucking now.

Chapter 92

The following morning Harry walked into Mel's office with a plan in his head and a look of determination on his face.

"Constipated?" Mel said in greeting as Harry entered the office.

"What?" Harry answered.

"You look like you're constipated or something," Mel said.

"Very funny," Harry replied.

Mel just looked at him.

"No, I'm not constipated and my dick didn't fall off in the shower this morning. Just got shit I need to do and it needs doing now," Harry said with an extra dose of emphasis.

"If you walked into the doctor's office and ran that pile of crap by him, do you know what he'd say?" Mel asked Harry.

"No, what would the doctor say?" Harry asked.

"Just do it," Mel replied. He then looked down at his beloved New York Times signaling their conversation was now over.

Constipation would have been much easier Harry realized.

~ * ~

"Yeah, Sherry," Harry said into the phone receiver, "I need to hit the road for a spell to work on a few things."

He listened, and listened.

"Sher, it's a short trip and I won't miss the kids Saturday," Harry told her.

He listened again.

"No chance. I'll be home long before next Saturday. I won't screw it up, Sher," he assured her.

Harry had to move the receiver away from his ear to save his hearing. That didn't stop him from hearing Sherry shout, "You won't screw it up. You won't screw it up like you screwed up how many Saturdays, and Mondays, and Wednesdays, and every other fucking day that ever existed."

The silence that came over the line was worse than the screaming fit he had just enduring from his loving ex-wife.

"I'll be back, I promise," Harry promised Sherry.

"Your ass had better be fucking back or, or I'll, or you'll, oh just get back and don't disappoint your kids, Harry."

With that, she hung up on him.

From the front of the office Harry heard, "Day getting any better, schmuck?"

"Up yours too, Mel," Harry shot back in retort.

Ten seconds later they were both laughing.

"Did you say hi to sis for me," Mel finally got out when he had stopped laughing.

"Ah, there didn't seem to be a good spot to get that in," Harry answered. "I'll be sure and tell her next time we have another one of our pleasant and overly joyful conversations."

"Thanks," Mel said as he went back to reading his Times, and not exactly silently laughing at Harry's expense.

~ * ~

To start the ball rolling on his plans, Harry dialed Ms. Timmons at Trundle Industries. Once he was done laying out phase one of his plan for her, he received the assurances he needed that he would have back end protection should it be necessary to bring in the troops to assist.

"Thanks, Timmons," Harry said.

"Not to worry, Harry," she said. "At Mr. Trundle's direction, the full resources of Trundle Industries has your back on this one. And Harry, I'm there for you, too."

He didn't know what that last comment meant, but he said, "Thanks, Timmons, I appreciate that."

And as usual, Timmons was gone.

Chapter 93

A road trip. Actually it was going to be a series of road trips strung together to properly align some ducks in a row. Harry's row that is.

The first stop in the Harry Mickey Shorts road trip to "Poker Case Fame and Glory" was the office of a most unlikely participant in his plan. He had called ahead and made an appointment using a bit of P.I. trickery to convince an executive assistant to move another appointment to make room for his high priority home office visit.

"It is of THE utmost importance that we keep this visit entirely on the hush-hush," Harry told her. "You do understand, don't you? I can't impress upon you how confidential this issue is. That means everyone including your boss. I must ask you to say you understand so there will be no screw-ups here. Any deviation could result in a disaster beyond monumental proportions. Say you understand…"

Certain she was about to piss in her executive assistant pantaloons, Harry heard, "Not a word to anyone at all. I swear."

"Great, you'll probably get a nice raise for your confidential assistance in this matter," Harry told her.

~ * ~

Upon his arrival, Harry introduced himself to the executive assistant and was brought immediately to the small conference room on the third floor.

"I didn't say a word to anyone, I swear," the executive assistant to the Vice President told Harry. "Not a single word to anyone," she repeated as she hurriedly left the room.

Two minutes later the door to the conference room opened and Clint's father stepped into the room. Seeing Harry, he said, "What are you doing here, Blanchard? What do you want? What in the hell are you doing here? I was told it was home office, very confidential, very hush-hush. It's not home office at all, it's you. I'll have you thrown out of the building…"

Harry put up his hand and showed him his Private Investigator license which had the effect of stopping Rensford in mid-sentence.

"Please sit, Mr. Rensford," Harry said. "I will explain why I am here and what I want. It will be very clear to you in a few minutes that our having this little talk is in your, and also Clint's, best interest."

"Two minutes, that's all you get. Two minutes and then I'm going to have you thrown out of the building and arrested for impersonating, for saying you were…shit, I don't know what for." Rensford said.

A half hour later, Harry left the building having been invited to the Rensford house for dinner that night. On his way out, Harry had thanked Rensford's executive assistance for her superb handling of this most delicate situation. He told her it was critical to keep the meeting to herself and he would be back to her if he needed anything else.

Satisfied with step one of his plan, Harry checked into a local motel with plans to leave the following morning on the next leg of his journey.

Good news—they left the light on.

~ * ~

Harry arrived at the Rensford residence promptly at seven that evening. He had stopped for a bottle of wine and ended up getting a red and a white not knowing what was on the menu for dinner.

When he rang the bell he was caught by surprise when Clint answered the door. Since they had agreed his visit would be kept quiet until he arrived at the Rensford house that night for dinner, Harry had naturally expected Clint's father to answer the door.

"What are you doing here?" was how Clint greeted Harry at the door.

"I invited Mr. Shorts to come for dinner," Harry heard Ray Rensford say from behind Clint. "Please come in Harry."

"Thanks, Ray. Hi, Clint," Harry said as he handed the wine to Clint's father mostly to get them out of his hands.

"But, Dad," Clint said turning to his father.

"It will be very clear why Mr. Shorts is here once we sit and have a talk," Clint's father said to his son.

Chapter 94

Clint, his father, and Harry were seated in the Rensford living room after Ray had gotten himself and Harry a beer. Clint had listened to Harry for ten minutes and his facial expressions had changed from joy, to dismay, to utter disbelief as Harry told his tale to Clint and his father. Ray Rensford had heard Harry's spiel earlier in the day but listened again just as intently the second time.

"Again," Harry said, "some of it is built on fact, some of it is an extrapolation from those facts, and some of it is sheer speculation generated by the first two."

"It was very disappointing to me to hear you could see the hole cards while you were playing online in the pokcolmon site," Ray Rensford said to his son. "I would ask you to confirm it, but Mr. Shorts assured me this piece of information was absolutely true based on facts he has in his possession."

Clint was still shell shocked from what he had just heard Harry tell him. His father's statement was just gravy on top of a pile of shit he was about to eat without a knife or fork.

Devastated to be knocked down seven or eight pegs in his father's eyes, Clint tried to redeem some semblance of his dignity and pride by saying, "But I didn't need to see the hole cards, dad. I was beating everybody I played with ease every time I went on the site. I didn't need any help; they told me it was for the good of the organization. What could I do?" Clint finished.

The hope of forgiveness was in his eyes.

"What could you have done? You could have said no. You could have said I don't need to cheat. You could have said I don't cheat, period. You could have walked away is what you could, and should have done," his father answered him.

Clint's eyes watered and he dropped his head in further devastation. His father had called him a cheat and a coward in the same breath.

"But, I understand the pressure they must have placed on you, what was at stake, and how you might not have known what to do in response. It's fixable, Clint. Rensford's don't hang their heads, son. We keep our heads high and we take our lumps if, and when, we have to."

Clint raised his head with a look of hope in his eyes that his dad could make it all better and fix it like he'd done throughout Clint's whole life.

Harry thought it was his clue to jump into the fray at that point.

"You were promised a piece of the action after college and you thought you had a source of income for the rest of your life. It's the 'you thought' that's the problem, kiddo," Harry told Clint.

"What do you mean," Clint said. "What's a problem?"

"BrianK had no intention of it ever getting that far. You weren't much more than another pawn in his chess game, a game he's a master at," Harry said.

"You mean there is no position in the pokcolmon.com organization after college. No riches at the end of the rainbow for me?" Clint asked Harry.

"I really doubt it, Clint. If I'm right, BrianK's a bad man and lots of people and kids are going to get hurt if he has his way," Harry told Clint.

Clint turned toward his dad and said, "I wanted to make you proud, dad. I wanted to show you I was capable of creating a future for myself at an early age just like you did. I wanted to create 'success' and be someone you could be proud of to call your son."

Ray Rensford looked at his son and said, "I've never been prouder of anyone in my whole life, son. You don't have to do anything to prove yourself to me. Just be someone we can all be proud of and I'll be the happiest man on this earth."

Clint went over and hugged his father. His father hugged him back just as hard, if not harder.

"Harry and I have discussed how we should handle this going forward, Clint. We, that's you and I, will do everything we can to assist Mr. Shorts and provide whatever he needs to make this right. To make everything right for as long as it needs righting. You with me?" Clint's father asked him.

"Rensfords don't shirk their responsibilities," Clint said sitting up ram-rod straight with re-found pride. "You bet I'm with you any way I can, or have to be."

"Good, that's my boy," Ray Rensford said. "Now your mother has prepared a fine meal and we're keeping it waiting. Let's show our guest what Rensford hospitality is like."

Chapter 95

There was an old movie Harry had seen some time back called the 'Boys in the Band.' If Harry has any say, the remake would be titled the 'Boys in the Basement' and he knew who would be starring in it.

Al and his brethren down below had provided the name, home address and phone number of another of the key players in this charade. That would be stop number two in the current Harry Mickey Shorts road show.

~ * ~

"Yes, ma'am, that is what I said. I'm Dan Weathers with the IRS. I can have your daughter brought downtown and investigated officially, or I can come to your home and we can chat unofficially to see if we can resolve this issue amicably without, well, you know," Harry lied.

"Oh, my," Mrs. Dawson replied.

"Time is of the essence, Mrs. Dawson," Harry continued. "I can be there when she gets home from school and we can resolve this in short order."

"Oh, my, I just don't know," Mrs. Dawson replied.

Knowing there was no Mr. Dawson, Harry said, "Perhaps I should discuss this with Mr. Dawson, ma'am. Where can I reach him?"

"Oh, my, I don't. Well, there is no Mr. Dawson, Mr.?" Mrs. Dawson replied.

"Weathers, ma'am. It's Dan Weathers. What time would be good for me to come by and get this straightened out, ma'am?"

"Well, Lizzie gets home from school at a bit after four, Mr. Weathers. She normally goes up to her room and gets right on that confounded computer she spends all her time on. Maybe if you're here at maybe three forty-five that would give me a chance to get you something to drink and some cookies before Lizzie gets home," Mrs. Dawson told Weathers. Harry. Both of them.

"That will be fine, ma'am," Harry told her. "I'll see you at three forty-five, and it would probably be best if you didn't say anything to anyone else about this. I could get in hot water if my superiors knew I was doing this for you and Lizzie without IRS sanctioning."

"I won't say a word," Lizzie's mother assured him.

~ * ~

At a few minutes past 3:45 that afternoon, Harry found himself seated in the formal living room of Mrs. Dawson's house drinking lemonade and eating the best homemade chocolate chip cookies he had ever tasted.

"Can I get you anything else, Mr. Weathers?" Mrs. Dawson asked Harry.

"No, ma'am," Harry answered her. "Do you mind if I ask you a few questions before Liz gets home?" he asked her.

"Oh, that might be hard, Mr. Weathers. I don't know too much about anything," she replied.

Odd response Harry thought to himself.

"Just one or two then if I might, Mrs. Dawson. Do you approve of Lizzie's playing on pokcolmon.com?" Harry asked.

"Oh, Lizzie is always playing on that machine of hers. It's all she ever does other than her school work which she's very good at you know. She's number one in her class second year in a row. She's very good at school and hardly tries at all. Not that she doesn't try I mean, she just doesn't work at it all that much with her being on that darn machine so much," Lizzie's mom said.

"That's interesting, ma'am. You must be very proud of her being number one in her class, plus having all that scholarship money set aside already," Harry said.

"Yes, I'm so very proud of her. Mr. Dawson, Lizzie's father that is, he would have been just as proud if he was here to see it."

"I don't mean to pry, Mrs. Dawson, but did you lose Mr. Dawson recently?" Harry asked.

"Lose him, oh no, I didn't lose him," she replied. "I don't know where he is, but I don't think that's the same as losing him. Do you, Mr. Weathers?"

"Um, no, I guess I don't, ma'am," Harry said not knowing how else to respond to that.

"Has Mr. Dawson been gone long?" Harry tried.

"He stepped out, but he should be back," she replied.

"How long ago did he 'step out'?" Harry continued.

"Oh, it's only been a little over six years," Mrs. Dawson replied. "At least I think it's been a bit over six years. I lose track of time now and again."

"He should be back any day now," Harry agreed with her as he put another cookie in his mouth so he wouldn't have to say anything more.

Chapter 96

Harry and Mrs. Dawson sat quietly for the next few minutes. Harry was afraid to ask any other questions not knowing what Mrs. Dawson might say in reply. Mrs. Dawson seemed content to sit and watch the front door waiting for her Lizzie to get home from school.

The cuckoo clock had just finished its fourth cuckoo when the front door opened and Lizzie Dawson entered the house. She dropped her books on the table just inside the front door and was starting toward the stairs that led to the second floor when she realized they had company.

"Come here, Lizzie," her mother beckoned.

Liz Dawson froze in her tracks. Harry could tell she was deciding what to say to her mom and the visitor.

"Lizzie, this nice man is Mr. Weathers. He is with the IRS and he's come to see you. I think he wants to ask you a few questions," Lizzie's mom said.

"Hello BobbyGirl," Harry said.

The surprise on her face surprised even her mother.

"Is everything alright, Lizzie?" Mrs. Dawson asked.

Regaining her composure, Liz said, "Everything is fine, mom. Why don't you let me talk to Mr. Weathers and then I'll help you get dinner ready."

"That would be nice, Lizzie. I'll just go upstairs and tidy up a bit before we start getting dinner ready," Mrs. Dawson told her daughter.

While Mrs. Dawson rose and walked up the stairs, Liz Dawson, or BobbyGirl in poker cyber space, neither moved nor said a word.

When her mom was safely out or earshot, BobbyGirl said, "Who are you and what do you want? Did you do anything to disturb my mom? Because if you did, you'll pay for it," Lizzie told Harry with a look in her eyes that could kill.

"Why don't we sit," Harry said trying to calm the situation some.

"I don't want to sit. I want to know who you are. You're no

IRS guy. That's bullshit. Who are you? What do you want?" she demanded.

"I could show you my credentials," Harry told her.

"Showing me your dick would be as good as showing me your credentials," BobbyGirl answered. "They're probably both bullshit!"

Harry liked her spunk. Spunk requires spunk in return.

"My name is Harry Mickey Shorts," Harry told her. "What's bullshit is BrianK, the entire pokcolmon.com setup, but not my dick."

At that, BobbyGirl smiled.

"And," Harry continued, "you're up to your ass in trouble and you better find a friend pronto fast if you're gonna come away from this shit with your troubled ass intact."

"Any cookies left?" she asked.

At that, Harry smiled.

"I saved a couple for you. Let's sit and sort this mess out," Harry said.

"Lemme make sure my mom is alright," Liz said. "She can get lost at times and I have to keep my eyes on her at all times. Sit tight and I'll be right back."

With that Lizzie headed up the stairs leaving Harry with nothing better to do than to sit and sip his lemonade. He had always hated lemonade.

Coming back down the stairs, BobbyGirl asked, "You want a beer Harry Mickey Shorts?"

"A beer would be great," Harry replied.

"Fine. I'll get it and we can talk. And by the way, now you have to stay for dinner. You don't stay and I'll have to listen to my mother for the next week asking when that nice man is coming for dinner. Your ass stays for dinner, no 'I don't think so' about it," she said with authority.

"I guess dinner it is then," Harry replied.

Chapter 97

"Thanks for the beer," Harry said as BobbyGirl placed it on the coffee table.

"Yeah, sure," she said as she sat on the couch opposite from Harry. "Now, who are you and what do you want? Have I seen you before someplace? I have, haven't I? You were at one of the tournaments. The last one I won I think it was."

"This makes it much easier," Harry interrupted. "You can ask the questions and you can answer them, too."

"Fuck you. Now answer the ones I didn't answer already," she spat back.

"The name's Harry Mickey Shorts, just as I said. I'm here to get your ass out of trouble and help you at the same time. And no thanks."

"No thanks?" she asked as a question.

"In answer to your "fuck you" offer, no thanks, I get enough already," Harry replied.

"That's funny. You know, I actually might get to like you, Harry Mickey Shorts," BobbyGirl said.

"There could be worse things in life," Harry replied.

"And you may think you get enough already, but when is enough really enough? And is what you're already getting as good as you could be getting? Guess you'll never know, will you Harry Mickey Shorts?" she told him.

"How old are you, BobbyGirl? And what is it you like to be called—Liz, Lizzie, BobbyGirl, or what?" Harry asked.

"How old am I?" she repeated. "Does it really matter sometimes? I've been taking care of my mom, going to school and running this house since my dad left. And no, he ain't coming back any time soon. My mother was loony tunes years before he went and found greener pastures somewhere else. He left me a note, forty-eight bucks, and told me to take care of her. I was eleven at the time but going on twenty-five. I'd been handling shit here for years before that, ever since I could see over the counter."

"Your dad?" Harry asked.

"When he was here, he wasn't here. He drank, he chased

skirts, he was always broke, and people were constantly in and out of here at all hours of the day and night."

"Not a pretty picture," Harry commented.

"It was what it was, it is what it is. I'm just lucky none of the scum he brought in here ever came after me. Thank god for small favors I guess," she laughed.

"What's wrong with your mother if I might ask?" Harry asked.

"You may. From what I gather she got caught up in the shit that went down here from day one. Booze, pills, grass and the all night fuck-a-thons. That's what I heard later on from my dear old dad. It's what did her in. She functions, but you saw how she functions.

"And, any or all of the above will do depending on where I'm at and what I'm up to. I guess if I had to choose one of them it would probably be Lizzie since it makes my mom happy; yep, that would be my choice if you put a gun to my head."

"Tough," Harry said. "Money?"

"We get by, always have. With some stuff I got going on and now BrianK's 'stipend' as he calls it from pokcolmon.com, I'm keeping us afloat for now. You gonna fuck with that, are you Mr. Harry Mickey Shorts?" she asked.

Harry told BobbyGirl what he knew and recounted his visit with Clint and his family. He told her the same thing he had told the Rensfords. "Some of it is built on fact, some of it is an extrapolation from those facts, and some of it is sheer speculation coming from the first two."

When he was done, BobbyGirl looked at Harry and smiled.

"I had the strange feeling it was too good to be true," she told Harry. "It's all going to shit?" she asked him.

"Not if I can help it," Harry answered.

"So, what do you want from me?" she asked.

Harry laid out his plan for her and what part BobbyGirl would play; that is if everything went according to plan. That is of course if she wanted to be part of the plan and help get BrianK and the rest of his scum-sucking shitbags.

Lizzie thought for a minute when Harry had finished, then she said, "Sure, why not. I have a lot to lose, but it might be fun at that."

"Good, I was hoping you would come along for the ride,"

Harry said.

"Might not be the only ride you get, Harry Mickey Shorts," Lizzie said with one serious mischievous grin on her face.

"I'm going to have to watch out for you, aren't I?" Harry replied.

"That you might, that you might indeed. Now let's get my mom fed and then you can tell me some stories, Harry Mickey Shorts."

Chapter 98

With Clint and BobbyGirl now on board for the ride, Harry set out on his path to stop number three on the HMS express. If things went this well the rest of the way, Harry was sure he would be home with plenty of time to spare before his planned Saturday with Max and Briande was upon him.

Hell, at this rate he'd have time to get in a little extracurricular sack time as well. With who was the question that was currently running through his mind.

Another dose of basement intel had provided the location of his next destination with all pertinent details included in the package he had received. With assistance like this, his job was getting much too easy.

Harry had used his P.I. know-how combined with some trickery and guile to navigate the first two pieces to his current puzzle. Stop #3 was going to be a straight on frontal assault. No trickery, no HMS hoodoo—knock on the door and get it on.

~ * ~

Harry was waiting for the right time to put Stop #3 into motion. He decided to call BobbyGirl on an issue he forgot to settle with her before he left. It was early enough and he was pretty sure he'd get her before she left for school, or…

When she answered the phone, Harry said, "I forgot to wish you a Happy Birthday before I left."

"Harry?" she asked hesitantly.

"Who else," Harry responded.

"What makes you think it's my birthday, or was my birthday?" she asked.

"The answer to that question is very simple, I believe. It's today if I have it right," Harry said. "And before you ask again, the card your mom got for you was really cute. That is if girls who are turning twenty-one consider puppies and kittens cute."

Silence, then, "I'm in high school. Harry. How could I possibly be twenty-one and still be in high school? You're mistaken," Lizzie responded.

"I don't think so, Liz. I don't think you're in high school, or your high school has a funny name. The ID card that's hanging from your bag said "Something Something Electric Company." I couldn't see all of it, but I saw enough. Second, your mom told me it was a big day with it being your twenty-first birthday and all. To be sure, I called my contact last night and he confirmed your date of birth—makes you twenty-one today. So again, Happy Birthday Elizabeth Dawson."

"Shit," was all Liz Dawson said in reply.

"Plus," Harry continued, "when you told me about your dad and you said, 'He left me a note, forty-eight bucks, and told me to take care of her. I was eleven at the time but going on twenty-five. I'd been handling shit here for years before that ever since I could see over the counter.' I knew you were lying about your age then. No matter how good you were, no kid at eleven could handle that kind of a load. Fifteen maybe. But eleven, no way, kiddo"

"Well, shit," Liz replied again. "What happens now?"

"One question," Harry said. "BrianK or one of his people come to you or did you go to them and propose this arrangement?"

"I've never been to high school, Harry. Under the circumstances, I home schooled myself and graduated right on time with the kids my age, which I am very proud of I might add. I'm taking night classes at the local CC and I do Community Theater down at the playhouse whenever I can fit it in with my class schedule. This dude approached me after rehearsals one night and the rest is history."

"What about the parental stuff? The credit card, and the required referrals needed to become part of pokcolomon.com?" Harry asked.

"When you run the show, shit has a way of getting overlooked or disregarded all together," she replied.

"Good enough," Harry said. "You have a Happy Birthday, Lizzie Dawson. And tell your mom I said hi. See you around."

"Thanks, Harry. And you'll be seeing more of me than 'just around,' you can count on it."

Chapter 99

Harry knocked on the door and waited. It was half past seven on a school night and Harry was fairly sure the people he needed to be home were home.

Knock, knock, knock Harry knocked again.

The door finally opened and a good looking lady was standing there in the doorway.

"Good evening," Harry started, "my name is Harry Mickey Shorts. I'd like to speak with you, your husband if he is home, and your son Kyle if I may."

The good looking lady, a Mrs. Pendrick by name, looked at Harry as if he had three heads and had just asked her to strip naked and do the hula.

"Who is it, Honey?" Harry heard from further inside the house.

The clothed Mrs. Pendrick didn't respond.

"Honey?" Harry heard from a voice that seemed to be approaching the front door where Harry and the dumbstruck Mrs. Pendrick stood.

When Mr. Pendrick got to the front door, Harry said, "Good evening, my name is Harry Mickey Shorts. I'd like to speak with you, your wife who I have just met, and your son Kyle if I may."

"Honey, go back inside," Mr. Pendrick said to his wife. "Honey," he repeated when she didn't move.

When she had finally unfrozen, she left them. Mr. Pendrick stepped outside and closed the front door.

"Who are you and what do you want?" he asked Harry.

"Good evening, my name is Harry Mickey Shorts. I'd like to speak with you, your wife who I have just met, and your son Kyle if I may," Harry repeated.

"You a wise ass, Harry Mickey Shorts? Get the fuck off my porch before I kick you off," Pendrick told Harry.

"Yes, I am, sometimes, and no you couldn't, ever," Harry responded.

"Huh," Pendrick responded.

"Yes, I am a wise ass, sometimes, when I choose to be; and

no, you couldn't kick me off your porch, ever," Harry told Mr. Pendrick.

Pendrick looked like he was about to try.

"Don't, you can't," Harry stopped him before he could give it a go.

"What do you want with us?" Mr. Pendrick asked Harry again.

"Paul, if I may call you Paul," Harry started. He then gave Paul Pendrick the Readers Digest version of what he wanted with the Pendrick family, and Kyle in particular.

~ * ~

They were seated in the family room ten minutes later—Paul Pendrick, Sandy Pendrick, Kyle Pendrick, otherwise known as BobbyBoy in pokcolmon.com circles, and the family dogs—Magic & Marva Pendrick—plus their cats Jethro and Ziggy.

Magic, Harry had just learned, was actually a Champion Airedale from the Victorianne Kismet line. She had been the pick of the litter from the first litter of puppies from Champion Victorianne Kismet Mirage, or Darby to her owner, who lived in Carlisle, Pa. Magic was part of the Beatles litter—all of the puppies were named after Beatles songs. Hence, her formal name Magical Mystery Tour was shortened to Magic. Her brother Max lived about a mile away.

Marva was the best looking Golden retriever Harry had ever seen.

Jethro was sitting on Harry's lap and Ziggy was cuddled at his feet like a little puppy cat.

Harry laid out for Sandy and Kyle the Readers Digest version of what he wanted with the Pendrick family, and Kyle in particular. Paul Pendrick had already heard Harry's spiel on the front porch.

When he was done, Harry said, "So, what do you think?"

Sandy Pendrick looked at her husband who quickly nodded at her giving his agreement. She agreed with the plan as well and she said, "I agree," to Harry.

"Kyle?" Harry asked.

Kyle looked at his dad obviously looking for some direction, or for his approval that Kyle should go ahead with Harry's plan.

"It's up to you, Kyle. You've worked hard on this and you

deserve some recognition for all your hard work. If it's something you want to do, then go for it. You know your mother and I will be there for you all the way to the end if it is what you want," Paul Pendrick told Kyle.

"And that's all there is to it? All I have to do is say yes and it happens just like that?" Kyle asked Harry.

"Just like that," Harry assured him.

"Well then, count me in," Kyle told Harry.

"That's great," Harry told the Pendricks. "I won't take up any more of your time. I'll be back to you with the final details as soon as I have them firmed up."

Looking down at the furry creatures on his lap and at his feet, Harry said, "I'll be on my way if I can get Jethro and Ziggy to set me free!"

The three Pendricks laughed and Paul walked over and removed Jethro from Harry's lap.

~ * ~

Harry left the Pendricks and was now headed home having completed what he considered an excellent road trip. BobbyBoy was Harry's boy now. He agreed to be the new 'front' person for pokcolmon.com when it all went down replacing the old front man, Clint. BobbyGirl and Clint had bought into Harry's plan hook, line and sinker and couldn't wait to put the plan in operation. The Fealtman's had been on board from the beginning and were necessary to start the ball rolling

Harry just loved when a plan came together. Of course they don't always come together, plans that is. But when they do, it is way past cool in Harry's eyes which are the only eyes that count in Harry's world.

Chapter 100

Harry had arrived home very late from his road trip and had fallen into bed without even taking off his clothes. He slept like a rock and woke to the sound of, what else, the ringing phone.

"Can't a body let a body get some sleep when he needs it?" Harry said to whoever had woken him up.

"I was driving by, saw your car in the driveway, and figured you were back," Sherry said.

"What the hell are you doing up so early, Sher?" Harry asked her.

"Harry, it's noon," Sherry replied.

"Oh," Harry said.

"I went shopping and bought some pastrami and those soft rolls you happen to like, Harry," Sherry told him.

"Pastrami," Harry repeated suddenly wide awake.

"That's what I said, Harry," Sherry told him.

"And the soft rolls with the caraway seeds?" Harry asked her.

"That would be the ones, Harry. Alpine Lace Swiss, too," she added.

"Ah, shit, you're killing me here, Sher," Harry said.

"Well, get your ass up and get on over here," she told him. "And, if you're a good boy, I'll give you one guess what's on the menu for desert, Harry?"

"What about the kids?" Harry asked.

"Can you say 'Class Trip,' Harry?"

"Till late?" Harry asked.

"Not before ten tonight," Sherry confirmed.

"How about 'Class Trip' and YUMMY, YUMMY," Harry said.

~ * ~

Later that night, after a delicious pastrami and swiss sandwich on one of his favorite rolls, and multiple portions of desert that involved a roll of a different kind, Harry was at the computer in Mel's office.

"Fealtman, check. Clint Rensford, check. BobbyGirl, check.

BobbyBoy, check," Harry said out loud. All checked and account-ed for after he scanned the updates he had just entered into the case file for the pokcolmon.com case.

Harry now had all the pieces in place to implement his plan. He knew what had happened, how it had happened, who had made it happen, and was pretty sure he knew what was supposed to happen from here on in. His job now was to make sure it didn't happen that way.

Confident he had done all he could for the time being, Harry shut down the computer and headed for the door to call it a night. As he was about to unlock the front door, Harry caught a glimpse of a shadow toward the right of the bar across the street from Mel's place. That shadow got larger as he stepped through the door and transformed itself into what looked like a black truck. Like "the" black truck. Like "the" black truck that kept popping up in Harry's life and Harry doesn't like shit like that. It disrupts the orderness of his life, or so Harry believes.

Harry ducked back into the office and re-locked the front door. He quickly went to the back of the office, grabbed the base-ball bat they kept in the rear of the office, and exited out the rear door. That enabled him to circle around the block and come up from behind the black truck that was still parked across the street from Mel's office.

Harry duck walked along the side of the truck aiming to put an end to this shit once and for all. He yanked open the door and drew back the bat ready to bash in the brains of whoever was fol-lowing him.

"Hey, yo!" somebody yelled as the guy he saw in the rear of the cab was hustling to get his pants back on. The chippy he was wrestling with was adjusting her skirt to hide what mamma said never to show to any dude in a big bad-assed truck.

"What the fuck?" the guy yelled at Harry.

"Oh, man, I'm sorry," Harry said as he quickly closed the truck's door and hightailed it around the corner heading for his apartment.

Better safe than sorry Harry said to himself as he walked up the block. Pretty nice ass on the chippy he also thought to himself.

Chapter 101

The following morning, Harry was sitting outside on his deck watching Sandy, his neighbor in the main house, working in her garden. He was enjoying a cup of coffee and some early Linda Ronstadt on the stereo while reading the paper. Ronstadt wasn't one of Harry's go to favorite listens. She was in the mix of lay back and let life roll on by Harry favorite listens. He was also enjoying watching Sandy who was nice to watch doing anything.

It also gave him the opportunity to put off deciding what to tell Max and his buddies now that he knew the truth about Clint, and about pokcolmon.com. It had to happen, but Harry just wasn't ready to tackle that chore just yet. It would have to be soon, not just yet was what Harry was trying to convince himself. Unfortunately he was losing the battle.

Once Harry was done reading the paper from cover to cover, sports pages first, he gathered up his stuff and headed inside. He couldn't pass up one last glance at Sandy who happened to look up at that moment, see Harry, smile and wave. Harry smiled and waved back.

Phone calls needed to be made. Back-up needed to be secured. End-game needed to be locked down solid. Harry needed to take one more peek at Sandy just for the hell of it.

~ * ~

"Yes, this is Harry Mickey Shorts calling for Ms. Timmons. Is she in?" Harry said as he began his phone calling.

"Ms. Timmons is not available," he was told.

"Will she be available soon?" Harry continued.

"No, Ms. Timmons is away on business and cannot be reached at this time," came the reply.

When Harry didn't reply, the voice said, "May I connect you with anyone else?"

"Yes, you may," Harry said. "Can you please connect me with Mr. Trundle's office?"

"Mr. M. Randle Trundle?" she questioned.

"None other," Harry answered.

"May I say who is calling?" she asked.

"You certainly may," Harry responded.

Silence.

After a few seconds, she said, "Sir."

"Madam," Harry replied.

"May I say who is calling, please?" she asked clearly annoyed now.

Harry was about to repeat, "You certainly may," when he thought better of it and said, "Harry Mickey Shorts."

"Please hold, Mr. Shorts."

Hoping for a catchy Muzak diddie, Harry heard nothing but dead air as he held.

Coming back on the line, the voice said, "Can you hold, Mr. Shorts?"

"Till the cows come home," Harry replied.

Dead air.

"Harry," he heard finally. "Are you in town?" Trundle asked.

Harry though he heard voices in the background and asked, "Are you in a meeting? Am I disturbing something?"

"No, Harry, it's just a board meeting for one of the Trundle Industry subsidiaries. They can wait. Are you in town?" he repeated.

"No, I'm at home, Mr. Trundle. I had called to speak to Ms. Timmons and was told she isn't available, so I asked for you hoping to catch you free," Harry told him.

"I'll be tied up here all day, Harry. I have an hour before I have to leave for a dinner at the Mayor's mansion tonight. Can you be here at six for a beer or two?" Trundle asked.

"Six it is, Mr. Trundle. If we hurry, we could probably have three."

"You are something, Harry," Trundle said. "I'll see you at six."

Chapter 102

Nicely framed, Harry thought to himself as he sat outside Trundle office at ten minutes to six that evening. He was speaking of the new work of art that had replaced the Renoir which previously hung behind the receptionist's desk outside the executive offices.

He was also speaking of the stunning blond presently manning said receptionist's desk. Her "framing" was also a work of art in Harry's eyes.

At one minute to six the door to Trundle's office opened just as Timmons stepped off the elevator heading for Trundle's office. Timmons went inside and the door started to close. Trundle stuck his head out of the opening and said, "Coming, Harry?"

Harry took one more look at the receptionist, shook his head, and then started for Trundle's office.

Trundle shook Harry's hand warmly and said, "Cool one, Harry?"

"She is, and I will," Harry replied.

Trundled smiled.

"Have a seat at the conference table while I get the refreshments," Trundle said. "Would you like anything, Wendy?" he added.

Timmons looked at Harry and said, "Yes, I would, Mr. Trundle."

"Your usual?" he asked.

Still looking right at Harry, she smiled and said, "No, something different might be nice. Surprise me."

Harry smiled back at Timmons, but he had no idea what they were smiling about.

Trundle returned to the conference table with drinks for everyone.

"So, Harry, what is it you needed to see me about? Or should I say us about?" Trundle asked.

"Well, I hadn't expected Ms. Timmons to be joining us, but no matter. It's always a pleasure to see Ms. Timmons' smiling face," Harry said.

"Time, Harry. Time," Trundle urged.

"Yes, time," Harry agreed. "I believe I have all my ducks in a row and I'm ready to proceed to the end game scenario on the pokcolmon.com case. You both know what has gone on up to this point and I've already laid out for you what I would like to have happen once I implement the end game. Is Trundle Industries in agreement with my proposal?"

Trundle took a sip of his beer and spoke first.

"Harry, I can confirm Trundle Industries is in agreement with the proposed plan you have provided to us. Corporately we are on board and prepared to implement, but we have been waiting on the final piece to solidify how we will incorporate this new entity into the organization. I believe the last piece is about to be confirmed, or at least I hope it is," Trundle said.

Looking at Timmons, Trundle said, "Ms. Timmons?"

Timmons looked from Harry to Trundle and then said, "To quote a famous, or maybe it's an infamous Private Investigator, I'm down wit it!"

Harry didn't know what Timmons was "down wit," but the smile on Randle's face told him that whatever it was, it was a good thing. Most likely a good thing for both Trundle Industries and Harry's plan as well.

"That settle's it then," Trundle said.

Trundle held out his hand to Harry and they shook. Timmons placed her hand on top of theirs to signify she was an integral part of the agreement.

Harry raised his glass in a toast and said, "To Trundle Industries, to M. Randle Trundle, and to Ms. Timmons for whatever she just agreed to."

"Here, here," Trundle agreed in toast.

"Here, here," Timmons mimicked.

They finished their drinks and Trundle said, "I have to go hob-knob with the hob-knob crowd and god knows one doesn't want to be late for that."

They all laughed.

Standing, Harry said, "Can I take you anywhere, Ms. Timmons?"

"Not yet, Harry, not yet," she replied.

Chapter 103

Harry was at home making himself some dinner when the phone rang.

"How you be, poppyson?" Max asked Harry.

"I'm fabulous, couldn't be better," Harry told Max. "How you be?"

"If I was any happier they'd be calling me Mary Poppins," Max replied.

"Huh?" Harry replied.

"We watched the movie last night. Never mind," Max said.

"Well, okay," Harry agreed.

"You ready for Saturday?" Max asked.

"If I was any readier they'd be calling me Mary Poppins," Harry replied.

"Good one poppyson. I guess I deserved it," Max conceded.

"You did. Nine as usual?" Harry asked.

"Make it a little earlier if that's alright," Max asked.

"Why earlier?" Harry inquired.

"Make it a little earlier if that's alright," Max repeated.

"Alright, I get the picture," Harry said. "Ten to nine be good?"

"Okee-my-dokee," Max replied.

"Anything special I'll need?" Harry asked.

"Bring your P.I. hat?" Max told him.

"My P.I. hat?" Harry asked.

"Testing...Testing...1,2,3...1,2,3... Bring your P.I. hat... Bring your P.I. hat... Testing...Testing...."

"Enough, Max, I heard you. I'll bring my P.I. hat," Harry said.

"Good. See you Saturday, pops," Max said as he hung up.

"Kids," Harry said to the dial tone.

~ * ~

Harry dialed the phone, waited for the message recording he expected to hear, and said, "The Giants made a huge comeback."

After he hung up the phone, Harry started counted.

One itty-bitty Mississippi. Two teensy-weensy Mississippi's. Three slightly bigger than miniscule Mississippi...

The phone rang.

"That was fast," Harry said when he answered it.

"Hello, Harry," he heard in reply.

"Hello back at ya, Robert," Harry replied.

"Lonely, or are you in need of my, of our services?" Robert asked.

"Hardly ever lonely, hardly ever enough," Harry replied.

"Same old Harry. Speak," Robert said.

"My pond is full of ducks and they are swimming in a line tighter than a virgin's..., well, you get the picture," Harry said.

"I get the picture, Harry."

"I'm going after BrianK and his operation," Harry told Robert. "Do you, or should I say yous plural, want a piece of what's left of him when I'm done?"

"Timing?" Robert asked.

"I can be accommodating to some degree," Harry answered.

"Give me a minute to check," Robert said.

Harry waited until Robert came back on the line.

"I need a week and then I'll need one day's notice to mobilize. That doable?" Robert asked.

"There's a schedule and yours is doable. For you, and only for you, it would be my pleasure to accommodate you in any way possible," Harry replied.

"Yeah, Harry," Robert said and he hung up on him.

Harry's mind started whirring and the permutations sped by his mind's eye like a time warp gone bad. It had all played out as he wanted it to and the end result pleased him. It pleased him mucho—for the kids, for Max, for Trundle Industries, for the ever-present Ms. Timmons, and for Harry.

Yeah, it was all there. And, Harry loved every mind's eye second of it. Every last one.

Chapter 104

Harry had to drive around the block once to get to the door at exactly ten minutes to nine the following Saturday morning. Once before, he had sat in the car at the curb to create the same effect, but Max saw him and chided him for his poor planning.

"It's quite embarrassing in front of mom and Briande," Max had told him at the time.

Harry had vowed to never let that happen again.

As he pulled up, Max came out the front door followed by his sister Briande. Sherry was following them.

"What's this rig?" Max asked.

"I love it, daddy," Briande chimed in.

Harry was standing on the other side of the car when Sherry said, "Harry, you've outdone yourself this time. I wish I was coming along just to ride in the, ah, I guess 'vehicle' is the best way I can describe it."

"It's a Rolls Royce Silver Cloud. It's hoity-toidy even for the Rolls Royce crowd," Harry told her.

Sherry's hunched shoulders combined with the elbows in, palms up gesture said, "Where in the hell did you get that ride and who'd you have to kill to get away with it?"

Harry had seen the same gesture before.

"Guy owed me for a thing I did for a guy who owed him for a thing he did for him. This is payback and I've been holding it for the right time," Harry told Sherry.

"For the kids?" Sherry said.

"Other than for you, Sher, is there anyone better?" Harry answered.

The smile on Sherry's face told Harry he had just scored a bunch of brownie points he would be able to cash in at a very opportune time.

"Let's roll," Harry told the kids.

"Yes, let us depart," Briande said in her best British accent.

"Pip pip and all that," Max contributed.

"Pip pip indeed," Harry said. "Later, Sher," Harry said as he ducked into the 'vehicle' as Sherry had called it.

"Master Max, Lady Briande, you may call me James if it pleases you. I will be you chauffer for today's journey," Harry said as he settled in behind the wheel.

"Oh, daddy, you're funny," Briande told Harry.

"Let's get a move on there, James," Max said. "Lady Briande and I have things to do, places to go, people to see. Pip pip then, James my good man."

"Where to then, Sir Pipsqueak?" Harry asked.

"To the Port," Max replied.

"The Port?" Harry repeated.

"Yes, the Port of Washington if you would," Briande said.

"Ah, yes, the Port of Washington. As you command," Harry said.

Harry, Max and Briande laughed together and they were on their way. Port Washington was the town due north of Manhasset on the water—the Long Island Sound.

"Will you be travelling across the seas then?" James asked.

"Very presumptuous of a mere hired car driver to inquire as to what we, clearly not of the same class as a mere driver, would be doing. Don't you agree Lord Max?" Briande said.

She clearly was doing all she could to hold back her continued laughter.

"Quite," Lord Max agreed with Lady Briande. "Next he'll expect us to actually pay for today's endeavors. The audacity of the man."

"Audacity this, Maxy. If you don't tell poor James where to go, your Lordship and Ladyship will be going around the Royal Block over and over again," Harry said.

Unable to hold it together any longer, Max said, "Hit that new boat landing in Port Washington. You know the one?"

"All over it," Harry said. "What are we in for?"

"A cruise," Briande told Harry.

"One of those Cruises to Nowhere?" Harry asked.

"No, a Cruise to Almost Nowhere," Max replied.

"Well that explains it," Harry said.

Chapter 105

Harry parked the Silver Cloud in the Cruise lot and he, Max and Briande got out and walked up to the main gate. Harry had heard there were some new activities going out of the newly renovated boat landing but had no idea what they were. A "Cruise to Almost Nowhere" was a new one on him.

"So, what's with this 'Cruise to Almost Nowhere' we are about to embark on?" Harry asked.

"It's the same as a cruise to nowhere, daddy, but they throw in a stop along the route to make it almost nowhere," Briande told Harry.

"Oh now, that surely clears it up for me," Harry replied.

"Just go with the flow," Max told him. "When we get on board the dude in charge will tell us what's going down. Or at least I hope he will," Max said.

"Even clearer than before," Harry said.

Briande elbowed Harry in the ribs and said, "Pay the fare and let's get on board or we'll miss the launch."

"As you command, Lady Briande," Harry said while paying the fare.

The boat was a pretty good size that Harry guessed could probably hold more than two hundred people. They got on board and grabbed seats so they would be close to the front and they could get a good view of the people in charge when they told them what was going to go down.

"It's mostly kids and their parents from Manhasset and Port Washington High Schools. Me and Bri know a bunch of kids who will be onboard and you might even know some of the dads," Max told Harry.

"Or moms," Briande chimed in.

Twenty minutes later a whistle sounded and Harry could feel the boat begin to move. The Captain appeared and put his hands up to quiet the group so he could speak and be heard.

"Hello everyone," he started. "Welcome to what we call our 'Cruise to Almost Nowhere.' I'm Captain Rollins and this is our cruise director Barb Birmingham. While I and the rest of the crew will endeavor to ensure that we have a safe and smooth journey today, Barb and her staff will make sure every last one of you has the best time you've had in a long time.

Everyone cheered.

"Barb, why don't you tell everyone what we have in store for them today," the Captain said.

"Hi, and let me welcome each and every one of you onboard today. We have a full day planned for you, so let me give you a quick rundown and then we can get started having some fun. This room we are in now will be the gathering place when we need to get everyone together at the same time. It's the Blue room—yep, the walls are painted blue. Upstairs you'll find the game room where we have a ten foot high Velcro Dart Board set up, a Roulette Wheel, and several other cool games to play. You will win points that you can use to purchase some pretty neat stuff before you leave later on today."

Everyone cheered at the news they will be getting stuff.

"In the room behind us, through the door at the back of this room, is the Pink Room. Can anyone guess why we call it the Pink Room?" Barb the cruise director asked.

A chorus of "Because the walls are painted pink" was confirmed by Barb.

"That's right, they're pink. And for being so smart, everyone gets fifty points to start you on your way."

Yup, as expected, everyone cheered.

"In the Pink Room you'll find twenty separate areas sectioned off with licensed Cosmetologists in each one. Anyone of the girls know what a Cosmetologist does?" Barb asked.

There were murmurs but nobody raised their hand to take a stab at it. That is among the girls. One of the boys raised his hand and Barb called on him.

"What's your name?" she asked.

"Todd," he told her.

"Go ahead, Todd, tell the group what a Cosmetologist does."

Todd hesitated and then said, "Cosmetologists are often the initiators of style and change. Cosmetologists can help you acquire a certain look with the right hairstyle and hair coloring, manicured nails, and Cosmetologists also shampoo, cut, color, and style hair and advise clients on proper hair care. They give manicures, facials, and do plenty of other stuff."

"That's perfect, Todd. Let's have a round of applause for Todd everyone," Barb said.

The room gave Todd a warm round of applause while his father tried to duck his head inside his collar.

"How'd you know that, Todd?" Barb the cruise director asked him.

"My sister's a Cosmetologist and I hear her practicing that speech all the time," Todd said.

"Well Todd, since you were brave enough to raise your hand and give the group a very good description of what a Cosmetologist does, you get fifty extra points."

"Cool," Todd said as his father raised his head from inside his shirt collar.

"All the girls are welcome to go in and have anything they want done for as long as they would like. I'd invite the boys as well, but I'm not sure I'd get too many takers. Any boys interested?" Barb asked.

From the back of the room a boy's voice was heard yelling, "For how many points?"

The room broke up in unison over that one.

Chapter 106

Order restored, Barb moved on.

"Sorry, no points for guys visiting the Pink Room. Some of you may have seen that breakfast is set up on the buffet tables behind me and we will be having lunch in the pier pavilion when we make our mid-day stop. The set of instructions and work sheets that were provided on the tables you are now seated at describe the lunch time activity we have planned. Josh will now give you some details."

"Welcome aboard," Josh said. "During our mid-day stop we will be playing a game that's part solve the mystery and part name that celebrity. Where? Well, we will be visiting Block Island which is a small island in the Long Island Sound and it is our one stop-over today. Hence, our 'Cruise to Almost Nowhere' as we call it. That is where you will have to search for hidden clues that we have placed both in the lunch pavilion and various other locations on the island. You have to find the clues and figure out what famous person, performer/singer or singing group the clues point to. Some are current and some go back a ways. Your parents will have to put their thinking caps on to come up with those. There are also clues hidden on this boat that are not all that obvious."

"How many?" someone called out.

"The work sheets in the information packet on your tables have space for fifty answers—you have to state what the clue is and what the answer is. Once you're back on board, you use the clues you found to name the fifty people that make up the "Who's Famous" list. The more you come up with, the more points you get. If you don't think you're going to be good at it, you can join forces with other kids and use a team approach, but we encourage everyone to try it on your own. You'll be surprised how easy it will seem once you get the hang of it. Your list is due to Barb or me by five p.m. At six p.m. we will announce the answers and the top ten winners. Any questions?" Josh finished.

Max whispered to Harry, "Got your P.I. hat with you, pops?"

"I'm wearing my invisible one," Harry assured him.

"Good job, poppyson," Max replied.

Barb took over again and said, "Thanks, Josh. A few last an-
nouncements before we get to the having some fun part. If you
brought your swim suits, we will stop while we are on our way
back after lunch. An hour has been allocated for swimming and
we have showers downstairs for those that indulge. And lastly, and
perhaps of most importance to the parents along for our trip today, on the top deck you will find a full cigar bar and grown-up
refreshment station to enhance your 'Cruise to Almost Nowhere'
experience while your sons and daughters partake in the young
people's activities. Enjoy."

The parents cheered that particular announcement.

Barb finished with, "Have fun everyone."

~ * ~

Harry made sure the kids had at least some breakfast before
they embarked on their activities of choice. Immediately thereaf-
ter, Max and his buddies took off for the game area intent on pil-
ing up as many points as possible. Briande headed for the Pink
room with her gal pals looking to be "made more beautiful" as
they explained it, emphasis on the more.

"May God have pity on the Cosmetologists, or at least may
they be paid a more than adequate fee for the torture they were
about to endure at the hands of fifty or more squealing teenagers,"
Harry said to the dad sitting next to him.

The dad agreed wholeheartedly.

Harry bullshitted with a couple of the dads he knew before
beginning his wandering in search of clues. By the time the kids
met up with him around 11:30 he had found fourteen different
sets of what he assumed were clues.

"You look much more beautiful," Harry said to Briande
when she emerged from the Pink Room. "Emphasis on the
'more,'" he added.

"Thank you, daddy," Briande told Harry.

"How'd you do, squirt?" Harry asked Max.

"The dart board was really cool," Max started. "We kicked on
the Roulette Wheel and I won the most points during Sports Trivial Pursuits. Overall, I'm getting "points flush" shall we say."

"I won Fashion Trivial Pursuits among the girls and almost
won the foam ring toss upstairs," Briande told Harry proudly.

When Harry told them how many clues he had found they

hugged him to the point of embarrassment.

"Enough," Harry yelled. "Let's hit that Block Island there, get us some grub, then gather up them there clues, young 'uns."

"Oh, daddy, you're so funny," Briande said.

Chapter 107

Lunch proved to be a half-a-feast with a very nice Samuel Adams White Pale Ale for the old 'uns in the group. Lemonade was provided for the wee ones. Harry thought the Boston Cream Pie for desert was excellent.

Harry, Max and Briande headed out after lunch and found twenty more clues in the first thirty minutes. The clues got a bit scarcer after that requiring more ingenuity on their part. By the time they had to head back to the boat they had found a total of thirty-one clues on Block Island. Max spotted two quarters in a small frame hanging over the entrance to the walkway back onto the boat.

"Good one," Briande commented.

"Two quarters?" Harry queried.

"Fidy Cent," Max said.

The light bulb went on over Harry's head and he got it.

Back on the boat the kids went off in different directions and came back with what they thought were an additional three clues Harry hadn't found originally.

They now had what looked to be forty-nine sets of clues. They set about trying to figure out what the clues meant and if they fit the game they were playing. By the time they had to hand in their work sheet they had figured out forty-one answers to the clues they had. Some of them were:

Max's two quarters for Fidy Cent

The direction the boat started in was eastward for Clint Eastwood

The room Briande spent more of her time in for the singer Pink

Harry figured out the penny and what looked like an old Sheriff's badge for the actress and director Penny Marshall

The stuffed turkey with the handkerchief bandana for Tom Hanks

A combination of a Red Rooster, the sun and peppers pointed Max at the Red Hot Chili Peppers

The picture of a man with his arm around a young girl standing next to a tree gave Briande the ex-American Idol Chris Daughtry

And maybe the one that clinched it for them, Harry figured out a fork resting on the Daily News was for the actress Tyne Daley

Briande was most proud when she figured out the picture of a bird, a legal document and a can of Yams was Robin Williams

In the end, they decided they had legitimate answers to thirty-nine sets of clues and handed in their work sheet as such. Max went back to the Blue Room to hang with his buds and Briande set off for another visit to the Pink Room. Harry ventured forth in search of the top deck and a refreshing libation.

The "Cruise to Almost Nowhere" had proved to be a major success in the eyes of the parents Harry talked to. They chatted and drank, some of the guys smoked cigars, and all agreed to make it an annual excursion for as long as their kids wanted to participate. Harry enjoyed his Absolute Gimlet on the Rocks, a fine cigar, and being a real honest-to- goodness parent type person at least for one day.

At 6:00 pm, everyone gathered back in the main room to get the results of the Mystery Clue Game as it had been officially named by the group. One entry had a grand total of three right answers and won the booby prize. When the winners were announced, Max and Briande jumped up and proceeded to do a victory dance that made Harry proud. They both hugged Harry and the whole crowd gave the Shorts a rousing round of applause.

Max's buds jumped all over Max.

Briande's friends congratulated her and hated her at the same time. It's a teenage girl thing Harry had learned.

Harry didn't know what the hell to do. He was saved when one of the mothers on the trip came over and gave Harry a congratulatory hug. The fact she said, "Call me, Harry," was something the rest on the crowd didn't need to know.

~ * ~

It was still reasonably early when Harry dropped the kids off at home that night. Sherry met them at the door and asked how the day went. Max showed her the Derek Jeter autographed helmet he got for his prize points and said, "Mom, dad was awesome today."

Sherry didn't know what to say.

"Mom, you and I are gonna have a blast when we go for the all day spa treatment I got with my points," Briande told Sherry.

Sherry didn't know what to say.

"You're the best, Daddy," Briande told Harry. She gave him a big hug and went into the house.

"Harry?" Sherry asked.

"Sher, it was one of the best days of my life."

"You are something, Harry," Sherry said. "I still don't know what, kiddo, but you sure are one hell of a something."

The kiss Harry got told him Sherry meant every word of it.

Chapter 108

"Well, well, well, if it isn't Harry Mickey Shorts," Dolly said to Harry as she walked up to his table.

"Hey, Dolly," Harry responded like all was good with the world.

"Hey, Dolly. That's all you have to say is 'Hey, Dolly?'" Dolly responded.

Harry didn't know whether to smile or run for the door.

"Hey, Dolly," she repeated. "After all that time, we go back to my place and get it on like we did and practically get me evicted over the racket we made, and all you've got to say for yourself is 'Hey, Dolly?' No call and you got the balls to say 'Hey, Dolly' and that's it?"

"Ah," is all that escaped from Harry's mouth.

"Ah," Dolly repeated. "Ah. That's it—ah. Harry Mickey Shorts, I don't know what the hell's going on in your life right now, but you had better get your shit in gear. The old Harry Mickey Shorts would have had me crawling away from the table swearing what you did wasn't so bad and pleading for forgiveness and another chance."

"Um," was the best Harry could come up with.

"I should, I aughta, you deserve…" Dolly said. Then she smiled and told Harry it was the best nights she had spent in as long as she could remember. You can shit on me more often if I can get a romp in the sack that good, Harry."

Harry sighed a sigh of extreme relief.

"What can I get you, Stud Man?" Dolly asked.

"After that, something strong, Dolly," Harry said.

"Make it two, Dolly" Robert said as he sat down across from Harry.

"For you, anything you want," Dolly told Robert.

"Harry," Robert said.

"Rowbear," Harry said dragging out the bear.

"Dolly one of yours?' Robert asked.

"Past history with a recent reoccurrence," Harry answered.

"Worse reoccurrences you could be saddled with," Robert

said.

"The saddle's available if you're looking for a ride," Harry replied.

"Dance card's full right now," Robert said. "But, if my rodeo comes back to town…" Robert let dangle.

"She can buck with the best of them," Harry told Robert.

"Been a while since I've been bronco busting," Robert said, "but one never knows when one's gonna need to relearn an old habit."

"A truer truth has never been told," Harry agreed.

"I've never been here before," Robert said.

"Patrick's Pub is as good as it gets," Harry told him.

"Seems to be, Harry, seems to be so far," Robert said.

Dolly appeared at the table with their drinks.

"Your GPS down?" Harry asked.

"Funny, Harry," Dolly said, "Actually, I was in the back getting a fresh bottle to make sure your friend here got a drink he would enjoy."

"And my drink?" Harry asked.

"I've had you, Harry. Gotta keep the new blood happy," Dolly said with a smile directed at Robert that could have lit up the whole place.

"Mighty nice of you, ma'am," Robert said

"Name's Dolly," Dolly told Robert

"Pleased to meet you, Dolly. I'm Robert," he responded.

"And I'm pleased to meet both of you," Harry said. "Now scoot Dolly so Robert and I can enjoy our drinks and talk."

"Later, Robert," Dolly said.

"Yeah, later, Dolly," Robert replied.

"Hey, man, you still married or what?" Harry asked.

"Harry, if I told you the answer to that question, I'd have to kill ya," Robert said.

Harry looked at him and they both cracked up.

Chapter 109

"So, BrianK," Harry said once they were done laughing.

"BrianK," Robert repeated. "Where are you with him and his organization?"

"Everything is set and ready to be put into motion. The "Big Twenty" tournament BrianK has been planning is now scheduled to go off next weekend. The people we need will be involved and they're all on board and raring to go," Harry told Robert.

"What do you need from us?" Robert asked.

"I provide the fireworks and you provide the manpower once the shit hits the fan. I can only assume BrianK will have his people there including our friend Frenchie," Harry said.

"And afterward?" Robert asked.

"I have a plan in place to deal with the current pokcolmon.com organization once we have BrianK secured and out of the picture," Harry said.

"BrianK's mine I assume?" Robert asked.

"All yours to do with as you please," Harry assured him.

"So, if I have this right, we sit back until needed and come in to clean up the riff-raff. And, we get BrianK and whoever else we want from the pokcolmon.com group?" Robert asked.

"That's right," Harry said. "And let's be clear on who the good guys are here. For their cooperation, immunity has been promised to Clint and BobbyGirl. BobbyBoy and this kid Fealtman are also part of the show and you have to promise hands off for them as well. Deal?" Harry asked.

"We can live with that," Robert said.

"Good," Harry said.

"And the money?" Robert asked.

"It's all accounted for and I have the means to get at all of it," Harry told him. "The after-the-fact set up is already in place and it will be a smooth transition to the new organization," Harry assured him.

"Name? Principals?" Robert asked.

"Let's leave something for a surprise," Harry said.

"Whatever you say, Harry. Once we have our boys and we're

gone the show is all yours," Robert told Harry.

"Cool. And just one more request if I may?" Harry said. "If Frenchie gets in the way, he's mine."

"Might be fun to watch," Robert said. "You sure you can take him?"

"Yeah, I'm sure," Harry said.

"Then he's all yours," Robert told Harry.

Robert tossed back his drink, got up from his chair and walked out without saying another word.

"Weird fucking dude," Harry said to his back.

Dolly appeared at Harry's table and asked if Robert was gone.

"Yeah, just left," Harry told her.

"Too bad," she said. "I kinda liked him."

"I wouldn't worry about it, Dolly. He's like the wind. If he gets the itch, one day he may blow in here and surprise the hell outa you. But, don't get too attached. As I said, he's like the wind and you never know which way the wind is going to blow," Harry told her.

"You would know, Harry. You would surely know," she said.

Dolly smiled, turned, and walked away. Harry tossed back his drink, got up from his chair and walked out without saying another word.

Dolly watched Harry walk out knowing he'd be back. He always came back. She was hoping his friend Robert would be back as well.

Chapter 110

The pokcolmon.com website contained all of the information about The "Big Twenty" tournament. Daily updates provided fodder for the legions of followers and the message board had been going non-stop for two weeks.

Over the past week, Harry had gotten Al to post vague messages concerning Clint and the "Under 18 World Championship of Poker" tournament. Nothing specific was included in the posts, just innuendo that there was more there than met the eye. It was now the evening before the tournament that was to be held the next day. It was time for Harry's boys from the basement to add another message of their own to the message board chatter. It was time for Harry to light the fuse and get the fireworks started.

But first he had to tell Max what he knew and what he intended to do.

Harry called Max and gave him the Readers Digest version. The conversation didn't last long. When Harry was done, Max asked, "Can I be there when you nail the scummer?"

Without hesitation, Harry said, "Get your scummer nailing duds ready cuz you got a scummer to nail."

With Max satisfied, Harry made the call.

"Go ahead, Al," Harry told the leader of the basement boys. "Post the email and make sure it hits front and center."

"Will do, Harry," Al confirmed.

Harry waited fifteen minutes and then logged onto the pokcolmon website using the dummy I.D. and password Lars had set up for him. Once he was in, Harry went to the message board and found the following message:

Reliable sources have informed us that Michael Fealtman's sister has admitted to poisoning our own Clint Rensford the morning of the "Under 18 World Championship of Poker" tournament to get back at him for what he did to her brother. She was quoted as saying, "You mess with my family, you mess with me," she had said. "Don't ever think you can fuck with Mike and somebody's not going to stuff it down your throat and pull it out your ass."

The message board was ablaze with follow-up messages trying to find out who posted the original message and was it true. Questions were being fired about fast and furious:

Who's this Mike Fealtman dude?

Is it true the sister worked at the tournament casino location?

What'd Clint due to Fealtman?

Why isn't Clint answering Fealtman's sister's bullcrap message with his own?

Is Fealtman in the "Big Twenty" tournament?

Hey BrianK—is this stuff true man?

Why isn't pokcolmon debunking this shit?

Harry was loving every minute of it. He was sure BrianK and his people must be running around like chickens with their heads cut off trying to figure out who posted the original message. And why? What does Fealtman have to gain from a message like this? What do they do to stop the follow-up messages? Do they answer the messages?

Harry saw nothing in reply from BrianK or any of his people. His only guess was that they were content to ride it out and address it the following day at the tournament site. If that was the case, then Harry was in hog heaven and the slop couldn't taste any better.

Harry called Al and told him to post the follow up message he had given him as soon as possible. He told Al to shut down after he was done and delete the I.D. he was using so there would be no way BrianK or any of his people could trace anything back to Al or his boys.

"You of course know that isn't necessary, Harry," Al told him.

"Yeah, I know it, Al. But humor me and delete it anyway. It's not like you can't create another one if we need it," Harry told him.

"Consider it done, Harry," Al said.

And it was. Two minutes later the following message was posted on the board:

The pokcolmon.com management team offers their apologies for the Fealtman/Clint post that hit the message board and will clear up any misconceptions before the start of the "Big Twenty" tournament that begins tomorrow at noon.

With that, the message board lit up again with hundreds of

posts trying to get something, anything more from the pokcolmon management team, Fealtman, his sister, or Clint. Of course, since BrianK hadn't sent the message and Harry was acting on behalf of the Fealtmans and Clint, nothing else would be forthcoming.

Saturday was going to be a blast.

Chapter 111

Harry picked up Max early Saturday morning in his vintage Mustang Mach I. If you're gonna go, you might as well go in style was one of Harry's oft' quoted mottos.

"Guess we be tooling in style," Max said as he got in the car.

"Class deserves class," Harry told him.

"It's about time you recognized it," Max kidded Harry.

"Shut up and eat your Egg McMuffin," Harry told him. "And you better not get anything on my car, squirt."

"Yes, sir. You betcha, sir man. Not gonna get nottin on the boss man's car," Max said.

"Shut up, squirt," Harry repeated and they were on their way.

~ * ~

The venue for the "Big Twenty" tournament was small, much smaller than the site of the last tournament they had been to. They were there early so they got a primo parking spot close to the entrance.

No sign of Robert or his troops when they got there. Harry didn't expect to see any.

No sign of Trundle or his entourage either. Harry thought he might see some sign of Trundle Industries being on the prowl, but it was still early he reminded himself.

As they entered the venue, Harry was surprised at the size of the hall's interior. It was much roomier than Harry would have envisioned from the outside. Besides the tables they would use for play, there was a bleacher section for the fans who would come to watch, a fairly substantial food court, a small stage with a podium, and the area Harry would call home for the day—the bar.

Three tables were set up in the middle of the room with seats for seven, seven and six players at the tables. Twenty players in all; hence the "Big Twenty" tournament. The top seventeen players currently participating in pokcolmon.com plus the special invitees—Clint, BobbyGirl and BobbyBoy would make up the remainder of the twenty participants.

A special rule had been established for this one tournament.

If your winnings after the tournament exceeded the maximum amount allowed for one individual per the pokcolmon.com by-laws, the excess winnings would only be distributed for post graduate programs at accredited institutions.

"I'm gonna see who's here and stake out my seat," Max told Harry.

"Cool," Harry replied.

"I assume you'll be situated in the small area in the corner?" Max said pointing to the far corner of the room.

"Ah, that would be a possibility," Harry replied.

"Have one for me," Max told Harry and he was off.

~ * ~

At 11:00 am, Harry made a full turn around the hall to see if any reinforcements had arrived. The parties he was expecting were nowhere in sight, but one person he had expected to see was now present and accounted for. Frenchie was in the house.

"Funny, but somehow I expected you'd turn up today," Frenchie said to Harry as he saddled up to where Harry was standing.

"I'm a funny guy," Harry responded.

"Yeah, real funny," Frenchie said. "Just don't think of trying anything funny today."

"Won't have to try too hard," Harry said.

"What's that supposed to mean?" Frenchie asked.

"That's for me to know and you to find out," Harry said.

Harry stuck out his tongue at Frenchie and walked away.

Chapter 112

By 11:30 the place was getting pretty crowded. None of the Big Twenty had made an appearance yet and Harry was starting to thing BrianK had them sequestered away someplace. He knew Clint, et al weren't with the others since he had orchestrated their arrival with them beforehand.

Max caught Harry a few minutes later.

"Where is everybody, pops?" Max asked.

"Who is everybody?" Harry countered.

"The players," Max said. "There's gotta be five hundred spectators here already and they're still arriving in droves. Me and my guys are dying to meet and talk to the players who are kicking butt on the pokcolmon.com site. And Clint, and BobbyGirl..."

"I told you on the way here you and your buds would get some time with Clint and a few of the others. Bide your time and I'll deliver. I promise, kiddo," Harry told Max.

"Alrighty, pops. I'm cool with that," Max said and he was off again.

~ * ~

The number seventeen money winner on the current pokcolmon.com board entered the room at 11:45 as intended. The buzz hit the room almost immediately. Michael Fealtman had made his appearance.

At exactly the same time there was commotion from the back of the stage area and the place lit up like Mardi Gras. The other sixteen top earners made their way into the hall from a back door behind the stage. Kids were yelling and running in every direction. They didn't know whether to run to get the scoop from Fealtman or mob the rest of the "Big Twenty" who were now heading for the tables.

Harry was absolutely loving the shit out of it.

There was someone now standing at the podium whom Harry hadn't seen before. That someone asked for quiet and had to yell several times before he got the room's attention. Finally they quieted down.

The Harry "Big Three" hadn't entered the room as of yet. It was less than fifteen minutes to show time.

With the room now quiet, the pokcolmon.com flunky simply said, "I give you BrianK."

As BrianK stepped to the podium, pandemonium reentered the hall as questions flew for all over the room.

Raising his hands to quell the uprising, BrianK said, "I would like to take this opportunity to welcome everyone, players and guests alike, to the first ever "Big Twenty" pokcolmoc.com tournament."

The place erupted in applause.

The room now quiet again, BrianK said, "Before we begin play, I feel it is imperative that we, pokcolmon.com and myself, address the message board activity of yesterday right through this morning. First, I will read a statement prepared on behalf of the organization and then I will also give you my personal view of this incident:

"The pokcolmon.com organization categorically denies any knowledge nor does it place any credence in the statements made on the pokcolmon.com message board as it relates to Clint Rensford's unfortunate illness at this year's "Under Eighteen World Championship of Poker" tournament. But, should said statements prove to be factual, we as an organization will do everything in our power to bring justice to bear on that individual."

The room was momentarily silent. Partially it was to wait for BrianK's personal thoughts. Partially because some of the kids and grownups in the room didn't understand half of what was said in the statement.

BrianK addressed the group again. "As for me personally, this is my view on the matter. If this individual has something to say to the pokcolmon family, let that person stand up and say it in our presence, to our faces. Don't hide behind a message board and make claims that can't be substantiated. Until that point, I, we stand by the account as originally reported.

"Unfortunately," BrianK continued, "it seems as though the person being discussed who could clear up this matter isn't hear to speak up for himself. As you all know, Clint was invited to participate in our inaugural "Big Twenty" tournament and has chosen not to appear…"

A loud cheer interrupted BrianK's ramblings at that point.

"Clint, Clint, Clint" could be heard from the back of the hall.

"I'm here to speak for myself, BrianK," Clint said loud enough for all to hear, "but we have a tournament to play first. Talk later. Let's play some poker!" Clint shouted and the place again erupted in a loud chant of, "Clint, Clint, Clint."

Following right behind Clint walked BobbyGirl and Bobby-Boy. Harry's "Big Three" were in the house.

The crowd exploded.

Harry looked at BrianK whose mouth was currently hanging open in disbelief. And, off to the right of the podium, leaning inconspicuously against a back wall, was the one, the only, Rowbear.

Chapter 113

Just as Harry had instructed, Clint, BobbyGirl and BobbyBoy had quickly moved to the tables within the now roped off area. They had found their places before BrianK's people could do anything about it. The crowd was electric.

Looking back at the podium, Harry saw BrianK was nowhere to be found.

With all the players now seated at the tables and the crowd back in the bleachers, or scattered around the outside of the hall, the same earlier underling went to the podium and said, "Let the tournament begin."

Surprisingly, Harry found himself longing to hear the words "May the cards light up your lives!"

Clint, BobbyGirl and BobbyBoy were seated at the three different tables to start. The other player involved in the ongoing Clint saga, Michael Fealtman, was seated at Clint's table. The other players in the event were new to Harry.

Since it was a one day tournament, the rules called for higher than usual starting blinds, stiff antes and accelerated blinds. Play was fast and furious from the first deal on. Ten thousand chips weren't going to last long if you took one "bad beat."

Time for a smidge of poker explanation:

In poker, bad beat is a subjective term for a hand in which a player with what appear to be strong cards nevertheless loses. It most often occurs where one player bets the clearly stronger hand and their opponent makes a poor call that eventually 'hits' and wins. There is no consensus among poker players as to what exactly constitutes a bad beat and often players will disagree about whether a particular hand was a bad beat.

Any hand that looked like a favorite to win can end up losing as more cards are dealt, but bad beats usually involve one of two not mutually exclusive scenarios:

The player who wins on a bad beat is rewarded for mathematically unsound play. Calling a bet despite having neither the best hand nor the right pot odds or implied odds to call, then winning anyway, is characteristic of this type of bad beat. It can also involve the inferior hand catching running cards when it requires two cards in a row to come from behind to win the pot. For example, catching cards on both the turn and the river that complete a straight or flush.

A very strong hand loses to an even stronger one. This type of beat occurs with some frequency in movies. In the films The Cincinnati Kid and Casino Royale, The Kid and Le Chiffre each lose with a full house to a straight flush. In this situation, it is possible that both players have played their cards well, and avoiding the bad beat could not have been achieved without committing a mistake. Such an occurrence is sometimes referred to as a setup or cooler in poker lingo.

The first hour was a feel everyone out period and there wasn't much challenging going on. As such, there wasn't much excitement either. The crowd was getting restless and looking for something to happen. They were waiting for the first person to make a move. They were waiting for the party to get started and the fun to flow free and easy. The crowd was waiting for some action.

Little did the crowd know the first move would be Harry's.

Harry looked at Robert and nodded. Robert nodded back. All was at the ready and it was again "Show Time."

It started as a low murmur from the back of the room close to the front door. The low murmur slowly got louder and before you knew it everyone was looking in the direction of the girl that had just entered the hall.

"Hey, that's Fealtman's sister. What the hell is she doing here? Why isn't she in jail?" BrianK's underling yelled.

"Yeah, look, it's Mikey's sister," someone else yelled.

Play had now stopped and there was movement all over the room. The pokcolmon.com people were descending upon Fealtman's sister. Frenchie appeared and was about to jump into the act when two very official looking guys wearing dark shades stepped between the girl and BrianK's people, including Frenchie. After a brief standoff, the pokcolmon people, including Frenchie, backed away.

Fealtman's sister spoke.

"Clint, you piece of shit, I poisoned you once and I'd do it again in a heartbeat. In fact, I will do it again. You can count on it."

The crowd was clearly stunned to silence.

"And where's that other piece of shit. Yo, BrianK. Come back out here you cowardly piece of human waste," she went on.

Everyone could feel it. THE confrontation everyone wanted was about to happen. It was THE confrontation that everyone had been waiting to happen. And, it happened. BrianK was back out in the open and back at the podium.

"Will someone please arrest that girl," he started. "Where's Frenchie? Take care of that girl, Frenchie," BrianK continued.

Frenchie was nowhere to be found.

A small scuffle had ensued around Fealtman's sister when a voice could be heard saying loud and clear above the rest of the crowd, "Leave her alone!"

Everyone turned their attention to the voice and the person behind it—Clint Rensford.

Chapter 114

"I said, leave her alone," Clint repeated.

From the podium, BrianK said, "Finally we will have some sanity in this hall. Go ahead, Clint, tell her to stop this. Tell everyone here what a lying bitch this Fealtman girl is. Clint, you go ahead and tell everyone what they want to hear. Tell our pokcolmon family the truth, what we all know as the truth."

All eyes went from BrianK to Clint.

You could hear a pin drop. There wasn't a sound throughout the hall as everyone waited to see what Clint was going to do.

Clint began walking toward the stage. The crowd parted to let their king through. The crowd was ready to have their Clint strike down the blasphemer and restore BrianK and pokcolmon.com back to its rightful place. The crowd wanted to believe in the truth.

The problem of course was the real truth.

As Clint stepped up onto the stage, BrianK took a step toward him and held out his hand to Clint. Clint walked right past BrianK as if he wasn't even there and stood before the podium.

"The truth," Clint started. "Yeah, it's probably time the real truth be told. Not BrianK's truth, not pokcolmon's truth, not Fealtman's sister's truth, and finally, not my truth. What I'm talking about is the real truth."

BrianK tried to get to the podium but Clint pushed him aside. The glare he gave BrianK told him don't try that again.

The crowd edged closer to the stage waiting to hear Clint make them whole again. They wanted to hear that all was going to be okay and pokcolmon.com actually was what they all thought it was. It wasn't to be. Not today, not now, not ever.

"The real truth has been in hiding for a long time," Clint started. "I wasn't poisoned by Fealtman's sister. That isn't the truth."

All eyes turned to the back of the hall, but she was gone. Michael Fealtman's sister was nowhere to be found. She had vanished.

"That's right," Clint said. "I wasn't poisoned by her or anyone else. In fact, the real truth, I wasn't even found unconscious on the morning of the "Under Eighteen World Championship of Poker" tournament. I was never unconscious. I was sitting up in my room watching the tube waiting for the tournament starting time to pass."

Upon hearing Clint's admission, BrianK rushed up to Clint and pushed him away from the podium. In a flash, two very large and equally official looking guys grabbed BrianK, dragged him off the stage and pinned him to the back wall.

Not a single pokcolmon person came to BrianK's aide.

It took nearly five minutes to restore order in the hall.

Back at the microphone, Clint continued.

"The real truth," Clint said again. "BrianK orchestrated the entire deal. He wanted publicity for his group, publicity for pokcolmon.com, and publicity for the 'Under Eighteen World Championship of Poker' tournament. He offered me what was, as they say, 'A deal I couldn't refuse,' and I took it. I now know it was a mistake but it was too much for an eighteen year old kid to pass up. He turned me into a cheat and a liar. The specifics don't matter. What matters is I let all of you down, I let my family down, and I let myself down. To everyone, I am truly, truly sorry."

Without saying another word, Clint turned and walked right off the stage and continued out the door in the back of the hall.

Again, the entire crowd had been shocked into utter silence.

Chapter 115

Once the crowd realized what had just happened, a minor state of bedlam ensued. Harry, Robert and Robert's people stayed out of the way to see what was going to happen. Harry kept his eye on his remaining "Big Two" plus Fealtman, and of course, Max.

"People, people, calm down people," the BrianK underling was yelling into the microphone from the podium. Everyone, please calm down and give me your attention."

He achieved some minor success with that try.

In a much louder voice he yelled, "Everyone, we have a tournament to play. We have money to be awarded. We have..."

He ran out of "we haves."

The voice of reason saved the day. Well, she may not have been the epitome of the voice of reason, but the two buttons she had unbuttoned unleashing the vision of reason got enough attention to quell the disturbance.

"I don't know what the hell that was, but I came here to play some poker and win some money. Pokcolmon invited us here, and we're here. So I say, let's get back in our seats and play," BobbyGirl told the crowd.

The voice and vision of reason had spoken, and play thus resumed.

After a brief time of player uncertainty, a flurry of deep bets, calls and subsequent ALL IN's brought the number of players left in the tournament to ten. BobbyGirl had garnered the most chips to that point followed closely by Bobby Boy. Mike Fealtman was sitting in a good spot in fourth place.

BobbyGirl polished off another player who had gone ALL IN with a pair of K's in the hole only to be knocked out when BobbyGirl caught an Ace on the River. She now had a commanding chip lead.

As the next hand we being dealt, BobbyGirl stood and walked to the podium. The girl contingency stood and cheered their star. The rest of the people in attendance wondered what was going to happen now.

That would be the rest of the people other than Harry. It was time for the next step in Harry's plan to be taken.

"Thanks girls," BobbyGirl said with a wave to her crew in the bleachers. "I want all of you to look up at the leader board. You see who's winning this invitation only tournament—it's me. BobbyGirl is winning fair and square. And for the longest time it looked like I beat all comers on pokcolmon.com the same way. But, I didn't. Yeah, I won, but not fair and square. BrianK offered me a deal just like Clint and I took it. He helped me win online and he helped me win the tournament most of you came to see. Just like Clint, I cheated. And just like Clint I let fame, glory and money get in the way of decency. BrianK is slime and whatever he gets he deserves. But you guys deserve better."

Without saying another word, BobbyGirl turned and walked right off the stage and continued out the door in the back of the hall.

Like déjà vu all over again, the entire crowd had been shocked into utter silence once more.

Robert's guys plunked BrianK off the wall, threw handcuffs on him and paraded him through the crowd toward the front door. He was hit, kicked, spit on and splashed in the face with more forms of liquid than one would have guessed existed in that particular venue. Funny, but the two guys escorting BrianK to the door never lifted a finger to stop them.

Chapter 116

Step three in the Harry Mickey Shorts master plan now hit the venue. Moving to the podium from behind the stage, Harry took the mike off the stand and went to the front of the stage. Taking a deep breath, Harry whistled into the microphone.

Some people dove for the floor, some hid behind chairs, and others covered their ears not knowing what the hell was happening.

When it was semi-quiet, "Hi," was all Harry said to start.

He let the crowd get ahold of themselves and urged everyone to sit.

"Hi, again," Harry continued. "You don't know me, but that's all right. I don't know myself sometimes either."

A few people chuckled. Others looked at Harry like he had two heads.

"Somebody needs to take charge right about now and that somebody is going to be me. First, and let me make this very clear, we are going to finish this tournament."

That brought a cheer from the crowd.

"Good," Harry said. "That's more like it. We are going to finish the tournament and distribute the winnings to the player's accounts. The money exists and each of you who are a part of pokcolmon.com should feel safe in knowing that your accounts are secure and will remain as such."

That brought an even more enthusiastic cheer from the crowd.

"But before we move on to the rest of the tournament, I want to let you in on what's gonna go down from here on in. BrianK is no more. He will be dealt with and will not see the light of day for a long, long time. What you knew as pokcolmon.com will be replaced by another entity run by a major New York conglomerate called Trundle Industries. The man I'm going to introduce to you I trust with my life. I would trust him with the lives of my kids. And, as pains in the asses as they can be, that's big for me."

The people in the hall laughed as they continued to warm up to this intruder who was commanding their attention.

"Ladies and gentleman, and pains in the asses of all ages, I give you Mr. M. Randle Trundle."

Trundle came from the back of the auditorium and slowly walked up the isle toward the stage. He was in no hurry and let the people in attendance see his confidence and warmth as exhibited by the big smile and the wave of his hand he gave everyone he passed.

He took the stage and stepped behind the podium. Before he began speaking, he looked out at the crowd and again flashed a huge smile for all to see.

"Hello. My name is Randle Trundle and I run Trundle Industries. On behalf of my company I have accepted the responsibility to keep what was pokcolmon.com running just as it did before. You will see nothing different when you log onto the site and the rules will remain the same."

That brought the most enthusiastic cheer from the crowd so far.

Pointing to an individual standing to the right of the stage, Trundle said, "This lady is Ms. Timmons. She is my assistant. No, she is much more than that. She is my right hand person who I trust with everything I do and anything that involves Trundle Industries. I value her as I value few others. Her values are my values. Her integrity is without question. When I tell you she will be your champion, she will be your champion."

Trundle looked at Ms. Timmons, smiled, and then looked at Harry standing in the background.

"Ms. Timmons will run Trundle Educational Enterprises (TEE) for the first year. She will act as company President with full responsibility to run it as need be. Once she has it running as we envision, she will then resume her position as my direct assistant.

"TEE will be based on the Isle of Mann for legal and tax purposes. We have the absolute support of the US Department of Education and the current government on the Isle of Mann. We will continue to utilize the same interpretation of an early United States law that the pokcolmon.com organization called upon. Together we envision a long and successful tenure for TEE that will provide you, the youth of today and the leaders of tomorrow, needed funds to reach your ultimate potential."

The place erupted with cheers, applause and everything else

you can think of that meant they were happy.

"Now," Trundle continued, "enough of me running my mouth up here. We have a poker tournament to complete."

Chapter 117

The players were so happy to be playing and assured they would keep the money they already had in their accounts they went nuts when play resumed. ALL IN's were the norm in every hand getting down to the final three players less than two hours later.

BobbyBoy led the three players with a chip stack equal to the other two players combined. A victory for BobbyBoy seemed to be all but in the bank.

Mike Fealtman was in second place on the chip leader board.

"Dudes," Fealtman said. "How about the three of us go ALL IN in the dark, right now, and get this gig over with quick like? Winner gets all the chips."

Two nods from the other two players and the hand would be played for all the marbles—in the dark.

The down cards were dealt and the Flop was placed on the board—Ace of Hearts, Ten of Diamonds and Four of Hearts.

Since Fealtman had suggested the ALL IN, he laid down his cards first—KQ of Diamonds. He had an inside straight draw and three cards to a diamond flush

The third player turned his cards over and showed the Seven of Spades and Three of Clubs. He had bubkiss.

BobbyBoy looked at his cards and dropped them on the table—King of Hearts and Nine of Diamonds. He trailed Fealtman's K and better kicker and needed Runner-Runner hearts for a flush.

The dealer tapped the table, buried a card, and turned over the Eight of Hearts.

BobbyBoy still trailed but had gotten Runner #1 toward his Heart flush. No help to Fealtman and player #3 was all but done. He needed a Seven or a Three—not a Heart.

The stillness was broken by a "Go Mikey" from the bleachers. That started an avalanche of "BobbyBoy" and "Get Em Mike" chants from the crowd.

Finally, quiet restore, the dealer tapped the table, buried a card, and turned over the River Card. It was the Jack of Hearts giving Fealtman his straight, but Runner #2 gave BobbyBoy his flush and the tournament.

He had da nuts.

"Way to go," Fealtman said.

The crowd rushed the final table and swarmed all over the three final players. BobbyBoy held up the hands of the other two players and flashes erupted from all angles.

BobbyBoy made his way to the stage where Trundle awaited holding the Tournament Champion's trophy. When he got there, Trundle shook BobbyBoy's hand and spoke to him quietly for a minute. When they were done, Trundle handed him the trophy and emulated BobbyBoy's gesture by holding his hand high in triumph. BobbyBoy then held the trophy over his head while cameras clicked everywhere.

Trundle went to the podium again and said, "Trundle Educational Enterprises gives you its first tournament champion—BobbyBoy."

The chant of "BobbyBoy—BobbyBoy—BobbyBoy" erupted again throughout the hall.

Trundle again took the mike and said to the crowd, "TEE is also proud to announce that they have an agreement in place, as of one minute ago, with its new spokesperson—BobbyBoy."

The chant of "BobbyBoy—BobbyBoy—BobbyBoy" again filled the hall as his crew surrounded the stage.

~ * ~

Harry had pre-arranged for Max to spend ten minutes alone with BobbyBoy when the tournament was over. Max met Harry near the front door smiling from ear to ear.

"That was cool, Dad," Max told Harry.

"No problem, Max. You ready to split?" Harry asked him.

"Yeah," Max said. "I gotta get home and get online so I can brag about the ten minutes I got to spend with the new spokesperson for Trundle Educational Enterprises."

"Good enough," Harry said. "You remember Robby's dad, don't you?"

"Sure. It's nice to see you again," Max said politely. He held out his hand for Robert to shake.

"It's nice to see you again, too," Robert told him.

As they went to leave, Robert said to Harry making sure Max

couldn't hear, "You sure you're good with this, Harry?"

"Yeah, I'm good," Harry said. "But, if it looks bad, shoot him."

"Will do," Robert told Harry.

Just before they got to Harry's car, a figure stepped out from behind a van and blocked their path.

"You fucked up a good thing I had going," the man said.

"I figured you'd think that, Frenchie," Harry replied.

"I can't have that happen and let it go without doing something about it," Frenchie said.

"I figured you'd think that too, Frenchie," Harry replied.

"He in this?" Frenchie said nodding in Robert's direction.

"Just me and you," Harry replied.

Frenchie squared off and Harry complied.

Frenchie took a step to his right, feigned a big right hand and let fly a left hook that showed Harry he knew what he was doing.

Harry caught it on his arm and kicked out the inside of Frenchie's right knee. He put a bit extra into it and Frenchie crumpled to a knee. He refused to quit and got up looking to hurt Harry bad. His stance said martial arts and his eyes said come on.

Harry straightened and bowed ever so slightly.

Frenchie didn't follow suit and tried to catch Harry off guard with a round house kick. Unfortunately, his bad knee didn't cooperate and it was a weak attempt. Harry came up under the back of the kick, grabbed Frenchie's balls in a vice grip, spun him and pinned him against the van. The crack everyone heard was the sound a nose makes when it meets an immovable object.

Harry let go and Frenchie slumped to the ground. It looked like Harry was going to add one for good measure, but he heard Robert say, "That's enough, Harry. I'll take it from here."

Harry stepped back. He asked Max if he was all right.

Max looked at Harry with that look a son gives his dad when he's more proud of him than anyone else in the world.

"You da man, poppyson, you da freakin man. And pops, that was da nuts!" Max told Harry.

Chapter 118

The sun was shining, a warm breeze blew in from center field, the hot dogs tasted great, and the fresh beer he had just gotten was perfect. Harry was sitting in Trundle's box watching the Bayport Schooners on their way to another convincing victory.

"Hello, Harry," Timmons said as she sat down in the seat next to him.

"Timmons," Harry said back without looking over at her.

"Good game?" she asked.

"Every baseball game is a good game," Harry replied. "The Bayport Schooners winning just makes it even better."

Timmons didn't reply and sat watching the game without speaking.

"Where you been?" Harry finally asked.

"There was a lot to do to get Trundle Educational Enterprises ready for launch. I've been back and forth to the Isle of Mann several times and put in some long days and nights when I was back here in the states," she replied.

"All work and no play…" Harry let hang.

As if she didn't hear him, Timmons said, "The results from the battery of tests we put BobbyGirl through came back really strong. She's a very bright young lady who obviously can also be very resourceful when she wants to. She's proved to be a real find and has functioned perfectly as my assistant so far."

Harry just smiled.

"But you already knew that, didn't you, Harry?" Timmons asked.

Harry smiled again and then said, "I had a feeling."

They sat and watched the game for a time.

Timmons broke the silence.

"You know, Harry, even though I knew BobbyBoy was going to be the spokesperson for TEE, and he was probably the best player of the three left at the end, I was hoping Fealtman would win."

Harry finally looked over at Timmons and then back at the game.

"Mike Fealtman will have his day in the sun, the North Carolina sun that is," Harry said. "With the sudden departure of one of their freshman pitching recruits due to a small "substance" incident, Fealtman was offered a half-scholarship starting in the fall. I'm sure the fact one of Randle's close business associates sits on the school's Board of Directors had nothing to do with it."

"That's good to know, Harry," Timmons replied.

"Yeah, I like that kid. His sister, too," Harry replied.

Again, they sat quietly and watched the spectacle that was baseball on a beautiful day.

This time it was Harry that broke the silence.

"Been that busy you say?" Harry asked.

"More than you can imagine, Harry," she replied.

"All work and no play…" Harry repeated.

~ * ~

The game ended with another convincing Schooner victory in the books. Harry and Timmons sat as the crowd slowly made their way up the aisles heading for the exits.

Harry turned and looked at Timmons. This time he looked directly into her eyes and smiled.

"Can I take you anywhere, Wendy?" Harry asked her.

"Yes, Harry, you can fly me to the moon."

About the Author

Rich Kisielewski has spent thirty plus years in the insurance industry and currently works in New York and Philadelphia. An uprooted New Yorker, he lives in Central Pennsylvania with his wife and collection of dogs and cats.

Visit his website at: www.richkisielewski.com

Other Books by Rich Kisieleswki
from WolfSinger Publications

da sticks

Not long ago, Harry had moved back to the town where his ex-wife and kids reside and was trying to rebuild his life. The "work hard and play hard" attitude that carries Harry through life is balanced by the softness evidenced in his dealings with his children. Once again, he was going to have to be away from them and the new life he had been trying so hard to establish.

Going undercover at MechInsCo, Harry gets exposure to executives within the company including his lifer accounting boss, the psycho senior finance executive and a frantic company president. They all paint the same picture-a company losing money with no idea how, or why. His stint at MechInsCo supplies Harry with some raucous times: large amounts of information, booze and ladies provide him with much more than he signed on for.

da bug

Harry Mickey Shorts gets a call from M. Randle Trundle, a New York business tycoon, who is in need of Harry's help. Without a thought, Harry drops what he is doing and races off to help his benefactor, and his friend.

Trundle is a part owner in Board Room Farms—a horse racing stable—which is run by his brother, Danny Trundle. He informs Harry the stable's stud breeding stallion was found dead in his stall and Trundle feels something is wrong. Harry agrees to help Trundle with the case and does what he does best by going undercover and begins digging into the world of thoroughbred horse racing. Having bet on more than a few nags before in his lifetime, Harry is comfortable around the track and blends in very smoothly.

During his investigation, Harry forms an alliance with the ranch's female vet—in more ways than one. She agrees to provide needed intelligence on the current and prior goings-on at Board

Room farms. Along the way, she becomes a serious love interest in Harry's life. Unfortunately, that conflicts with Harry's renewed part-time interest in his ex-wife that may prove to be a "pick one" dilemma, sooner, rather than later. His love for, and continued attempt to become part of his two children's lives, remains paramount in Harry's thinking.

Investigate these other Mysteries
from WolfSinger Publications

The Dolmen – Matt Bille

When attorney Julie Sperling's fiancée is murdered while re-searching a controversial museum exhibit, she calls on her ex-lover, science writer Greg nightmarish pursuit as very real preda-tors from ancient folktales try to hunt down anyone with knowledge of their existence.

For Greg and Julie, the City of Angels has become the gate-way to hell...

In Adam's Fall – Phoebe Wray

Old New England towns are infamous for their odd murder stories, but that had never happened before in Halton, Massachu-setts.

When history teacher Nikki Sheridan trips over the dead body of a young Muslim girl in her backyard she finds herself at the center of a murder mystery. A mystery that will take her on a perilous journey with the police, the FBI, a nervous town ready to point fingers at neighbors who seem different, and a man calling himself 'the Patriot': a dangerous zealot whose hateful agenda could destroy the small town or bring them even closer together as they face a homegrown terrorist in their midst.

Murder Most Howl – Margaret H. Bonham

Dog Mushing Can Be Murder

For Stephanie Keyes, noted sled dog racer in Colorado, sled dog racing can be dangerous enough. But when a fellow musher and rival is found murdered and she's a prime suspect, Stephanie races to find the killer before he can strike again.

Missing sled dogs and deadly goals abound in this super sleuth tale—or is it tail?

www.ingramcontent.com/pod-product-compliance
Lightning Source LLC
Chambersburg PA
CBHW051143030726
47504CB00004B/1018